Titia Sutherland was brought up in the country and has spent much of her adult life in London. She had a patchy education at various day schools, and English was the only subject in which she received a good grounding. As a child she started many novels which were never completed, and she and her brother wrote and acted in their own plays. In her late teens she spent two years at the Webber-Douglas School of Drama and a short period in repertory before marrying a journalist. The birth of a baby put an end to acting. Following a divorce, she had a series of jobs which included working as a part-time reader for a publishing firm, and designing for an advertising agency.

She started to write when the children were more or less adult and following the death of her second husband. Her other novels, *The Fifth Summer*, *Out of the Shadows*, *Running Away* and *A Friend of the Family*, are also published by Black Swan. She has four children, enjoys gardening and paints for pleasure when there is time.

Also by Titia Sutherland

THE FIFTH SUMMER
OUT OF THE SHADOWS
RUNNING AWAY
A FRIEND OF THE FAMILY

and published by Black Swan

Accomplice of Love

Titia Sutherland

BLACK SWAN

ACCOMPLICE OF LOVE
A BLACK SWAN BOOK : 0 552 99574 6

First publication in Great Britain

PRINTING HISTORY
Black Swan edition published 1993
Black Swan edition reprinted 1993
Black Swan edition reprinted 1994
Black Swan edition reprinted 1996 (twice)

Set in 11/14pt Linotype Melior by
County Typesetters, Margate, Kent

Black Swan Books are published by Transworld Publishers Ltd,
61–63 Uxbridge Road, London W5 5SA,
in Australia by Transworld Publishers (Australia) Pty Ltd,
15–25 Helles Avenue, Moorebank, NSW 2170,
and in New Zealand by Transworld Publishers (NZ) Ltd,
3 William Pickering Drive, Albany, Auckland.

Printed and bound in Great Britain by
Cox & Wyman Ltd, Reading, Berkshire

In memory of Arnot, with love

Acknowledgements

I would like to thank David Ellis-Jones, Annabelle Ruston and Jonathon Dodd for their expert advice on the world of art, and if I have made any mistakes, I apologize.

Aesthetic emotion puts man in a state favourable to the reception of erotic emotion. Art is the accomplice of love. Take love away and there is no longer art.

Remy de Gourmont, *Décadence*

Chapter One

Claudia died six months ago. I find I have to remind myself of the fact constantly as I follow the familiar route out of London to Sussex, past the Robin Hood gate at Richmond Park and on to the Kingston by-pass; and still my mind has difficulty in accepting the truth, deluded as it is by the agonizingly clear vision I have of her. I see her emerging from the front entrance of her house, where the door is seldom closed in summer, her hair bright against the dark interior. Pulling down a strand of climbing rose and holding it absently to her nose, she waits for the car to crunch slowly to a halt in the drive, the smile breaking on her face and sweeping upwards like a wave on the shore. She is completely relaxed, genuinely careless of our deception, while my heart is thudding like a sledge-hammer from fear of discovery and the effect she has on me. This is how it is each time: or rather, how it used to be. An unheroic man and a generously confident woman in the throes of an obsession, greeting each other conventionally outside the family home. Her home and that of Josh, to whom she is lawfully married. In my imagination, despite a fondness for him, I would get him to absent himself conveniently for the entire weekend, so that Claudia and I could have the place to ourselves. In reality, of course, he was always there, bursting with noise and restless energy, silent only at work in his studio. Today it will be Josh alone; it is unbelievable she will not be in the doorway to meet me.

My daughter Sophie is beside me, blissfully unaware of my inner torment; her profile serene and slightly turned away to watch the suburbs retreat and become country. Out of the corner of my eye I can see the tip of her uptilted nose gleaming in the sunshine. She holds her face near the half-open window to catch the breeze, like a dog. She is wearing a white T-shirt and a minuscule strip of denim which I presume to be a skirt. Her hair is loose today, dark and shiny over her shoulders, strands of it parting in the draught. I like it best twisted into its ballerina knot, showing the pure lines of neck and head. I wonder what she is thinking: I never know with Sophie. It does not matter; she has a lovely uncomplicated personality so I am not unduly worried. However, since losing first Jane and now Claudia, I have become nervously protective towards her: the only jewel left in my crown.

We have not spoken a word since we started, but it is a comfortable silence: she is the most restful of companions, like her mother, but without Jane's disconcerting air of secret amusement. I wonder sometimes whether this easy-going nature of Sophie's is an asset in a dancer. The technical perfection is undoubtedly there, although I am not expert enough to judge. It strikes me, though, when I have watched her perform, that a little more fire would not come amiss. But who am I to criticize when the English National Ballet have offered her a place, the only one of her year to be chosen? And she is young, not quite eighteen. Secretly I suspect the spark I am looking for will be supplied by a lover. I shy away from the idea, the fastidious father: shy away from the thought of lovers in general.

She turns to me. 'Has Josh started painting again?'

'I really don't know,' I answer truthfully. 'The fact that he's asked us down this weekend seems encouraging. After so long,' I add.

'Why did he give up all of a sudden? Was it to do with Claudia?' she persists.

The day seems to be growing hotter; my hands are clammy on the wheel. I fumble for a handkerchief.

'I never discovered. He wouldn't talk about it,' I reply. 'Retired into his shell and refused to come out.'

'Odd, that, isn't it? I thought you were great mates. I mean, you'd done so much for him. You sort of made him a success, didn't you, by exhibiting his pictures?'

I suspect that whatever I did for Josh has been more than cancelled out by my treachery. I made him and destroyed him. I answer obliquely.

'I imagine what's happened is he's had some kind of mental block. It happens to artists as it does to writers. The trouble is, the longer you sit around doing nothing, the more difficult it becomes to start again.'

'Like losing your nerve?' Sophie asks sympathetically.

'Exactly.'

'Poor Josh.' She yawns and stretches, flexing her long arms and legs like a cat. 'He's had a horrible time, with Claudia dying and everything.'

Studying her charming reflection in the mirror above her head, she adds, 'I'm surprised he's asked me, too. It's ages since I last met him.'

'He remembers you, and it was only about eighteen months ago. But you were a mere child then, of

13

course,' I point out, teasing her, and she makes a face at me.

'I don't suppose he's asked us down for nothing,' she says. 'I think he's planning a surprise for you.'

I feel a nasty stab of apprehension. 'Such as?'

'A whole studio full of new paintings, waiting for your approval? All this time he's been working in secret because he doesn't want any interference from outside. I can understand that,' she says placidly. 'It's not possible for dancers, but sometimes I wish that it were.'

'Nice if you were right, but I'm afraid it's unlikely,' I say, managing a smile, my nerves subsiding gratefully. 'Although I mean to use a little friendly persuasion on him if he's amenable.'

'Oh, we'll cheer him up,' Sophie says with the breezy confidence of a games mistress. 'I think it's going to be fun.'

I am reduced to silence by this youthful optimism and touching innocence. Left to my own thoughts, they turn apprehensively to the possible motives behind Josh's invitation, delivered out of the blue without explanation. There has to be a motive, for the man has been a virtual recluse for six months, turning his back on the art world; on myself in particular, if my instincts are right. They may have led me astray, however: I am riddled with guilt, which is misleading, and I am working in the dark. I have no idea how much he knows about my affair with Claudia, if indeed he has any concrete evidence. I was careful in the extreme, but I cannot vouch for Claudia. No outsider can tell what happens within a marriage; she was good at pretence, but he must have sensed the difference

14

in her. Most likely she did not bother to hide it. I loved her and I knew her inside out, inclusive of faults. Besides, they had started to have rows, which bears out my theory; not their normal, enjoyably unimportant spats, but bitter warfare on a grand scale that eventually precluded my weekends with them. At the very least he suspects duplicity if he does not know for certain, and the prime suspect is myself, judging by his abrupt ending of all communication between us: the unanswered letters, the blank telephone calls – the complete shut-down.

I dread the moment of eye-contact on arrival. This will be our first meeting since he more or less refused to see me. I am full of trepidation, for what sort of reception can one expect from a man whom one has cuckolded? I hope very much he has not brought me all the way down here to punch me on the nose. I would be useless at retaliation; I am a pacifist, a self-confessed coward. I loathe the sight of my own blood. Josh would be quite capable of it, he is not a subtle man. I can but pray that his son Sam is with him; I don't believe he would resort to physical aggression in front of an eleven-year-old. Words are more likely: one almighty row, perhaps, to clear the bitterness from his soul?

It is my own fault, I was not forced to accept. I could have made excuses: spent the weekend in a far more compatible manner. A mixture of things drove me to put my head into this idiotic noose. The letters were a strong- incentive: my letters to Claudia. I asked her more than once not to keep them, to flush them down the lavatory or stick them in the boiler. But Claudia had a contempt for caution. She merely smiled that

15

curly, sphinx-like smile of hers and assured me they were perfectly safe, that no-one could possibly find them.

They prey on my mind; I wake in the night sweating at the thought of Josh reading them. My panic is not entirely self-centred: genuinely, I do not want to be the cause of any further suffering on his part. God knows whether I shall ever find them, but at least I will have the chance to search. Knowing Claudia, it is highly likely they were stuffed in a kitchen drawer amongst old recipes, or left lying around by the telephone to be used as doodling pads; in which case I am, as they say, undone. Josh will have found them long ago.

I would dearly love to redeem myself. Bedding a friend's wife is probably beyond redemption: besides, you cannot have redemption without repentance and I do not regret Claudia, it is an impossibility. But the killing of a unique talent as a result, now that is a different matter, and a far greater sin in my view. Josh is not merely a friend, he is my one great discovery. The emotions this induces are not to be guessed at, they have to be experienced to be believed: pride, elation, deep affection, a sense of achievement and extreme nervousness in case something adverse should happen to disrupt this amazing run of luck. One becomes as possessive of one's discovery as an old-fashioned nanny of an only child in her care. One runs around practically clucking in an effort to guard his interests. One does not, unless unhinged, go to bed repeatedly with his wife.

To rekindle his belief in himself would be the most satisfying act of atonement I can imagine: it would render even this traumatic weekend worthwhile.

'Is Josh a *great* painter?' Sophie asks, and I am surprised her mind is still on the subject, as if she has read my thoughts.

'What constitutes great? In my opinion, yes, without doubt,' I tell her. 'Others would disagree, he's not everyone's cup of tea. Do you like his work?'

'I like the straightforward ones, the ones I can understand. And I love the colours.' She frowns. 'One or two of them worry me, where he seems to be painting women's parts, only they're disguised as something else.' She looks at me. 'Am I right?'

I laugh. 'Paintings aren't meant to be dissected so minutely.'

'Neither are women,' she says, unperturbed. 'I prefer a whole, unhidden nude, personally.'

Darling Sophie; she has not much appreciation of the visual arts.

We are coming into Ripley, and there on the left is the Talbot Arms which reminds me once again of Claudia. I pull off the road impulsively and into the car-park on the pretext of needing to pee, and decide to risk my licence with a glass of white wine. I drink it slowly under Sophie's disapproving eye while she sips tomato juice. The wine does little for me. I need something a great deal stronger to dispel the ghosts and the misgivings, and the habit my mind has of slipping back in time.

I have not spoken directly to Josh about this visit. He telephoned the Gallery last Monday while I was at lunch, and left a message with Zelda. I am normally out to lunch, as he well knows: obviously he wanted to avoid explanations at that point, for which I was thankful. Zelda delivered the message on my return in her usual expressionless tone, although Josh is one of her favourite artists. She enjoyed arranging his private view, shows enthusiasm for his pictures and is more than a little in love with him. She must have been secretly burning with curiosity about his resurfacing after a year.

The news shook me. 'I'll ring him back later. We'll be busy with Mr Van de Beer for the next hour or so.'

Zelda lifted her head briefly from a pile of catalogues.

'He said not to bother unless you weren't going, just to arrive in time for lunch: and bring Sophie, if possible.'

Message given, she directed her hideous horn-rimmed spectacles back to whatever she was doing. Charm of manner is not one of Zelda's assets, but the Gallery would fall apart without her; so I was brought up to believe and have since discovered for myself.

'How did he sound?' I asked, to disturb and exasperate her.

'Like always. Ebullient, possibly inebriated, but only slightly.'

I said reluctantly, 'I'd better ring him anyway.'

'He gave the distinct impression he would really rather you didn't,' she said without bothering to raise her eyes.

So I did the same as I had done a thousand times before, and followed her advice. Receptionist, secretary, PA, Zelda has organized the family-owned Siegler Gallery for forty-five years.

I have a hazy but shameful recollection of my mother, who was director at the time, taking me there for my first glimpse of what I was to inherit. I must have been about six, I suppose, and I could not understand why it was empty of furniture apart from a huge desk at the far end. I cannot recall what style of painting was being shown, but the pictures frightened me; and behind the desk Zelda was seated, a young woman in those days, but with the same cropped hair and an identical pair of outsize glasses. Zelda dislikes children intensely and I must have sensed antagonistic vibes because I wet my pants. I did not see the inside of the Gallery for some years after that: until I was considered old enough to control myself, I presume. The second time around the pictures fascinated me and I was hooked for life; which was just as well as my career had already been decided for me: I was to follow in the footsteps of my Siegler forebears. God knows what scenes would have ensued had I chosen to become an accountant or an actor: but the question is hypothetical. I became an art dealer, and the owner and director of the Siegler Gallery since Mother reluctantly relinquished the reins. She is seventy-five and as dictatorial as ever, interfering when the mood takes her like the worst of back-seat drivers.

The Gallery was my maternal great-grandfather's creation. He gave it his name and, from a modest start, he built it into one of the most prestigious galleries in the West End, occupying spacious rooms in Albermarle Street. It passed to my grandfather and so in due course to my mother, there being no sons of that generation to inherit. It has seen incredible changes, survived two world wars and, judging by photographs, looks much the same as at the turn of the century; a single carefully-chosen canvas on an easel in the elegant plate-glass window, 'Siegler' in discreet gold lettering above the entrance. Zelda also has changed remarkably little, except that the dark cropped hair has turned to white: life and the world have altered around them.

It seems to me that we lived in astounding luxury in those early post-war years: a vast dark flat in Lowndes Square, thick pile carpet wall-to-wall, highly-polished antiques and servants to cook and serve quantities of expensive food. My childhood was passed in the two extremes of female-dominated comfort at home and the spartan confines of boarding school. I was bullied relentlessly; the fact that I was pale and undersized with dark curls and long lashes only served to exacerbate the problem of my Jewishness. Anti-Semitism flourished as strongly in Britain after the Holocaust as before it, even encompassing the Upper Fourth at prep school. Fear communicates itself and my fears were endless: of the dark, dogs, cats, swimming, climbing trees, Nanny and, most of all, my peers. I wished passionately I had inherited my Gentile father's healthy Anglo-Saxon looks instead of being cast in the Siegler mould. I wished it still on occasions as an adult: until Claudia killed the complex for good. No-one desired by Claudia could hang on to an inferiority complex. There is a lot in me that has not changed from childhood, but I have cut my list of fears considerably, and learnt to circumnavigate trouble rather than face it head-on, which should serve me in good stead for the next forty-eight hours.

We have reached Haslemere; we will be there in half an hour, Sophie informs me happily, setting my nerves freshly on edge. As usual in moments of stress, I call on memories of Jane who always had the power to soothe: whereas, whatever effect Claudia had on me, it was far from tranquil.

In retrospect, nothing momentous happened to disturb the easy flow of my life until Jane's death. I had married her, Sophie was born, the Gallery continued to succeed and I was absorbed in all three of them. There was no reason to suppose this satisfactory state of affairs should not continue into the unforeseeable future. I took it for granted: that was my mistake. Smugness is an offence punishable by the Fates; I should have known better.

She died by falling downstairs with a loaded tray in her hands, tripped by a heel caught in the hem of her dressing-gown. The accident was so unlikely, so tragi-farcical, such a sheer waste of life, that for a long time my anger at her stupidity battled side by side with grief. The tray was Sophie's, who was in bed with 'flu. Sophie's grief was the worst to bear because it was chiefly silent, and she felt illogically responsible for the tragedy; as did I, even less logically. Our mutual guilt and misery faded with time, as inevitably it must do. I speak for myself: I do not know for sure how long or how deeply Sophie suffered at fourteen. She buried herself in her exams and her dancing: possibly inordinately so. I tried to talk to her frequently about Jane so that the subject should not become taboo. But Sophie was the same then as she is now: delightfully open on the surface while divulging nothing of herself.

I miss Jane greatly to this day. I miss her crooked smile, the way she looked as if something I said or did amused her; her serenity; her fine blonde hair and deep blue eyes that took in everybody and everything, but judged without condemning. She was good for me and I owe her so much; for giving me Sophie and preventing me from becoming a cynic, a trap into which I am apt to fall for refuge; and for laughing me out of pomposity. I owe her for years of entertaining tedious clients and for great pleasure in bed; and in a strange way, because she made me believe in myself, I owe her for Claudia. I loved Jane, and I love the memory of her no less; Claudia has not crowded her out or diminished her. My love for each of them is quite separate; it is easy to keep it that way. They were very different people, one might say complete opposites, generating in me a widely different set of emotions.

A month or so before meeting Joshua Jones, I bought one of his paintings. It caught my attention in the Fulham Gallery: 'Girl with Cat', a view through a doorway of a nude dressing, her auburn hair the colour of the cat curled asleep on a cane chair. Several things about it gave me pleasure: the quality of light and line, and a kind of innocent eroticism. I gave it to Jane for her birthday, to fill an empty space on the bedroom wall; it is a perfect bedroom picture. The buying of a Joshua Jones set off a shattering train of consequences. It never ceases to amaze me, the reverberations resulting from a harmless and isolated action such as this. For without doubt, his name would have meant nothing to me when I was introduced to him, if it had not been for 'Girl with Cat'. We would have passed a polite word or two and gone our separate ways. As it was, I was immediately interested, it having been in my mind to find out more about him.

Jane and I went with reluctance to the party at which I met Josh and Claudia; only her insistence on good manners drove us to put in an appearance. It was given by a dreadful woman who collects people from the art world as others collect snuffboxes, jamming them together in a confined space. The result, without relief from members of an alternative profession, is terminal boredom. That evening proved to be no exception. Jane was parted from me immediately and I spent a quarter of an hour talking shop and drinking indifferent champagne, trying hard to stop my mind from going to sleep. Over to my right I noticed a bear-like man talking to no-one and helping himself at regular intervals from a dish of smoked salmon canapés on the table beside him. His face expressed the kind of aggressive vulnerability of one who feels he should be better treated but is damned if he will let it show. He wore a black velvet jacket slightly strained across broad shoulders and a tie which had worked itself askew, and looked unaccustomed to either. My hostess appeared beside me on a wave of Dior's 'Poison' and shrieked in my ear: 'Oh, Lord! Joshua Jones is on his own again,' and, gripping my arm, she shunted me towards the smoked salmon eater. 'So talented!' she assured me knowledgeably.

'Leo, I want you to meet Joshua Jones. Josh, this is Leo Kinsey, director of the Siegler Gallery. Oh dear – two empty glasses. I'll send someone over to you.'

Josh stared at me with embarrassing reverence.

'Very nice to meet you, Mr Kinsey,' he said, shaking my hand painfully and relapsing into silence.

'Well, I'm delighted,' I told him. 'Delighted. I have a

charming painting of yours, bought about two months ago.'

'You have?'

I was not yet acquainted with the rapid changes in his facial expression: like clouds and sun alternating across a hillside. Now was the sun's turn as pleasure, amazement and hopefulness battled for dominance.

'Which one is that?' he managed to say.

' "Girl with Cat". It was a present for my wife, as a matter of fact. The best I've ever given her, so she claims. It hangs in the bedroom – the ideal place for it.'

'Great, great. I'm glad you've got that one. One of the ones I was reasonably happy about.'

I could tell he was beginning to ease up but the conversation still had to be nursed along. Our glasses were refilled; Josh halved his at a gulp.

'Wonderful hair, the girl in the painting,' I said.

'That's my wife, Claudia.' He smiled. 'I don't get her to model for me as a rule: she's hopeless, can't hold a position for two minutes. I used her for that one because of the hair blending with the cat's fur. You must meet her, she's here somewhere.'

He glanced around him, making a vague gesture with his arm and slopping his drink on to the pale carpet.

'What are you working on at present?' I asked. He told me, his words gathering momentum as he warmed to the subject. The effect of the champagne and my obvious interest in him was reducing his inhibitions considerably. I let him talk, giving him only a gentle prod of encouragement now and then with a question of my own. A definite metamorphosis occurred as I listened; his voice, from being husky with awe, grew in volume, the accent which had puzzled me became pronouncedly Welsh and the arm gesticulations increased wildly to emphasize a point. The original expression I had seen on his face as he stuffed it with food seemed in all likelihood to sum up his personality: flamboyance and insecurity oddly mixed.

He was an arresting man physically: thick-set, earthy and handsome, his features exaggeratedly strong. Nostrils and mouth curved extravagantly, jaw and cheekbone jutted like a primitive carving. His eyes were a true, fierce green and his skin pockmarked, which merely completed the picture of animal attraction. He exuded a kind of nervous vitality. I remember thinking, somewhat maliciously, that he was a housewife's dream of 'a bit of rough'. Afterwards, I knew that to be envy on my part; for even then, before I had become involved in his life, I felt myself pale into insignificance beside him, shrivel up inside, saw myself for what I was: a slight and sallow-skinned introvert with grey-tinged hair receding at the temples. No matter that in my field I was held in respect: Joshua diminished me. I did not allow this inner discomfort to show; I merely countered his volubility by doubling my own suavity.

'I'm talking too much,' he said at last. 'I'm boring you.'

I shook my head, gave the briefest glance at my watch. 'On the contrary; just keeping an eye on the time. We have to be somewhere at eight-thirty. In fact,' I said, 'I'd be very interested to take a look at your work. I was about to suggest a visit to your studio, if you agree.'

He stood quite still, his glass stalled halfway to his lips.

'Agree?' he said in disbelief. 'I'd be more than delighted, Mr Kinsey.'

Sunshine fairly poured across his face, closely followed by a cloud of doubt.

'I don't mean to sound presumptuous,' he added diffidently, 'but I'm not sure my style of painting would be of interest to you: from the point of view of the Siegler Gallery, I mean. You have an Impressionist tradition, surely?'

'That's so. But it's our policy also to have maybe one or two contemporary shows a year. I'm not promising anything,' I told him, 'until I've had a look. Shall we make a date?'

'Of course, of course,' he said, slapping his pockets. 'Diary, diary. Claudia's whom we need, she's the organizer. Where is she now?'

'Here I am,' said Claudia, materializing by his side.

Josh put an arm round her waist and pulled her close to him. 'My saviour,' he said. 'This, darling, is Leo Kinsey, director of the Siegler Gallery, and he's kindly offered to come to the studio and view the pictures. Claudia, Leo Kinsey.'

She put a cool hand into mine. 'Leo, how nice,' she said, dispensing with the 'Mr Kinsey' nonsense: and then she smiled.

I do not consider myself to be a particularly lustful man. I have never felt the need for stimulus provided by pornographic literature, or the necessity for extra-marital sex, apart from one unimportant incident. I was of that rare species, the genuinely happily-married man; in those days, Jane was the cherished provider of all I wanted. I have, of course, had occasional licentious thoughts about women fleetingly glimpsed – what heterosexual man has not? But on the whole I am boringly monogamous, preferring my sex to be cosy rather than adventurous. So what exactly happened to me that evening as I exchanged social niceties with Claudia in a crowded room? Why did I experience a weird sensation of being drawn unwillingly towards a predestined conclusion?

I did not take to her. She was the type of woman I find particularly intimidating: confident of her sexual powers and happily convinced that no man would fail to succumb. That was the impression I had; such tactics have an adverse effect on me: I want to turn and run. She could not be called pretty, she had none of Jane's willowy softness; striking, perhaps, for she was as tall as her husband and had a mane of hair the exact colour of dark, coarse-cut marmalade. I felt that the charm, so blatantly directed at me for the moment, was an accoutrement, as easily discarded as her earrings: and yet, when she smiled, it was as if the whole of her went into it, like a promise. I know now what I suspected then, that her motives for charming me at the time were based on the advancement of Josh's career: only a minute portion of that shining promise was for me alone.

Her eyes were a wide-open, innocent blue, and she had a way of never taking them from one's face, of concentrating intently as she talked. They were inappropriate, those eyes: the cat's eyes of Josh would have suited her better. I found them desperately unnerving; in turn I concentrated on nothing, swivelling my gaze frequently to include Josh, while my hands and feet twitched and shuffled with a nervous, tingling life of their own. God knows what I said to her; I felt my normal urbanity desert me entirely, only vaguely aware of having committed myself to some date which she was scribbling in her diary.

I caught sight of Jane seconds later, standing in conversation with a group of people a few feet away; and I saw by her expression and the slow smile of private amusement that she understood something of my discomfiture. She never mentioned it or showed signs of mistrust. But for a moment I felt as if I stood naked and visible to her eyes only. That night I carefully avoided looking at the painting of Claudia hanging in the bedroom: I would never feel at ease with it again and thanked God that Josh had depicted her back view, so that her penetrating gaze was turned away.

Some weeks later, when we had reached the stage of meeting Josh and Claudia on a social basis, there was nothing to distinguish those occasions from similar ones with other friends. The initial impact of the original evening did not last; I managed to get myself under control. Jane discovered an unlikely rapport with Josh: she had a great capacity for enquiring into people's lives without appearing inquisitive, and Josh loved to talk about himself. He grew extremely fond of Jane in the half-year he knew her. In fact, it would have been easy to imagine them taking their intimacy a step further, had I not known better; she was far too deeply in love with me to look elsewhere. As for myself, my one act of unfaithfulness was of such insignificance – (a rather drunken one-night-stand while on business in Florence) – as to hardly count. I would like to believe that had Jane lived, the affair with Claudia would never have taken place. In my heart of hearts, I doubt whether I would have had the strength to resist.

A yelp from Sophie brings me sharply back to the present: I have missed the turning to the village, driven through Midhurst and out towards Chichester on remote control. Backing the car, I swing to the left by the signpost marked Lower Pelling and we wind slowly down the lane to the valley. On our right the hill unfolds in gentle gradients, and below us on the near side the stream flows our way, leading us with unnerving inevitability to our destination. Sophie lowers the window and breathes in the smell of the country.

'Wonderful!' she sighs.

I wish to God I could agree with her. This narrow road, the banks of summer foliage brushing the side of the car, the trees in their fresh blatant green: all these are reminiscent of an intense longing. A very different sensation has taken me over now, brutally invading my breathing and my digestive system. The feeling is vaguely familiar; I cast around in my mind for its origin and all at once it is there: the cold and sickening fear of being driven back to school.

Chapter Two

The house looks the same. Why should I expect it to be otherwise? Houses remain as they are until they change hands: only the lives of the occupants are altered by circumstance, shifting them like so many grains of sand.

They must have lived here for thirteen years: Josh was twenty-seven and Claudia thirty-one when they bought the place. She had been left a modest amount of money in her mother's will, enough to cover the price of two adjoining farm cottages in bad condition which they had knocked into one. The result from the outside is pleasing: a low building of weathered brick and pale criss-crossed timbering. The interior is not so satisfactory, the narrow upstairs corridor intersected by a lethal series of small steps and the bedrooms a hazard of beams to anyone of average height. It has its charm: from the upper windows you can see the river at the bottom of the garden. But for me the house has always had a faintly sinister atmosphere: there are too many dark cramped corners. Claudia liked to give the impression that they rebuilt it with their own bare hands, but this I know to be just one of her fantasies. She designed the layout, according to Josh, got it all wrong and fell back on the services of a student architect anxious to cut his teeth on the project for peanuts.

We roll slowly to a halt, my heart beating at twice its normal rate. There are three cars already parked in the drive: Josh's old Ford, a mud-caked Landrover and a sleek red Jaguar. The latter is out of keeping with Josh's life-style, and the fact that there must be other guests calms me miraculously: it precludes me having to face Josh on my own. The front door is open as usual: an open void with no-one to greet us.

'Just look at that rose,' Sophie murmurs, meaning the pale-pink climber clustered halfway up the house and around the entrance. I turn my head away, tears burning my eyes, to stare across the garden. This is genuinely Claudia's own creation; the sloping lawn, the herbaceous border, the pergola by the lily pond, the spread of wild daffodils in March. She started from scratch, from nothing but a field and with little help. Josh ploughed things up initially with a borrowed mini-tractor and that was that as far as he was concerned, the idle sod. The making of a garden did not interest him. Sometimes I firmly believe he deserved what he had coming to him.

Tucked away to the left I can see the potting-shed, very much Claudia's domain, and the stretch of lawn ending in trees which she called her little garden. Everywhere I look is a reminder of her, but nothing so acutely painful as the empty doorway. Amongst the group of trees near the river there is a large hornbeam; I seem to remember a tree-house hidden in its silvery depths, built by Josh for his small son, Sam. And now, as if I have conjured him up from the past, Sam's figure appears over the incline of grass, instantly recognizable by a thatch of flame-coloured hair, and approaches slowly. He is intent on something he is

31

holding and has not noticed us; reaching the lawn's verge, he steps carefully on to the gravel without looking up. At close quarters he is very grubby, jeans covered in mud, and T-shirt in green stains of either grass or lichen. Sophie and I climb from the car and wait for him.

'Hallo, Sam,' I say clearly before he collides blindly with my legs.

'Hallo, Leo.' He raises a freckled face to mine and smiles, unsurprised.

'It's been a long time. I thought you might not remember me.'

'You haven't changed much. Anyway, Josh said you were coming.'

'You haven't forgotten *me*, have you, Sam?' Ever demonstrative in her affections, Sophie spreads her arms wide for a hug. 'We used to play pooh-sticks on that little bridge over the river.'

'Careful,' warns Sam, stepping backwards. 'Mind my owl.'

For the first time I notice the bird's head peering over his two hands, its huge eyes yellow and mal-evolent.

'Sorry,' he adds, 'but I don't want him squashed, you see. You're Sophie, aren't you? You look different somehow.'

'Well, so do you: much taller.' She squats down to get a better look. 'Isn't he lovely? Where did you find him?'

'Under a tree.' Sam smooths the bird's pale-brown feathers with a thumb. 'I think he'd been rejected by the parent birds. He's only half-grown and there's something wrong with one of his wings. It's not broken, just weak; he ought to be flying by now. That's what I've been doing this morning, encouraging him, but he won't fly.'

'I expect he will when he's bigger. May I stroke him?'

Sam nods. Sophie touches the downy head with a forefinger.

'He's a barn owl. When he's fully grown he'll be pure white,' Sam informs her. He turns to me. 'Do you want to stroke him, Leo?'

'I think the poor thing's had enough, thanks, Sam,' I suggest politely. It might have fleas, for all I know, and its beak looks highly dangerous.

'I'll put him back in his cage for now.' Sam wanders off, stops, says over his shoulder, 'Like to see the rest of my zoo?'

'This afternoon, perhaps. Do you know where we can find Josh?'

'They're out at the back, in the garden. I was meant to tell you but I forgot; sorry. He said to go straight through.'

I watch him walk away, thinking: he is all Claudia, her eyes, her hair, her smile. His chunky build is the only thing inherited from Josh.

'I do like Sam,' remarks Sophie. 'Has he always been mad about animals?'

'As far as I know,' I answer, 'he only had guinea pigs the last time we met. Proper little Gerald Durrell, isn't he? I dread to think what loathsome creatures he has locked up by now.'

'Don't be such a killjoy, Pa!' She slips an arm through mine. 'You and your antipathy to wildlife. Come on, let's look for Josh. I'm dying to find a loo.'

We get no further than the cool dark hall before a door bangs and Josh appears as suddenly and noisily as the Demon King.

'Leo! You old shyster!'

He flings brawny arms around me and thumps me on the back several times. I cannot recall him embracing me before; in our closest moments, there was always an element of reserve between us. Who am I to grumble? I am deeply relieved to find affection where I had expected animosity.

'Thought you'd deserted me for good,' he tells me loudly and reproachfully, as if the separation is my fault; and he turns to Sophie, standing cool and smiling behind me. There is a tiny silence.

'Dear God,' he says, 'she's grown up,' and he kisses her on both cheeks. 'I *am* glad you came,' he adds quite quietly; and then he is himself again, grabbing the overnight bags and leading us up the steep staircase, saying over his shoulder, 'I'll show you where you're sleeping and then come on down for a drink. Marcus is here, and Da. You haven't met Da, have you?'

'Who are they?' Sophie asks me when we are alone.

'Da is Josh's father; he's a retired mineworker who refused to let his sons work down the pits. Don't you remember Marcus, Claudia's son by her first marriage?'

'Oh, *that* one,' says Sophie without enthusiasm.

A shout of laughter bellows out from below my bedroom window and we make a move to join them. I realize Josh has not let me get a word in edgeways beyond a polite murmur. Whether he, too, feels a certain amount of embarrassment at this reunion, I cannot be sure: but I am more than ready for a drink, and that is a commodity one can count on in this household.

'Anyway,' Sophie hisses as we descend, 'Josh is definitely painting again.'

'How do you know?'

'Traces of paint around his fingernails,' she says with the triumph of a Miss Marple.

There is a fly-blown looking-glass on the chest of drawers in my room. It would be comforting to think this is distorting my post-prandial reflection, causing the bags beneath the eyes, the perspiring sallowness of the skin. God! I look unhealthy compared with Josh, swaggering around in faded blue shorts, a mass of tanned muscle. How does he turn that colour? Whatever Sophie claims, it is not achieved closeted in a studio. I do not believe he is working; on the other hand, neither does he give the impression of a man suffering from a nervous breakdown. The last two hours have been an endurance test comprised of alcoholic intake, inedible food and an uneasy assortment of family; and Josh, ebullient as ever, at the heart of it all. He has not flagged yet: I can hear his undiminished voice in the garden, talking to his father, while I, with indigestion, have grabbed at half-an-hour's solitude.

I can see no difference in Josh, and I am in a quandary. The fulsome welcome I received should, by rights, have lulled me into security. Nevertheless, stretched out on the bed, heartburn mingles with a minor qualm. I have been given the worst room in the house: the one where the water pipes gurgle all night and the lavatory flushes with the thunder of Niagara Falls close to one's reclining head. It is dark and pokey: I remember Claudia saying it was only suitable for unwanted guests. I am aware this is not a palace and Josh has a full house, but it would not do young Marcus any harm, for instance, to slum it for a weekend and give up his comparatively spacious accommodation to a senior visitor.

Sophie, I note, is to sleep in the double spare bedroom next to Josh; grudgingly I must admit it is more suitable for a girl, with its chintz and muslin. There is a bathroom between the two rooms, and women like their facilities close to hand. I was never given the feminine spare room in times past and was secretly thankful. It was painful enough imagining Josh and Claudia in the same bed, let alone having to listen to the outcome.

The effects of Josh's food ease gradually. I glance at my watch. It would be delightful to sleep the afternoon away but politeness dictates otherwise: Josh has suggested a walk, just the two of us. Sam has taken Sophie for a row on the river. She is the easiest of creatures, perfectly happy to fall in with whatever plans are made. I could not help feeling enormously proud of her as we walked into the garden before lunch; the sheen of her hair in the sun, the long straight back and slender limbs. Josh and his father were lolling in ancient deckchairs, a litre bottle of wine between them; Marcus was sprawled on the grass scowling absently into space. Josh rose with alacrity: his father remained where he was, apparently mesmerized by Sophie's legs.

'Sophie, this is my da,' Josh said, holding her lightly by the elbow. 'Da, Sophie; Sophie, Da.'

He pulled an extra deckchair closer and gave the recumbent Marcus a prod with his foot. 'You all know this idle specimen. Get to your feet, boyo, and find another chair.'

Marcus shot him a look of intense dislike before loping away.

'He's sulking,' Josh said, 'as usual.'

'Come and sit by me, girl, and tell me what you do,' Da ordered.

Sophie gave him a friendly smile and sank down gracefully beside him.

'Please don't get a chair for me,' she said. 'I'm happier on the grass.' As she sat, the mini-skirt became invisible.

Da was a shrunken first edition of his son; the same carved features, the same build. Knowing little dark eyes shone beneath a thick crop of white hair. His leathery skin was a network of wrinkles, and a scar by his left eye gave the impression of a permanent leer. Josh poured out wine and handed us glasses. Marcus returned dragging a chair behind him listlessly and glanced round him.

'We had enough of these already. Typical,' he muttered bitterly. He erected the one he had fetched. 'Why don't you have this, Leo?' he suggested, and collapsed on the ground exhausted.

'Thank you.' Such extreme lethargy made me wonder whether he was either anaemic or drug-addicted. He did not look well, but then he was the fragile type physically, the sort that women cluck over; not unlike Rupert Brooke, had he been moved to wear his hair in a pony-tail. There was nothing of Claudia in her first-born that I could see. I felt an unaccountable stab of sympathy for him.

'Weren't you aiming for drama school when we last met?' I asked, holding out my glass to be topped up by Josh.

Marcus shot me a look of wary interest. 'I still am. I took an audition for Central.'

'Any luck?'

'Still waiting to hear,' he said, pulling up tufts of grass.

His voice when not mumbling was clear and beautiful.

'And until then,' Josh said, 'he'll be like a bear with a sore arse. Cheer up, chickadee, and fetch me another bottle of this from the fridge, will you? Best to keep him busy,' he explained to me loudly when the boy was scarcely out of earshot.

There was a pause, in which Josh drained his glass and refilled it. 'And how's the Gallery going, Leo?'

'As well as can be expected.'

He smiled down at me. 'Don't tell me the recession has hit you? Not Siegler's, surely?'

'I don't know why you should imagine we would be immune,' I said with a touch of hauteur.

'Sorry,' he said, wiping the grin off his face. 'Didn't mean to get you on the raw.'

'That's all right.' A little of the old affection for him welled up in me. 'The truth is, I've been working flat out recently and I'm quite tired.'

'Do you ever wish,' he asked slowly, 'you could throw it all up and do something different?'

'No, never. I love what I do, always have, always

will,' I added. 'And you, Josh? Is that what you want? It would be a crime, in my opinion.'

I stared up at him, my vision blurred by the sun so I could not read his expression. But I saw his eyes glinting, as if with tears or anger.

'We've got a lot to catch up on, Leo. Later, eh? We'll take a walk along the river, perhaps, just the two of us.'

Marcus reappeared at that moment, a second litre of Muscadet was opened, and Josh padded around us in bare feet, saying, 'Come on, plenty of drinking time before lunch.'

I looked anxiously at Sophie but I need not have worried: she was talking animatedly to Da, her knees drawn up to her chin.

'Do they still take canaries down mines? And those poor little pit ponies?' I heard her ask.

Da was sitting up straight, delighted by the attention. I noticed his yellow polo shirt had 'Lacoste' embroidered on the breast, the pale linen trousers had a knife-edge crease, and I could have sworn the moccasins on his feet were Gucci, or at least an expensive equivalent. I wondered where the cash came from and whether he had accrued it by saving the fruits of his labours or by more dubious means. The Jaguar in the drive tied in nicely with his image and made him a diverting puzzle. The Welsh sing-song of his voice was soporific in the middle of a hot day: under half-closed lids I watched the heat haze dancing at the end of the lawn, smelt the not unpleasant muddy smell of the river, wondered when on earth we were going to eat.

I must have dropped off: the next thing I knew was Sam saying, 'Lunch-time, Leo.'

Stepping blindly from the sun through the open

doors and into the comparative dimness of the kitchen, I had the shocking illusion of seeing Claudia standing there, her hands outstretched: then I realized it was Sophie holding a large bowl of salad. Josh's family were already seated, Da opening a bottle of wine, Marcus running his fingers languidly through a flop of dark hair, his spine curved over the scrubbed wood table. Touches of Sophie's industry were evident in the jug of wild flowers in the centre, and the colourful salad reeking of garlic into which she was busily mixing a dressing. Her actions were so evocative of Claudia that I was unable to watch her, and slipped into the chair beside Sam feeling shaky and dis-oriented. The fact that Josh had shown no aggression towards me allowed me to indulge in nostalgia: to do a little secret mourning of my own. Lucky Josh, able to grieve openly from the beginning, to achieve some sort of peace.

My mouth tasted sour and my head ached dully: wine before meals does not suit me. Da came round the table with a bottle of red and filled my glass before I could stop him. Josh had taken an unevenly cooked pizza from the Aga and was slicing it up and shovel-ling the pieces on to familiar willow-pattern plates.

'Everybody start while it's hot,' he ordered. His voice had increased in volume, the only sign he ever gives of being halfway drunk.

'Pizza again?' queried Marcus mildly.

'Perhaps *you* would like to organize the meals from now on?' retorted Josh with heavy sarcasm.

'I don't mind how often we have it,' Sam said, already attacking his helping, the grime of the morning still on his hands.

'It's very good,' I lied. 'Home-made, Josh?'

'You must be joking.' He grinned at me. 'You know me and kitchens.'

'I don't mind trying my hand at a paella one of these days,' Da said. He sipped his wine delicately, little finger extended. 'Ever been to Spain, Sophie?'

'Once, to Madrid and Toledo.'

'You want to go south, girl. That's where the life is.' He smacked his lips in memory of unknown delights, culinary or otherwise.

'You'll be off any moment, won't you?' Josh said. 'You'd better get busy with the paella. He goes every year,' he said pointedly, 'squandering our inheritance.'

'There's grateful for you,' Da said placidly. 'After slaving away underground for forty years to put him through college—'

'On a scholarship, Da, if you remember—'

'—he begrudges me a bit of fun, is it? *And* sun,' Da said, appealing to Sophie. 'Sun's what you long for when you've lived like a mole for all your working life.'

'I can imagine,' Sophie agreed tactfully. 'Which part do you go to?'

'Benidorm,' Josh told her annoyingly.

Da rose to the bait. 'There's stupid you're talking. A touch of class is what I'm after, not fish and chips and football hooligans, which is what Benidorm amounts to.'

'In fact,' Marcus suggested gravely, 'it's the pits.'

I held my breath at this appalling joke, but nobody else appeared to have heard. Da was too busy describing to Sophie the little hotel he had discovered up in the ills above Marbella, Josh was examining the piece of singed pizza on his plate with distaste, and Sam, who seems to live in a dream world of his own, was several steps behind the conversation.

'Not quite like a mole,' he said pensively. 'Moles are blind, and there's nothing wrong with your eyes, is there, Gran'da?'

Josh snorted. 'Not when it comes to women and money, there isn't.'

'And what's wrong with that?' Da replied. 'There's sense in that,' and his small black eyes roved over Sophie. 'She's lovely, this girl of yours, Leo, but she needs feeding up: skin and bone, she is.'

'You have to be,' Sophie explained, 'if you want to dance.'

'Not in Spain, you don't. You should see the flamenco dancers: there's a tidy armful for you.'

'Bugger Spain!' Josh announced. 'Leave her alone, Da; you ought to be past lechery at your age. Did you see the El Grecos when you were in Toledo?' he asked Sophie.

'Yes, I did. I thought they were rather depressing; all those sad, elongated faces.' She looked at me and smiled. 'Pa thinks I have no taste in art, so my opinion doesn't count for much. The colours were wonderful, though; very like the colours you use, Josh.'

'You noticed that?' He seemed inordinately pleased by the comparison, his whole face lighting up in smug pleasure. 'The girl's observant, Leo. What d'you mean, she has no taste?'

'I never said any such thing,' I protested.

'You don't have to, Pa; I always know what you're thinking.'

'And she makes a great salad,' Josh said, helping himself liberally. He raised his glass. 'A toast: to

42

Sophie, a pearl among swine, and to Leo, my erstwhile guide and mentor, the hunter home from the hills.'

If ever there was a coded message, it was hidden in the last six words: Leo the predator, Leo the wife-stealer. Adrenalin flowed back into my system, prickling the palms of my hands. No-one else noticed, of course.

'To Sophie and Leo,' they echoed obediently, looking puzzled.

'Open the other bottle, Josh bach,' said Da, who had managed to keep pace unobtrusively with his son's liquid intake.

'It's about time,' said Josh through gritted teeth as he drew the cork, 'that *you* contributed something to the cellar. You're flush enough.'

'If I am,' Da replied, 'it's not from sitting on my bottom contemplating my navel, see? When did you last sell a picture, boyo, tell me that? It's pinning my faith on you, Leo, there's what I'm doing,' he added. 'Talk some sense into the boy, get him motivated. Seems to me he's given up on himself, wasting his talent.'

'You haven't the least bloody idea whether I'm working or not working,' Josh said with surprising tranquillity. 'And Leo's down here for a peaceful weekend: we've a great deal to catch up on. So kindly keep your inquisitive old nose out of it.'

'I wouldn't dream of pushing Josh. Artists must be allowed to work at their own pace,' I said firmly, thus establishing my rôle as uncritical protector. I would learn nothing of him by any other method.

'I know he's painting, anyway,' Sam said unexpectedly.

43

'Oh, you do, do you?' Josh stared at him in amusement. 'And how's that?'

Sam returned the stare with a bland, blue one of his own. 'I can smell the turps,' he said, 'and there's paint on your fingers. I suppose you *could* be decorating, but I don't suppose you are because most of the time you're in the studio and there's nothing to decorate there. Does anyone want that last bit of pizza?' he enquired politely.

No-one did: Josh put it on Sam's plate and there followed one of those silences that need to be broken.

'I remember there was a dinghy when I came here last,' Sophie remarked brightly. 'We rowed on the river. Does that still happen?'

'I do, sometimes,' Sam told her. 'Not so much now, though, because of my animals.'

'I'd like to do that this afternoon,' she said, 'only I'm not too good at rowing, I just go round in circles. How about you, Marcus? Would you come with me?'

He looked at her nervously, as startled as if she had suggested they dance naked on the lawn.

'Er – sorry. I've promised to meet someone for a ride.' He uncoiled his backbone and half-rose, saying, 'Do you mind if I go now, Josh? Otherwise I'll be late.'

'And who do you suppose is going to wash up?' Josh demanded.

'I'll do the supper things,' Marcus promised on his way to the door. 'I must get the Landrover back to Desmond or he'll kill me.'

'Desmond, Desmond!' mimicked Josh. 'The boy's life revolves round that old poofter.'

'I'll do the dishes,' Sophie said. 'It won't take a moment.' She started to clear the table.

'Are you going to help, Sam?' Josh asked.

'Yes, if I can have some of the salad for the rabbits. And then I'll take you out in the dinghy, Sophie.'

'I don't mind lending a hand,' Da said, putting an arm round Sophie at the sink.

'No, you don't.' Josh gave his father a push in the direction of the garden. 'I want a word with you. Meet you in half an hour, Leo, and we'll take a walk, OK?'

I stood for a moment, watching Sam put oily lettuce leaves into a plastic bag, and Sophie lift plates from the water to the rack in rhythmic movements: a Degas girl, her feet in the second position, her hair knotted now on the crown of her head. I had one of those waves of apprehension for her future which, much as I try, I cannot always control. Out of the four males in the house beside myself, only Marcus seemed unaffected by her charms; and she was totally unconscious of the fact. I would not be there to guard her forever.

The moment passed. She refused my offer of help, giving me a glance of compassion out of those doe eyes of hers: the compassion of the young for the old.

'Put your feet up, Pa, you look flaked.'

I am forty-nine; nine years older than Josh, five years older than Claudia, not exactly in my dotage. But I can see now what she means when I look in the spotted mirror. It's the turmoil that causes it; luckily she has no idea of the strain I am under.

Funny: I cannot recall her going to Madrid or Toledo.

My watch says three-twenty. I had better get myself off this bed, which dips like a hammock in the middle, and unpack the few things I have brought with me.

The wardrobe door swings back with a banshee-like yowl against the wall. The key has burrowed a hole in the plaster from many previous encounters. The furniture in this room, including the wardrobe, is of the dark, heavy kind: Claudia must have bought up a job lot in a sale. It lists perilously forwards, as if poised to fall across the bed, pinning the hapless occupant to the mattress. I hang up my suit tentatively, knowing perfectly well it will not be needed, but I cannot cure myself of the life-long habit of never travelling without one. The picture over the bed catches my eye: a blue and white jug of roses, inexpertly painted in oils and set in a heavy, gold travesty of a frame, but cheerful nevertheless. I wonder whether it is one of Claudia's efforts from her painting phase. She had many sudden enthusiasms – there was a potter's wheel in the potting-shed for a while – but no staying power, and the whole of the house is strewn with the mainly unfinished results of her labours: curtains without pelmets, cushion covers missing their zip-fasteners, half-embroidered rugs, a glazed mug patterned on one side only. I find it endearing and it makes me want to cry. I peer at the canvas, but there is no signature.

In the bathroom there is no toothglass, one towel that might belong to anyone and a spider in the bath. I return my sponge-bag to the bedroom, deciding that since this is now a bachelor establishment, such defects are natural and should be overlooked. Both the small lattice windows are open, but the room with its low ceiling is hot and airless. Leaning my elbows on the sill, I gaze out on the daisied lawn which slopes down to the river and remind myself of the reason they bought this place. A glint of water can be seen between the willow trees. Swifts curve and swoop in tireless flight against a pale-blue sky; the hill opposite undulates softly like rich velvet in the sun. There is silence apart from the distant crooning of wood-pigeons, and the air smells of grass and roses.

Three figures appear from below me and walk towards the river: Sophie, Sam, Josh, heading for the dinghy which is pulled up on the bank. Sam is carrying the oars. A black and white cat crosses the lawn after them, following like a dog. I had forgotten the cats. There used to be two of them: with any luck one should be dead by now. They are amongst the phobias I failed to conquer and Claudia used to shut them away when I was staying. I don't suppose I can expect the same consideration from Josh, although he has been almost unbelievably affable so far.

I am beginning to think he knows nothing about Claudia and myself: that I have built up an absurd neurosis over his imagined ostracism of me. Bereavement takes people in different ways; quite probably he shunned the company of all his friends and sheer guilt has made me take it personally. One thing is certain: he can't have read the letters. I wish to God that I could convince myself that Claudia had destroyed them, but I know her too well: she hoarded things like a squirrel, and besides, I remember the expression on her face when I asked her. Somewhere in the periphery of the house or garden, they exist. No point in looking for them blindly. Besides, I hadn't expected a household of people; I don't want to be caught scrabbling in drawers or peering into disused storage jars. I need to think logically: no, no time. I need to put myself in Claudia's mind, which was not in the least logical: to imagine her choice of hiding place rather than mine. The task seems virtually impossible and, on the other hand, imperative.

Josh appears reasonably stable. I hate to think of his ignorance being shattered this late in the day. What happened between myself and Claudia is behind us: it cannot be undone and I love her still, but it is past history. It is Josh's future that matters; I would hate to see that talent peter out from neglect. One thing is for sure: no subsequent artist will fire me with the same enthusiasm, the same excitement of discovery. From that first visit to his studio in Hornsey, I found little need to stop and consider the pros and cons of his work; only business sense made me wait a week or so before coming to a firm decision.

Chapter Three

Josh's studio was on the top floor of a Victorian house which had been divided into flats. I found him waiting for me on the doorstep, anxiety written all over his face and in the rigid set of his jaw.

'The entry-phone's out of order,' he explained as he led me up the dark stairs, the smell of cabbage and vindaloo curry accompanying us as we climbed.

The studio itself was north facing and reasonably large; some half dozen paintings were already hung, the residue stacked against the walls. A trestle table holding brushes, paints and the usual tools of the trade was pushed into a corner to give the maximum viewing space. Everything was neat and orderly, including Josh himself, in a pink shirt and black jeans. He had the unnaturally scrubbed look of a child on its first day at school, and his nerves showed through in a rush of jerky, half-finished sentences.

'—not seeing them to their best advantage – they need more space – hung the lastest ones – anything else you'd like to see I'll put on the easel – bloody light's bad today, of course—'

It was: a steady downpour of summer rain under sombre skies streaked the windows. It did not matter: I could see well enough to realize that I was looking at a talent in a league of its own. I did not announce what was in my mind immediately; he had to take me as seriously as I was about to take his paintings. I wandered round calmly, asking a question here, making a comment there, while the excitement over what I was seeing rose in me steadily. A little of his nervousness left him as he busied himself putting picture after picture on the easel for my benefit. Later, when I had seen the collection, he made us mugs of coffee and we sat talking for some time.

Poor wretched artists, living in constant expectation of rejection: I see it frequently, the suspense in their not-daring-to-hope expressions. I try to put them out of their misery one way or the other as swiftly as possible, to leave the unacceptable with a few grains of encouragement: suggestions as to which galleries might be interested in their work and so on. There is great satisfaction in being able to offer something to the outstanding one or two. But I could not remember experiencing the unbridled conviction of success felt in that hour with Josh's work. I did not promise him an exhibition there and then: I knew I had to think it over carefully before committing myself. Many would think me mad to risk a show for a comparatively unknown artist at a time when galleries were playing safe.

'I love them,' I said, quite simply, of his paintings. 'I'm very impressed. I would like to arrange something; give me a few days to go into it and I'll come back to you.' Seeing the painful look of uncertainty in his eyes, I patted him on the shoulder. 'Don't worry, I'm not going to let you slip through my fingers. I mean what I say.'

I left him then. Within three days I had been through the Gallery's commitments for the next twelve months, overcome my misgivings and come to my decision. I telephoned Josh to give him the gist of it, and returned to the Hornsey studio on the Friday. It was raining once more, the whole week had been wet, but nothing could drown Josh's barely-concealed delight. We sat on two upright chairs while I explained the policy of the Gallery, the percentage taken and the way in which we organized our exhibitions. I prepared him for the disappointment of selling a minimal number of pictures; forty-five per cent was considered high in the present recession. He had exhibited elsewhere, had painted for twenty years; much of the information I gave him may have been superfluous, but there was no harm in making things clear from the beginning. He listened, black eyebrows lowering above his eyes in a frown of concentration, nodding from time to time. It took roughly a year to arrange an exhibition: he would have completed new work during that period, and the final choice of paintings would be made quite close to the set date. It was some while before the implications of what I intended sank in.

'Are we,' he asked slowly, 'talking about a one-man show?'

I smiled. 'We don't talk about anything else at Siegler's.'

'My God!' he said quietly. 'That's wonderful. Thank you, Leo.'

He wrung my hand painfully, the colour rushed into his face and he started to cover his depth of feeling with a show of exuberance, insisting on fetching a bottle of vodka and mixing us Bloody Marys. Even in those early days I noticed his emotions lay uncomfortably close to the surface; I felt from then on a curious responsibility towards him.

'Champagne would be more appropriate,' he was saying, 'but we don't run to that, I'm afraid.'

By the time Claudia appeared, the bottle's contents had been halved, I having drunk a token splash since I was driving. I had quite truthfully forgotten about her. She came in accompanied by a small boy, a Sainsbury's carrier bag in each hand.

'What a pig of a day,' she said breathlessly, closing the front door with a foot. 'We're soaked through. Hello, Leo, nice to see you.'

She kissed me as if she had known me for years, her face damp against mine and devoid of make-up. She looked tired and very nearly plain, and less predatory than the way I remembered her: no longer a threat.

'Sorry if we've interrupted, but we couldn't stay out any longer. We'll get out of your light in the bedroom. This is Sam, by the way. Say how d'you do to Mr Kinsey, Sam.'

The boy put a bulky parcel he was carrying on the floor and gave me a small warm hand and an endearing smile; after which he disappeared under the work-table and began the unwrapping.

'Don't you dare let them out,' Claudia warned him.

'Let what out?' Josh demanded.

'Guinea-pigs,' she said, peeling off her anorak.

'You must be mad!' he roared, but without rancour. He was too steeped in euphoria to mind if Claudia had brought home an elephant. 'In six weeks there'll be a dozen of them. And they eat their babies – a disgusting habit.'

'They don't,' Sam said flatly. 'Not if you feed them properly, they don't.' It was obvious he was a born pragmatist.

'Don't take any notice of him,' Claudia told Sam, and eyed the vodka bottle. 'Ah, I thought so. Starting early, I see.'

She sounded unsurprised; it struck me that she treated Josh and Sam with the same fond resignation, as if they were of equal age and status.

'You don't expect Leo to leave without a drink, do you?' Josh said piously.

'I doubt whether Leo's had the lion's share.'

She smiled at me. Behind the smile, I caught sight of a nervous apprehension, perhaps over the outcome of my visit. Were they, I wondered, entirely dependent on Josh's art?

'Celebrating or drowning sorrows?' she asked lightly. 'No, don't tell me. I'm going to put all this in the kitchen,' and she turned to go.

Josh, who was probably only used to announcing his failures, seemed stuck for words and looked pleadingly at me.

'Oh, celebrating, definitely,' I told her, 'speaking for myself.'

'Leo,' Josh said gruffly, 'has decided to exhibit my paintings.' He glared at his feet, cleared his throat. 'A solo – a one-man show,' he added, trying hard to sound matter-of-fact.

Claudia's face lit up and became immediately beautiful. She dropped the carriers and went to put her arms round him.

'How wonderful!' she said, echoing his words. 'That is the greatest news – I can hardly believe it.'

She looked at me over Josh's shoulder and gave me a wholehearted smile, and I wished she had not because it stopped me from thinking coherently.

'I can't imagine how to thank you properly, Leo,' she said.

A guileless remark which only a fool like myself could interpret differently. 'The chance to exhibit Josh's work will bring its own rewards, I'm confident of that,' I replied, aware of my own pomposity and, in my mind's eye, Jane's gently mocking smile.

'He *is* good, isn't he?' said Claudia, giving Josh a kiss. 'He deserves a break.'

She became brisk all of a sudden. 'Goodness! Is that the time? I must get on: we're going down to the country after lunch. To the cottage,' she explained. 'It's our base. There's no room for all of us here.'

Sam stuck his head out from under the table, where he had been temporarily out of sight and mind.

'If Josh sells enough pictures, can we keep the cottage?' he asked. 'Then I can start a guinea-pig farm.'

I left them shortly afterwards. They asked me to stay for spaghetti bolognese but I was due to meet Jane for lunch.

'I didn't realize you were married,' Claudia said. Another time, they urged, anxious to repay me in whatever way possible: come for supper, soon, both of you, they added.

I drove home slowly in the early weekend traffic, my mind entirely taken up with Josh and what I had let myself in for. Such qualms are par for the course: however convinced of a talent one may be, there is no guarantee of its commercial success. I have no partners, no-one with whom to argue and discuss; decisions are mine alone, as are the triumphs and the failures.

It is impossible to say which quality within a work of

art captures the eye and the senses. I remember reading a newspaper interview of a celebrated writer in which he was asked a puerile question about the source of his inspiration. He claimed he could not give an answer: the origin of his thoughts and how he committed them successfully to paper was outside his control. It was a mystery, and what was life without a touch of mystery? So it was in the case of Josh's painting. I could not define the magic, attribute it solely to the brushwork, the excellence of line, the contrast of light and shade, the subtlety of colour. But for me the magic was there, and the mystery as well. I felt compelled to show his work: that it would be a sin to keep it under wraps. I had never had such a compulsion in my life before.

Claudia did not enter into these thoughts once *en route* from Hornsey to Chelsea; it seemed it was only her proximity that occasionally disturbed me. Such mild straying of the libido might just as easily happen sitting opposite a stranger in the tube: or so I decided later, poor deluded bugger that I was.

'I thought I might move Joshua's nude from the bed-room,' I said carelessly. 'Would you mind?'

Jane peered at me over the rim of the bath, her face pink from the steam.

'I'd mind very much. Why?'

'I like to switch things around every so often; you know how it is.'

'What were you thinking of putting in its place?'

I had not expected this opposition. 'The Lowry from the dining-room?' I said off-the-cuff. 'I'm particularly fond of that and we hardly get to see it.'

'Well, I'm particularly fond of "Girl with Cat" and I'd never get to see *that*, would I, if you move things around.' She studied her toes sticking out of the water and added unarguably, 'It's my birthday present.'

'So it is, darling.' I rinsed the toothpaste from my mouth and gave a self-deprecating laugh. 'All right, I'll tell you the real reason. I suppose you'll think I'm mad but it's the cat I can't take.'

'The cat in the painting?' She stood up, little blobs of foam clinging to her anatomy. 'Hand me the towel, would you?' She looked at me pityingly. 'You're mad,' she agreed.

'I can't help it. I've got a phobia about them,' I muttered sulkily.

'Real ones, yes, I can understand,' she continued over her shoulder, padding from bathroom to bedroom. 'But a cat in a picture – honestly, Leo. Come here and look at it.' She dragged me to stand beside her. 'I mean, honestly, you can hardly tell what it is: a small marmalade blob of paint half-hidden by the woman's arm.'

'You're right,' I said. 'You win. Let's forget it.'

'I can't think why you bought it in the first place, if that's the way it affects you.' She gave me a curious look. 'But I don't believe cats have anything to do with your wanting to remove it,' she said mildly.

I could have kicked myself for ever mentioning the subject. It did not produce a row – Jane was one of those people with whom it was virtually impossible to quarrel – but there was an unusual silence, more thoughtful than antagonistic.

Fortunately Sophie came in shortly afterwards and lay on the end of the bed, anxious to chat. She had one of those built-in braces on her teeth that give children the appearance of psychopathic murderers: apart from that, she was potentially beautiful at fourteen, with her straight dark hair and long limbs. I watched the faces of these two women of mine absorbed in their conversation and thought how lucky I was to have married the one and created the other. The three of us formed a small community of our own in the soft glowing comfort of the bedroom; an inviolable charmed circle. I was insufferably smug at moments such as these; but perhaps it was excusable. There had been a curious lack of warmth in my own upbringing.

Jane was listening to what Sophie was saying with a rapt expression. Her hair was tucked behind her ears; tiny, pretty pink ears. I had a picture of the little bits of bath foam adhering to her nipples, and wondered how long my daughter was to be allowed to yatter on. I could hardly say: time for bed, I want to make love to your mother; although it was the kind of statement Josh would have had no inhibitions in making, come to think of it, given the same situation.

If I had had my way, we should never have begun to see Josh and Claudia on a regular basis. I am not keen on getting too close to the artists with whom I am connected; I find it creates problems. One loses a certain amount of authority: they are apt to take advantage of a social relationship, start to demand a say in how their pictures are hung, query the lighting, and argue about commissions and all manner of details that are best left to the experts. They are like school-children in that respect, ideally managed by a mixture of tact, firmness and a modicum of friendliness. Not that I expect to be held in awe: but normally an invitation to the Gallery followed by a good lunch, and a further meal nearer the time their work is to be shown, satisfies everyone concerned. There is a fine line between regulated socializing and the forming of a solid friendship, and we stepped over it in this case. We drifted into it: there was the first time and after that, like most socializing, it became a habit.

I blame the women, which is strange when I consider Jane: Claudia, I well know, had her motives. But Jane had always been the perfect wife where business was concerned: there beside me looking beautiful when the occasion demanded it, staying out of it when not needed, never interfering in things she did not understand but invariably lending an ear and an opinion if asked. Even now I do not know what motivated her to push this friendship the way she did. Women never cease to surprise me.

It was she who said, after Claudia had asked us twice for supper and I had made excuses: 'We must go, darling. It's churlish not to when they're obviously trying to thank you.'

She was arranging flowers as perfectly as she did most other things. I can see her now, dressed in a deceptively simple mint-green frock, blonde hair swinging when she turned her head.

'I can't think why you're so against it. You're apparently excited about discovering him, and I thought you rather liked him,' she added, stripping a delphinium of its leaves.

'I find it rather embarrassing,' I confessed.

'Why, for heaven's sake? I find it even more embarrassing to keep saying no. When they ask us again, which they're bound to do, I'll go on my own if you refuse. Anyway, I'd like to see his paintings.'

'Don't be ridiculous,' I said crossly, acknowledging defeat. 'If you want to know, I'm certain we'll eat out; there's no room at the studio, and we'll have one of those dreadful arguments about who picks up the bill.'

'You'll have to let them,' Jane said calmly. 'Pride and all that.'

Eventually we went, and I was proved right; they had booked a table at a small Italian restaurant round the corner.

'I can't cope with cooking in this place,' Claudia admitted as we had drinks in the cramped kitchen. 'And the only place to sit comfortably is on the bed.' She gave Jane the benefit of her smile and her guileless gaze.

We became separated: whether by design or circumstance it was hard to tell. While Jane stayed behind to look at the paintings with Josh, Claudia and I walked to the restaurant: to claim the table, she insisted, before they gave it away. Her wide silk trousers made a soft swishing sound as we walked, her arm lightly and naturally linked with mine, and the scent she was wearing came and went in little waves on the warm night air. The restaurant was of the check-tablecloth, candles-in-wine-bottles variety; we sat diagonally, which gave me relief from those unrelentingly direct eyes. I ordered a bottle of the house red which the waiter brought accompanied by a bowl of crudités. Claudia bit into a carrot thoughtfully, as if there was something on her mind. I noticed several things about her before she decided to speak. Her mane of hair was held back sleekly by two tortoiseshell combs, her nails were painted red and her face carefully made up. She had made an effort, for some reason. Her teeth were very white and the incisors rather pointed, but those details had presumably been there all along without my noticing.

'This *is* nice.' She took a sip of wine and turned to me. 'You didn't want to come this evening, did you, Leo?'

Everything she said in those first days unnerved me. I made murmurs of denial.

'I can understand it,' she went on. 'You don't like mixing business and pleasure; I'd probably feel the same in your position.' She put a hand over mine where it lay on the tablecloth, and I could not figure out how to withdraw it politely. 'But I'm very grateful you're here. I wanted to have a chance to talk to you alone.'

(*Oh, God!* I thought, breaking out in a sweat.)

'About Josh,' she said.

'Really?' I replied neutrally, strongly opposed to hearing a string of marital confidences.

'Josh,' she said in a reassuringly practical voice, 'is beautifully organized in his studio and hopelessly disorganized when it comes to everyday life. When it comes to keeping appointments, or signing things, it might be best to get in touch with me. I keep the diary and run the business side of things. I sound bossy, don't I?' She smiled at me. 'Perhaps it's not necessary to tell you, but I don't quite know what's involved in the organization of an exhibition on this scale.'

'Nothing too arduous for the artist, but it's as well to know,' I said, my voice hearty with relief. 'If you could give me your country number.'

It makes me laugh to recall this conversation: Claudia was only marginally less chaotic than Josh, as it transpired. She wrote on the back of a card advertising the restaurant and decorated with a floral design. I have it still, tucked in an envelope with other memorabilia.

'The cottage number,' she said. 'I'm there most of the time with Sam. And you've got the studio one. We're making a studio in the barn beside the cottage so Josh can paint there as well.'

'It sounds idyllic.'

'It is. You must come and see it for yourself one of these days: unless, of course, that would be over-fraternizing?' she suggested, and I had the impression she was laughing at me.

'You really have the wrong idea about this evening, Claudia,' I started to protest. I realized it was the first time I had said her name aloud: Claudia. It rolled off my tongue with a rich, smooth sound.

'Josh unwinds down there,' she observed, ignoring the protestation. 'He doesn't drink so much.'

'Is that a problem?'

'Occasionally. It causes rows; he gets bad-tempered when he's had too much, not woolly and amiable like some people.' She selected a radish from the dish. 'He's a very insecure man,' she said.

'A lot of artists are insecure,' I told her. 'It goes with the job.'

'Oh, it has nothing to do with his work. He never loses faith in that. He's convinced he's good, and presumably he's right, isn't he, since you've chosen to exhibit his paintings?'

'More than good,' I said.

'It's something to do with his upbringing as a coal-miner's son growing up in a mining community. I suppose it was a tough childhood in a way, what with the constant grime, and tension over pit accidents and closures, and so on. Nothing has changed much since D.H. Lawrence's day, apparently. All the same, why be ashamed of it? It's a perfectly honourable way to earn a living: rather noble, to my mind.'

I watched her turn the radish between two vermilion nails, her face momentarily shadowed by introspection, and thought of my own childhood, of the protective luxury on the one hand and the bleakness on the other. I wondered whether Josh's boyhood environment, for all its drawbacks, had provided a kind of rough love and family solidarity which mine lacked.

'Is there anyone who *hasn't* got some sort of chip about their upbringing?' I suggested.

'I haven't,' she said, fixing me with wide-open eyes; and I believed her at that moment in time. She oozed confidence and, I decided disapprovingly, lacked a certain understanding for those who did not.

'I'll tell you something,' she confided, 'I'm not looking forward to the next twelve months: the build-up to Josh's exhibition. He'll become impossible as the time draws near, riddled with nerves and quarrelsome with it. He sees forty as a terrible milestone,' she added, 'past which, if he hasn't made a name for himself, he'll be doomed to mediocrity.'

'A perfectly normal supposition for creative people,' I pointed out.

Her negative attitude was beginning to irk me. The wretched man needed someone behind him to dole out calmness and sympathy, not impatience: someone like Jane, for instance. 'I'm sure,' I said firmly, 'you'll manage him splendidly. And I'm quite sure he isn't going to sink into obscurity.'

'I love him,' she said. 'I love Josh very much. Supposing he doesn't sell a single painting? Tell me that isn't possible.'

'Nothing can be guaranteed,' I sighed, 'but I would be extremely surprised, not to mention deeply disappointed.'

She searched my face as if to find a more reassuring answer stamped across it. Presumably some of my irritation showed instead, because she said, 'I shouldn't have bothered you with all this. Now you're cross,' and she gave me the full force of her curving smile. Those large eyes were disconcerting in their innocence, which I already felt to be unreal. One of her combs fell on the table; absently she ran it through the flop of hair before fixing it in place. God knows why this seemed to me an incredibly sexual gesture: I gazed longingly at the entrance, willing Jane and Josh to arrive – why the hell were they taking so long?

Claudia said, 'Well, if he sells nothing, I might just have to leave home: life wouldn't be worth living.' And then she laughed, to show it was meant as a joke.

When the others joined us finally, Jane was bubbling with enthusiasm for Josh's work and he was all sunshine with self-esteem. Always intuitive, she sensed my mood – (I tried to glower at her lateness, but I never succeeded in being out of temper with Jane for long) – and set about being quietly agreeable to Claudia. I comforted myself with the thought that this was merely one evening out of a lifetime, not necessarily to be repeated, as I ate indifferent pasta, drank more than usual and tried to match Josh's ebullient humour.

I was wrong in my thinking, of course; it was only one of many such meetings that were to stretch over the next few months. There were aspects of Claudia which infuriated me in those days. It was wearing on the nerves to be violently attracted to someone you were inclined to dislike and forced to endure her company. I do not imagine Jane realized she was putting me through a form of refined torture, and in any case there was little I could do about it: she had become enamoured with them and was determined to turn them into a cult. Every so often I dug my heels in and refused to see them: but Josh's art and therefore his well-being mattered to me. I felt duty bound to keep an eye on him from time to time since Claudia seemed a doubtful asset as a partner.

A month later I invited Josh for the statutory lunch, to look round the Gallery and to meet Zelda.

Zelda does not approve of our one or two exhibitions a year for contemporary artists: neither does she take kindly to the artists as a rule. She is apt to treat them as very junior members of an exclusive club, reducing some of them to pulp. What Zelda thinks should not matter, but unfortunately she is indispensable when it comes to the administration and the smooth running of Siegler's.

Before he arrived, I talked to her severely about Josh.

'He's special, Zelda. I have great hopes pinned on this one, so please treat him like a human being.'

She eyed me coldly. 'I have no idea what you mean, Mr Kinsey.'

I am addressed as 'Mr Kinsey' only in moments of extreme displeasure.

'I mean,' I said firmly, 'smile, be nice to him, make him feel at home, instead of like a dubious stranger who has stepped in something nasty and brought it in on his shoe.'

She does not smile easily; the most she achieves is a curious twitching of the lips like cracking ice on a puddle. When this happens, it shows that one has managed to tap a minute vein of humour. Her lips twitched now; 'Really, Leo,' was all she said, but it was a good omen.

As it transpired, I need not have worried: Josh delighted her and she fell in love with him. I would not have thought it possible at the time. Now I know him through and through, it no longer surprises me: Josh can charm the birds off the trees when he sets his mind to it. Even I was not immune; only by degrees did I come to realize his basic selfishness and how I had misjudged Claudia. I had told him something of Zelda: he arrived with a dozen yellow roses and spent almost as much time chatting her up as admiring my elegant Gallery. It consists of two rooms divided by double doors; I folded these back for him so that he could get an idea of the complete space it offered. This subdued him considerably and he wandered in deep thought along the pale grey walls, studying some of the lesser-known Impressionists that we were showing currently: stopping finally in the centre of the room and spreading his arms wide.

'My God, Leo!' he said, looking at me apprehensively. 'Are you intending to use the whole place for my pictures? They won't cover the half.'

'You'll be surprised,' I reassured him. 'They need to be widely spaced: we don't hang our pictures on top of each other. Besides, you'll have completed some additions by that time. How many, do you imagine?'

He ran a hand through his already ruffled hair. 'Four? Six? I don't know exactly. I don't paint quickly,' he said nervously.

'Don't worry about it,' I soothed him. 'Leave that to me. Come upstairs to the office and we'll have a drink before lunch.'

On our way out he scooped one of Zelda's square practical hands off the desk and raised it to his lips, making her flush. It was the nearest I had seen her come to simpering. He relaxed rapidly under the influence of a large vodka and a bottle of wine with our meal: I had chosen an unpretentious restaurant on purpose as an antidote to the awe-inspiring effect of the Gallery.

These informal get-togethers are designed to unwind anxious temperaments, not to impress, and I try to avoid talking shop. There is little to discuss at this stage before an exhibition. Instead I entertained him with a potted version of Siegler history, a ploy as statutory as the lunch itself and one which invariably has a calming effect. Josh was no exception: he listened in silence, nodding occasionally and obviously engrossed, since he seemed lost in another world. I caught him smiling once or twice which puzzled me: I could not remember saying anything particularly humorous. For a moment I had that unpleasant sensation of dwindling to insignificance in the face of a more powerful personality, and wondered whether I had banged on about the same subject a little too long.

Siegler's is admittedly one of my hobby-horses.

I ordered brandy for us both, asked a few questions and was rewarded with an untheatrical account of his childhood which belied Claudia's theory. I suppose my surprise showed through because he laughed suddenly, watching my expression through narrowed green eyes.

'You've been talking to Claudia,' he remarked without malice. 'She loves to invent complexes for me, to explain my drinking habits. I like drink and that's all there is to it.'

'I think she only mentioned that life was tough in a mining community,' I said diplomatically.

'I loved it. It isn't all coal and grime; the country around is beautiful.' His accent became stronger with his mind on home. 'There was rugger, we all played, even the girls until they got too large in the chest. I wanted to work down the pits when I grew up, so did my brothers: it seemed a brave and grand thing to do. Ever been down a mine, Leo?'

I shook my head.

'It's a world apart, dark and mysterious; primeval, really.' He grinned. 'I wouldn't look at it like that now, of course: I'd see it as uncomfortable and bloody dangerous. My da wouldn't let any of us work there: he was an ambitious old bugger, still is, but he was right. I liked drawing, used to draw the miners coming up from their shifts; that's how I got started. There was this art teacher at school, Miss Griffiths, had a bottom like a rhinoceros, but she encouraged me: she told Da I should go to art school, try for a scholarship.' He drained his glass and shrugged. 'So I did,' he said, 'and I got it.'

'The birth of a figurist; I'm glad we didn't lose you to the mines. Do you still have the drawings?'

He nodded. 'Claudia found them, put them together in a folder.'

Claudia went up a notch in my estimation.

'They're childish scribbles, no more than that,' he said.

'Never mind: one day they'll be of value.' I ordered a second brandy. 'Do you ever go back to your roots?' I asked.

'Not often.' He paused, then added, 'But I'll have to go before long. My mam's dying.'

'I'm sorry,' I said.

'Yes, thanks. By rights it should be Da on his last legs from emphysema, but there's nothing wrong with him.'

I had the impression this would have been a preferable tragedy. 'At least you have Claudia to go with you,' I suggested by way of comfort.

'I doubt it. Someone has to stay with Sam.' He finished his cheese and sighed with satisfaction. 'That was good, Leo: a great change from Chinese take-aways. Besides,' he added, 'Claudia's never got along with my family. Da's all right, he's a sucker for women; Mam claims she puts on an act, but it's my having married a divorced woman that really gets to her. She's staunch Chapel, is Mam.'

'Claudia was divorced?'

'It was a long time ago.' He brushed it away. 'Long before I came on the scene.'

'Whoever you married,' I said, gesturing for the bill, 'I suspect she wouldn't have been good enough in your mother's eyes.'

' "Why can't you find yourself a nice natural girl?" – that was her one cry.' He leaned towards me across the table, confidential with food and wine. 'Someone like Jane would have gone down well with her,' he said. 'She has all that lovely tranquillity and tact. Claudia doesn't have either.'

He gave a bellow of laughter, indicating the second brandy had been a mistake. Heads turned: it was time to leave.

'But Claudia's right for me,' he added. 'I need pushing, and she pushes like a bloody bulldozer. I'm a lazy sod at heart.'

I saw him safely on to the correct bus, where he raised an arm in salute through the windows: a bear-like figure with tie askew and shirt parting company with trouser waistband. I felt a small surge of warmth towards him. The lunch had been enjoyable: a chance to get to know him without the disruptive effect of women. At that point I was tiring of Claudia's company playing havoc with my emotions.

When I got back to the Gallery, Zelda had got a firm grip on her emotions and obviously regretted the brief airing she had allowed them. The roses were in a vase on her desk.

'Isn't he charming?' I asked her blandly.

'If you like the extrovert type,' she said, her eyes hidden safely behind her glasses. 'It's his competence that counts, rather than his social graces.'

She realigned an already immaculate pile of papers.

'In this case, it's more than competence,' I said. 'Wait until you see what he produces.'

'Do you have photographs?' she asked, trying not to sound intrigued.

'No, that wasn't how I discovered him. But I own one of his paintings. Come and see it this evening,' I suggested, 'if you'd like to.'

'Very well, then,' she replied surprisingly. 'I will, thank you.'

The way my memory has taken me, it might be supposed that life revolved round Josh and Claudia. This is not true: they formed only a minor part of it in those first months. Days went by without my giving them a second thought. Being back here in their cottage has made them assume an exaggerated importance in the normal contented progress of my everyday existence.

Sometimes, like now, I almost resent their intrusion. It messes up the otherwise unsullied vision I have of that summer: Jane's last. A good English summer for once, when everything flowered profusely at the right time, the Gallery was running successfully despite increasing economic pressure, the brace came off Sophie's teeth and I watched her dance Aurora in her end-of-term production of 'The Sleeping Beauty', tears wetting my cheeks. I am unable to watch her dance without crying; gripped by hopeless sentimentality inherited, I suspect, from my German forebears. Jane seemed to blossom during those months: a second blooming that reminded me of our first falling in love, the same kind of radiance about her. The mood was infectious and our sex life, always good, took an adventurous and exhilarating turn towards the erotic. At one point I wondered whether she was pregnant, hardly daring to hope, for this was how the start of Sophie had affected her: forgetting, in my hankering after a son, the difficulties this would present. There were complications with Sophie's birth and she had been advised not to have another child. But my wild surmise was proved wrong, and after a brief stab of disappointment I settled for the bliss Jane provided without questioning the reason. Thinking back, I see it now as a concession, this sudden extra zest for living, to compensate her death.

I cannot remember seeing much of Josh and Claudia in the summer. Either I have forgotten or life was absorbing enough to make their company irrelevant. Certainly Claudia's presence no longer threw me into a state of nervous tension when we happened to meet. Occasionally I needed to discuss some detail or other with Josh, in which case I telephoned her to arrange a date for us to get together; and she had joined Jane on a picture-framing course, so that the relationship between us all seemed to have slipped into satisfying normality. Three occasions have stuck in my mind: a private view at the Gallery to which Josh and Claudia were bidden for his enlightenment; a day spent with them in the country – (my mind's eye can see Claudia and Jane now, standing together at the end of the lawn, and Sam chasing Sophie in some game or other) – the only time Jane was to visit them; and lastly, a disastrous evening shortly after our return from holidaying in Greece, when we invited them to supper.

I am glad about Greece: it was the highlight of our year and I have grateful, tender memories of it. We sat around the kitchen table, Jane and I trying not to be boring about what we had seen and done, and uncomfortably aware of our tanned skins against Claudia's noticeable pallor. From the moment they arrived I could sense an undercurrent of dissension: Josh was unusually subdued and Claudia distracted by some private reverie. Even with a liberal flow of wine the conversation flagged. Towards the end of my description of a Cretan monastery, Claudia interrupted with an arresting non-sequitur.

'I'm going to have a baby,' she announced cheerfully.

There was a short, stunned silence, broken almost immediately by Jane.

'What wonderful news! Congratulations; well done, both of you.'

I thought she sounded a little too emphatic.

'Wonderful!' I echoed, feeling deeply envious. Claudia smiled at each of us. It appeared to me that she had softened, become less dynamic, as if nature was already slowing her down.

'Thank you,' she murmured.

'When is it due?' Jane asked.

'Bang in the middle of the exhibition,' Josh said sarcastically. All eyes turned on him, his distemper blatantly apparent. 'A baby was *not* on the agenda. Someone,' he added, eyebrows meeting each other, 'has been inexcusably careless.'

He glared at Claudia. She glared back. 'You, perhaps?' she suggested.

Intervention of some sort, I felt, was urgently needed before a full-scale row developed. I looked helplessly at Jane who was generally so skilled in diplomacy, but she was staring fixedly at her plate.

'Come on, Josh,' I said. 'You'll be over the moon when it arrives, you know that; and it won't make the slightest difference to the exhibition, except Claudia may not be there for the private view.'

'Exactly. And I want her there, not pushing and moaning on a hospital bed.' He was pouting his sculpted lips like a spoilt child. 'All those nappies and sleepless nights,' he groaned, 'and we can't afford another brat, anyway.'

'Shut up, Josh,' Claudia said automatically, as if she had been through all this before. 'You're embarrassing Jane and Leo.'

'There'll be no peace: constant mewling and puking. I shan't be able to *work*,' he remarked petulantly. 'At the most important crossroads of my life, this has to bloody happen.'

Claudia leant her elbows on the table, rested her chin on clasped hands and looked at him with the calmness of a Madonna. 'I'm quite prepared to leave you, if you like,' she said.

'I think I'll make some coffee,' said Jane.

Josh lowered his head and stuck out his jaw belligerently, but his eyes avoided Claudia's.

'You're too old for child-bearing,' he muttered, 'in my opinion.'

This statement was his final undoing. Claudia pushed back her chair and rose abruptly, her face stony with anger.

'Right,' she said, 'I'm going.' She turned to Jane. 'Sorry, Jane, to ruin the evening, but I can't listen to this selfish bastard a minute longer. As for your opinion,' she told Josh, 'you can stuff it.'

She kissed both of us on the cheek and went swiftly to the door. 'And don't bother coming home tonight,' she said over her shoulder. 'The door will be bolted.'

'Claudia!' Josh roared. Her footsteps could be heard running up the basement stairs.

'Claudia, wait.' Jane disappeared after her. There was the noise of a car revving up and shooting away in the street outside: then silence.

It needed an enormous effort to disassociate myself from their situation. Friendliness towards Josh was out of the question: I retreated into the kind of cool civility at which I excel when necessary. Out of common courtesy we offered him a bed but mercifully he bumbled away on his own into the night, covering up sheepishness with bravado; arrogantly confident that Claudia would relent with a little persuasion. I had longed to go to her, to put my arms round her purely in a gesture of comfort. His words, his attitude, belonged to a part of him I had not known existed: all the less acceptable to me because I was acutely envious of their so-called mistake. From this evening onwards, although I was not aware of it, my involvement in their lives was being built around me, brick by invisible brick, corralling me in until escape became impossible.

Jane was unusually quiet as we cleared up and went to bed. There was none of the animated discussion we normally indulged in, happily picking over the bones of the evening's entertainment. I made one or two remarks about Josh's boorish behaviour while I dried the glasses and I remember her reply. She had her hands in the sink and did not turn her head as she spoke.

'He's frightened for her,' she said simply, without elaborating.

I was amazed at her remark: even if there was a grain of truth in it, it should not excuse him. I wondered whether she had thought about another child with the same longing as myself. We did not talk about it and perhaps we should have done so; she never quite recovered her sudden burst of enthusiasm for living. I cannot completely absolve Josh and Claudia from blame for putting out that light; after all, it stemmed from their disruption. A month later, Jane was dead.

I cannot think about her death, and yet I cannot blot it out from my memory. The inability to forget, to put a veil over it, is a punishment for subsequent crimes: I know it. Outside the sun is shining, Josh is about to summon me for a walk, and still I have to run through the whole sequence of events like some compulsively horrible video. (Why doesn't he shout for me, break the continuity?)

Sophie in bed with 'flu, and my saying goodbye to her before leaving for the Gallery: that is how it starts. The traffic is bad. I reach the Gallery late. Zelda, factual but pale as death itself, is at the door with Sophie's hysterical telephone message. The journey home is a blank. I can recall nothing of it: one minute I am with Zelda and the next standing inside my front door staring down at Jane sprawled by the foot of the stairs. One arm is thrust forward, the other one flung back; she looks as if she is doing the crawl. Crockery, some of it in pieces, lies scattered around her; an open honey jar spills its contents in a golden pool; a tray has slid across the parquet as far as the drawing-room. The scene is faintly ludicrous, and as unreal as a country house murder: I remember thinking that, unable to believe in her death long after the experts had confirmed it and taken her away.

And then there is Sophie, sitting on the top step of the stairs; not crying, making no sound, but shuddering uncontrollably. I pick her up and put her to bed and bring hot-water bottles, and still the shuddering continues. The doctor gives her a sedative: she sleeps. The cleaner weeps as she clears up the mess in the hall. Suddenly the place looks spotlessly normal, mocking me in its sameness, inviting me to picture Jane's imminent return from some shopping spree or one of her classes: and Jane has gone, vanished inexplicably and forever because of a heel caught in a dressing-gown.

How can one accept such a thing? For days, nights, weeks I struggled with my unacceptance. I watched Sophie struggling also and, braver than I, winning. Sleepless, I would beat at the pillows with my fists and shout: 'Where are you, damn you? How dare you do this to me?' It is not time but exhaustion that heals in the end, so far as healing goes. The mind gets worn out from grief. I believe Sophie literally danced her pain away. As for myself, one might think that Claudia was the ultimate healer, but it was not so; Jane and she remained quite separate entities.

In fact, after the paraphernalia of bereavement, the funeral, the flowers, the letters of condolence, was behind me, it was Claudia who sought me out for solace and reasons of her own. I did not know it at the time: her telephone call some weeks later was ostensibly to enquire after my state of mind. Had I guessed at other motives, I might well have withdrawn, acted with the instinctive caution she had always instilled in me. But my instincts were blunted; I was living in what can best be described as a vacuum: working, eating, communicating automatically. It was out of this blurred no-man's-land that I asked her to lunch. How much stress and confusion could have been avoided if I had not done so: and how much I would have missed.

A rap on the door jerks me sharply out of my reverie: Josh is demanding to know if I am ready. I have not changed my beautifully comfortable loafers for those trainers which are considered more suitable for country walks and which frankly hurt because I have not broken them in. I put the past away for the time being and reluctantly prepare myself for the present. I can't think what the hell we are going to talk about.

Chapter Four

We cross the lawn, passing Da stretched out asleep with his torso in one chair and his feet on another: a newspaper covers his face and he is snoring gently. There is a narrow path that runs by the river, and we strike off to the right, in single file by necessity. Josh's back view looks uncommunicative.

On either bank the weeping willows bow to their reflections in the water; glimpses of hillside appear between them, curving softly upwards towards a light-blue sky, with two riders crossing the slope like flies. I do not know this route well: it arouses no nostalgia in me. Claudia and I used to walk in the opposite direction whenever we had the chance. There is a beech wood before one reaches the village where delightful hollows are lined with moss and fallen leaves as comfortable as a feather mattress. I have no wish to go that way: Josh's company would embarrass me.

The path is getting more and more overgrown as we progress, a tangle of tall grasses interlaced with wild flowers brushing our legs. I recognize only the poppies. Josh is carrying a cleft stick which he uses to whack at the undergrowth. He is wearing the same shorts as before and I notice his dark hair has grown long over his neck; staff in hand, he looks like some muscular prophet. I find our silence oppressive.

'What are these mauve flowers called, Josh?'

'Haven't a clue,' he says over his shoulder. 'You know me; I can't tell a tulip from a daisy, let alone the wild flora. Claudia was the one for that.' He stops so suddenly I almost run into him, and peers at the plant in question. 'It's probably "Milkmaid's Tits" or something similar: they all have extraordinary names.'

He gives a bellow of laughter before marching on; the feeble joke seems to have lightened his mood.

'We'll cross by the plank bridge,' he says, 'and walk to the top of the hill. Think you can manage that?'

'Of course,' I reply, stung by the veiled disparagement of my physical ability. The trainers are already beginning to pinch.

A tub-shaped dinghy appears, turning circles on the river with Sophie at the oars, and Sam in the stern giving instructions. She shouts, 'I'm no good at this,' giggling helplessly, and waves. An oar falls overboard and starts to float downstream. Sam, wearing bathing pants, leaps after it, the boat rocks hectically, Sophie shrieks. They are in no danger: the river is little more than a broad stream. I am glad one of us is enjoying ourselves: she has a foot firmly implanted still in childhood, and I am happy for her.

'I should take those shoes off,' Josh says mildly. 'Let them dry out a bit.'

We have, to my amazement, reached the peak of the hill and the relief of reclining on warm springy turf is enormous.

'I'll never get them on again. There must be better routes than through a bog,' I point out tetchily.

'If you'd followed me, you'd have been all right.'

'I did, more or less. It looked like grass, anyway, where I was stepping.'

'Those are the boggiest bits,' he explains, hands behind his head, gazing at the sky.

'So now he tells me.' I stare at the peat-brown, soggy shoes, thinking what a ridiculous conversation for two grown men: but safer than some topics.

'Poor old Leo.' He studies me lazily, his eyes green slits under heavy lids, and laughs softly. 'You never were made for the country exactly – the "Good Life" – were you?'

'On what do you base that assumption?'

'Well, your clothes, for instance,' he says, grinning.

'What's wrong with them?' I am genuinely hurt by this remark. There are some people whose clothes continue to look new however well-worn, and I am one of them. This weekend I have tried hard to get it right: my oldest lightweight trousers, casual shirt, these bloody trainers.

'I honestly don't know,' he says in puzzlement. 'I think it must be you: the man making the clothes rather than the other way round. Whatever you wore, the effect would be urban.'

Below us the house, the river, the village and the woods are laid out in perfect composition. The spire of Lower Pelling church rises above the trees, a grey index finger fringed with young and brazen green. The river is a pale snail's thread trailing from one side of the canvas to the other. For I find myself admiring it with an art-expert's eye as I would a Constable, which it resembles markedly. Josh is right: I can't appreciate the country for itself alone; I am an urbanite at heart, and the sight of this particular patch shouts 'Claudia' at me unbearably.

'Nothing wrong with that,' he says, luckily misconstruing my silence. 'It's an acquired taste, the country.'

'Well, at least I can't compete with your father when it comes to sartorial perfection.'

Josh snorts with laughter. 'Dresses like some old poofter in the South of France, doesn't he? Now *he's* acquired an ex-pat's mentality.'

'And the means?' I enquire, curious to know.

'Enough for his little luxuries. He saved: not your sock-under-the-mattress saving. He did it the conventional way, stashed so much away a month in a building society. When Mam died, he started to play the stock market: saver-turned-gambler. None of us knew until recently. Now he lands himself on all his children in turn and lives the life of Riley. I get more than my fair share of him.'

'A dubious compliment,' I suggest.

'Oh, he's not a bad old bugger,' Josh admits grudgingly. 'Seems to think it's his duty to keep an eye on me, for some reason. Even offered me a loan the other day.' He grins sardonically. 'A loan, mind you, not a share of the profits.'

He appears to ponder in silence the vagaries of his parent, while I study my feet and wonder how long it will be before I can remove the soaking footwear.

He sits up abruptly. 'I'm not being much of a host, am I? Dragging you through bogs, hiking you to the top of hills. I expect you miss Claudia.'

My heart and stomach leap together in panic.

'Home comforts,' he adds pleasantly. 'She knew how to provide them; I don't.' Innocent words, innocently spoken. 'Sorry about the room, by the way, but there wasn't much choice with the mob I've got staying.'

I pull myself together with an effort of will. 'It's fine, Josh. Everything's fine. Isn't that Marcus over there, in the distance?' I observe quickly.

Away to our right the riders have dismounted and are sitting engrossed in conversation, the reins looped over their arms. Josh swivels his head.

'Oh, God! So it is. With Desmond, dreadful old queen.'

'Who is Desmond exactly? What does he do?'

'Chases boys like Marcus.' He snorts in disgust. 'He runs the livery stables, and Marcus likes horses for some unknown reason, as well as Desmond.'

'Marcus isn't gay, is he?'

'I don't know. What do you think?'

'He doesn't strike me that way.'

Josh sighs. 'Frankly, I don't like being responsible for him. Don't know why he comes down here so often; he's got a perfectly good father of his own.' He slaps morosely at a persistent fly. 'He irritates me; I can't help it, I'm no good with teenagers, they're so bloody idle.'

'Sam will be one eventually,' I point out.

'That's different. He's my own; I love him.'

I think: simple as that; poor Marcus.

'And Sophie,' I add, 'is a teenager.'

'Ah, Sophie,' he says. 'She's a creature apart.' He pauses in thought. 'I don't *dislike* Marcus, although I get the feeling he's taken a scunner against me ever since Claudia's death. Maybe he blames me for it; I don't know.'

'How could he logically do that?'

'Feelings aren't always logical.' His mood, I can tell, has become introspective, the effects of the lunch-time drink having worn off. 'I don't pretend to be a good stepfather; I wasn't a particularly good husband. I used to think I was a good artist. Now I'm far from sure—'

'You know my opinions on that,' I tell him firmly. 'Look at the success of your exhibition; the number of pictures sold should have put paid to any doubts you may harbour about your ability.'

He does not answer; it seems an ideal moment to ask him about the future.

'It takes time to recover from someone dying; a long time. I should know—'

He lifts an eyebrow. 'Jane?'

'Of course.' It seems an odd question.

'Of course.' He nods.

'Creativity naturally suffers under depression.' I must find the right words. 'People are beginning to ask what happened to you, Josh. It would be a tragedy if your talent were never to see the light of day again.'

'I'm working in my fashion,' he says. 'I've never stopped working, if that's what you mean.' He gives me a peculiarly mirthless smile. 'Let's talk about it later, Leo. I'll be more fluent on the subject with a drink inside me.'

The figures of Marcus and the despised Desmond have risen to their feet. Eying them, Josh says, 'We'll start back now, if you're ready, in case they come drifting over. I'm not in the mood for chat.'

We return the way we came, my shoes squelching and slithering on the cropped grass. Going downhill brings a whole new set of muscles into play.

'It wouldn't surprise me if the boy's gay,' Josh says suddenly. 'He was mad about his mother; followed her round like a dog when it was her turn to have him here for the holidays. A touch of the old Oedipus, I should think. It annoyed me; I suppose in a way I was jealous.'

He laughs, swinging his stick at a thistle. 'Don't know why I minded; I should have been used to half the male population being in love with Claudia.'

I make no reply, uncertain of being in control of my voice. High above us a skylark sings, a speck in the blue. Nearby a larger bird, a hawk of some kind, hangs motionless on spread wings, then dives without warning. For a second I imagine the lark as its prey, but it sings on unconcerned while the hawk plummets earthwards with the speed and precision of a missile on some wretched fieldmouse. No time to run, to hide: it would not stand a chance against the accuracy of those long-distance, callous eyes. I shudder slightly, my distaste for nature confirmed.

Josh leads me back a different way through the garden; we approach between a beech tree and the hornbeam where Sam has his house.

'See that?' he says, pointing upwards into the branches at the wooden platform and the rope ladder. 'I'm proud of that; it's lasted well.'

We move up the slope towards the wall which borders the north side; two outbuildings built of the same soft red weathered brick stand at right angles. One is Claudia's domain, the potting-shed; the other houses Sam's zoo, so Josh informs me, quickening his step. I sense a sudden restlessness in him: but then his moods have always fluctuated, unpredictable as the weather.

'Better see if he's boring the pants off Sophie,' he says. 'She'll have had enough of him by now.'

'She likes younger people,' I protest. 'She won't mind.'

All around us I see evidence of neglect: the same goes for indoors, where fingerprints pattern the dust on table-tops and curtains sag forlornly from lack of hooks. But then Claudia could not have been called house-proud; the garden was her spiritual home on which she lavished hours of hard work and attention. The grass where we are walking, once a lawn as smooth as the one that runs down to the river, is now a hayfield; the herbaceous border under the wall a mass of overgrown plants, mostly dead or dying from thirst. The giant purple clematis growing over the potting-shed has a few pathetic flowers amongst a tangle of old and rotten wood. It saddens and angers me: this place of all places should be kept as her memorial.

'You'll need a scythe for the grass if it's allowed to grow much longer,' is the only comment I make: but it is enough to get Josh on the raw.

'Bloody hell, Leo,' he snaps, swinging round on me. 'What d'you think I am – Superman? I shop, I cook, I look after Sam. I run the fucking show, there's no-one else. Something has to give, and it has to be the garden because to me it's the least important.'

'Look, I'm sorry, Josh. It was a stupid remark under the circumstances; I wasn't thinking.'

I mean what I say, rattled as I am by his outburst and hating to be shown up as insensitive.

'It's OK, it's OK,' he says shortly, and knocks a few

heads off plantains with his stick. We take a pace or two in uncomfortable silence before he stops again and sighs.

'There is another reason,' he admits, looking around him. He appears deflated, as if his anger has vanished with the sigh. I notice lines beneath his eyes for the first time. 'I don't like coming here more than is necessary: it reminds me of Claudia.'

And that is the curious difference between us: he shuns the memory while I cling to it.

'I understand,' I lie to him reassuringly. 'Don't you have any help in the house? What's happened to – what was her name? – Mrs Morse?'

'She comes in when I need her: roughly once a week to do an almighty clean-up. And she'll still take Sam for the night if I'm away, which isn't often.' Glancing at his watch, he moves on. 'Can't afford her on the old basis,' he says. 'I'm not exactly flush. D'you realize, I've sold only one picture in the last six months?'

'Have you tried?' I am suddenly exasperated by his defeatism and the cloak of mystery surrounding his present work. 'Doors were opened for you: we saw to that. They're still open. Why,' I ask at last, 'haven't you contacted me?'

He pauses, leans against the wall of the potting-shed.

'Why not?' he asks thoughtfully of himself. 'It was the obvious answer, wasn't it? Carry on as before under the wing of my friend and benefactor, as if nothing had happened. Continue to paint to the same approved recipe: like mother's chocolate cake, every one a winner. Sorry, Leo,' – my face must register shock – 'if that sounds ungrateful, because I'm not. It was a great temptation to get hold of you: how easy and comfortable to let you deal with my renaissance. But events had changed me, the way I painted, my outlook on life. I preferred to blunder around in the wilderness and work it out for myself.' He grins at me, his teeth white in a sun-browned face. 'You were the only temptation I've ever resisted, Leo. Extraordinarily difficult to manage, isn't it? Or perhaps you wouldn't know.'

He speaks softly: in the shadow of the shed I feel all at once chilled to the marrow.

'By the events that changed you,' I say, clearing my throat, 'I presume you mean Claudia's illness and death?'

'Those, and others that gnaw away at your vitals,' he agrees. 'You know how it is.'

'I don't much care to be viewed in the guise of the devil,' I remark in an attempt at lightness.

'Oh, don't take it to heart,' he says, clapping me on the shoulder. 'It was just a simile, that's all, to illustrate a point.'

'Point taken,' I tell him a little sourly. 'I'm curious to know, though, what moved you to lift the telephone and dial me eventually?'

'I found myself missing you.' He looks at me with simple sincerity. 'Above all, I count you as a friend and it seemed ridiculous to lose you. Besides, I'm getting rather tired of the wilderness,' he adds. 'I reckon I've done my forty days and it's time to move on.'

From the direction of the zoo shed, the murmur of voices can be heard, and Sophie's infectious giggle.

'Let's go and dig them out.'

'Josh.' I put a hand on his arm. 'I'd like to see what you've painted recently. Despite this emotional maze of yours, I might still be of help; you never know.'

'All right,' he says carelessly. 'But you won't approve; it's not your scene, Leo.'

The inside of Sam's menagerie smells like most zoos: clean but nonetheless pungently of animals. Three sides are occupied by wire cages of varying sizes, and to the right of the door a long shelf is fixed to the wall and stacked with tins and paper bags. Everything is very neatly organized, and there are two buckets, a scrubbing brush and a bale of straw beneath the ledge.

I take in the spartan lay-out, consider it as a possible venue for hidden letters and discard the thought immediately. The place is unsuitably orderly for secrets: Sam would have discovered them long ago. Supposing he has already done so? My heart misses a couple of beats: I find the idea particularly distasteful.

We are alone now, he and I, Josh having taken Sophie away on some unspecified ploy. I am quite sure he is showing her the studio: it aggravates me that she should be granted the privilege freely where I have to beg. Typical of Josh's arrogance; he will find he can go too far with that attitude. My livelihood does not depend on his work, thank God. From the open doorway I can see their figures heading in the direction of the barn, his hand resting on her shoulder; ostracized, I give my attention to Sam. He is putting a rabbit into its cage; all along the stretch of wire netting, sharp bright eyes glitter balefully at me from their enclosures.

'Isn't it rather unkind to keep them shut up?' I query.

'They've all been injured.' Sam looks at me as if I am slightly retarded. 'I wouldn't do it otherwise.' He fixes the hook on the rabbit's door. 'When they're well enough I let them go. Look.'

He leads me slowly from cage to cage. 'That's the barn owl you saw this morning. He's ready to fly but he's a bit lazy. And this is my cub. He's called Troy.'

The creature is curled up asleep, nose to bushy luxuriant tail, the colour of autumn leaves: an attractive specimen as animals go. 'It's a fox cub,' I remark intelligently, and Sam gives me another of those glances.

'Why the name "Troy"?' I ask hurriedly.

'Well, he's only got three legs, and "trois" is French for three, but it's difficult to say, so I've made it Troy. You can't call someone "Three", can you? It sounds daft.'

'It certainly does,' I agree. 'What happened to the other leg?'

'He got it caught in a steel trap. They're illegal, but poachers use them sometimes.' Sam scowls, oddly contorting features better designed for good humour. 'I'd shoot them if I could catch them. It was in the woods: luckily I found him, Troy I mean, before he died or got killed. The leg was already chopped off.'

I feel queasy: how can children be so matter-of-fact about murder and mutilation?

'Shooting a poacher wouldn't be worth the trouble; perhaps it's as well you don't have a gun.'

'Josh has.' He moves on to the next inmate.

'He has?' Josh with a gun is unimaginable. He hates loud bangs.

'He doesn't use it, but it's there. It's a burglar-scarer, in case anyone breaks in.'

'Good Lord!'

'Come and look at my toad, Leo.'

I do so with reluctance; frogs and toads are particularly abhorrent, in my view. There is no straw in the cage; instead, Sam has built a kind of rock-pool, in the middle of which sits this hideous creature, covered in warts and liver-coloured spots, blinking and gulping as if regurgitating an ample meal. It is a caricature of a human gourmand. Luckily this is the last of the cages: I have run out of spurious comments.

'You're bleeding.' Sam is staring at my feet with interest. The back of the left trainer is tinged with red. 'Does it hurt?'

'Yes.'

'I expect it's a burst blister,' he remarks. 'I'll bandage it for you, if you like.'

'I think I'll go back to the house, thanks all the same, Sam; find some elastoplast.'

'There won't be any. Josh never remembers to buy things like that.' He stretches out a hand unerringly and lifts a tin box from the other objects on the shelf. 'Sit on the step and take off the shoe and I'll do it for you.'

The shoe has rubbed a hole in the sock: I remove both gingerly while Sam opens up a surprisingly comprehensive First Aid kit and proceeds to clean my heel with disinfectant and cotton wool.

'What's that?' I ask suspiciously as he unscrews the top of a jar of ointment.

'It's stuff for healing wounds: I use it for all the animals. It doesn't sting,' he assures me coaxingly.

'No ointment, thanks, Sam. Just a bandage or whatever.'

He looks at me sternly. 'Don't blame me if it goes septic,' he says.

'Oh, all right, then. But only a little.'

Ten minutes later we are standing beneath the tree-house; I have been persuaded there against my inclination, but it would seem churlish to refuse. My foot is comfortably protected by a firm wad of bandage, and the ointment proves soothing.

'Where did you learn your medical skills?' I ask him, knowing it was unlikely to be Claudia.

'The vet lets me watch sometimes, when he's not too busy. I helped him once, when his assistant was away.'

'Is that what you want to be – a vet?'

One foot on the first rung of the rope ladder, he swings slowly to and fro. 'Oh, no. I'm going to be a zoologist and travel a lot, and photograph animals in the wild.' His eyes are cloudy with distant visions. 'I've never been anywhere except here and London, and Wales twice. We haven't got the money, you see.'

'It's a problem,' I agree.

He shoots me an astute glance. 'Did Josh sell his pictures for lots at that exhibition in your gallery?'

'His paintings fetch a good price, yes,' I say guardedly.

'How much?'

'It's up to Josh to tell you that,' I say firmly, feeling illogically guilty about my forty-per-cent commission.

'I don't suppose he'd tell me. Not unless I get him in a good mood. The best time –' Sam pushes himself in motion with a toe '– is after he's had two drinks.'

'Exactly two?'

'Exactly: I've noticed that's the best time.'

I am more than a little shocked at the way in which this child of nature has been forced into precocity;

although he seems none the worse for it. A picture of health and serenity, he peers at me between the ladder rungs with a face emotionally unscarred and heart-rendingly like Claudia's.

'Will you do another exhibition for him, Leo?'

'I very much hope to, one day. It depends on Josh to a great extent, you see. Since your mother—'

I stop, wondering how much the loss has affected him. But he merely says, unperturbed, 'He's in the studio most of the time, so he must have painted masses. He won't show any of us, but he's bound to show you, isn't he?'

'Is it so important to you?'

'Very, because if Josh doesn't sell his pictures he'll sell this house and I'll have to give up the animals.' He stops swinging and adds perspicaciously, 'I know you're not into animals, are you, so it's probably difficult for you to understand.'

Taken aback, I wonder how I have given myself away. Was I born with this antipathy, or was it a result of my upbringing? Recollections of childhood return, sharply etched in my memory: walks with Nanny in Hyde Park, running on fat, toddler legs to pat a dog larger than myself; Nanny's admonition: 'Don't touch strange animals, dear, they may bite you.' And the mansion flat with its sombre furnishings and its acres of dark corridor muffled by pile carpet. Never so much as a goldfish was entertained as a pet; in my mother's view such things were unhygienic and superfluous. My father disappeared to the country at frequent intervals, but that was for the sole purpose of stalking, chasing and killing, and in any case he never took me with him. I suspect he considered me a wimp and full of Siegler squeamishness. An uncle took me once to the London zoo where both of us were bored, and I was sick from too much ice cream behind the monkey enclosure. It strikes me now quite forcibly that I had nothing of my own to love, fondle and play with in that strange atmosphere of spiritual bleakness; even the stuffed toys were banished to the back of a cupboard at an early age. No wonder I have made the most of women as wonderful substitutes in later years. I don't remember thinking consciously about these things before: Claudia's child has dragged them to the surface.

'I never owned an animal at your age. I didn't have a chance to get used to them,' I explain, and find I am talking to thin air. Sam's face gazes down at me from the tree-house, his red hair dappled by sunlight through the leaves.

'Like to come up, Leo?'

'Some other time, I think.'

'The only other person to come up here was Mum. She used to sit and read.'

'You must miss her.'

He pauses, answers indirectly. 'She wasn't like a mother,' he says, 'anyway, not like the ones I've met. You know, the sort who bake cakes and tell you to wash your hands. She was fun: she had weird ideas and made up great stories.' His eyes show vividly blue in the subdued light of his hideout. 'People being dead's unreal, isn't it? You can't believe it. Mostly I don't think about it when there's lots to do: I miss her in bits and pieces, suddenly, and then I pretend it hasn't happened, that she's somewhere else like the kitchen or the studio. It sort of works.'

I swallow hard, my vision blurred. 'It makes good sense,' I say with difficulty. For me, nothing works.

All at once he swings off his platform and down the ladder. 'I don't miss the rows, though,' he says cheerfully, dusting his hands on the seat of his jeans.

'Between Josh and your mother, I take it?'

He nods. 'The old rows were all right, the silly ones, when Mum used to throw mugs and things and Josh caught them. Those were like a sort of game they played. But then it all changed, just before Mum got ill. The rows were different, really frightening. Hey!'

He grabs my arm and points in the direction of the river. 'Quick! Come and look!'

He is off like an arrow from a bow: I follow, bowing my head beneath low-slung branches, until I am standing beside him on the bank.

'What am I supposed to be looking for?' I ask; and then, quite suddenly, there is a streak of brilliant colour skimming the brown waters: lost for a moment amongst the reeds to reappear like a tiny jewelled meteor darting downstream. The blue is heart-stopping, exotic and incongruous against the neutral backdrop of an English river: I can only suppose some rare tropical bird has escaped from captivity.

'What is it?'

'It's a kingfisher,' breathes Sam.

'I've never seen one before. It's beautiful.'

'He was here two years ago and now he's back. Perhaps there's a nest.' He looks at me exultantly. 'I bet you've never seen that colour blue in your life, Leo.'

'Only in oriental illustrations and paintings.'

'Oh, paintings,' he says with scorn. 'They're dead things: this is alive.'

I feel put in my place, accused of worshipping idols. There is no sign now of the kingfisher; we turn and walk slowly back, deep in our own thoughts, stopping by the tree-house.

'Thank you for showing me the animals, Sam, and the kingfisher: I wouldn't have missed that for the world.'

'It was great, wasn't it?'

'I think I'll wander back now. Are you coming?'

'Not for a bit. I have to feed the animals first.' He glances at my foot. 'I shouldn't take the bandage off, not till tomorrow.'

'All right. You're the doctor.'

'I expect you'd like a drink,' he says with a return of sophistication. 'If Josh isn't there, the bottles are somewhere in the kitchen.'

I lift a hand in salute and make a detour that leads me past the potting-shed. The door does not yield to my turn of the handle. Peering through dirt-encrusted windows, shading my eyes from the reflection of the evening sun, I can see the relics of Claudia's labours; garden tools, flower-pots, plastic rubbish bags. In contrast to Sam's establishment, it is a glory-hole, a place of infinite secrets amongst the jumble. I reach up to run a hand along the top of the door-frame in search of a key.

'Looking for something?'

Heart leaping up my throat, I jerk round to face Josh's parent, who has crept up on me soundlessly in those vulgar moccasins of his. For an instant I could commit murder; startled out of my wits and riddled with an exaggerated sense of guilt.

*   *   *

At times there is no substitute for whisky. The tumbler on my rickety bedside table is full of the golden brown liquid: my second, the first having been drunk in the kitchen in the company of Josh's father. It was several seconds before I could talk to him as we walked from the shed to the house. A dislike of being crept up on, and an absurd feeling of having been caught in some nefarious act made me resentful. 'Just having a look around,' I said in answer to his question. The last thing I wanted was to be dragged into conversation with him, but I had no choice since he followed me into the kitchen. In retrospect, sitting on the side of my bed, I have to admit that what he had to say was enlightening, if far from reassuring.

I found my house present of a litre bottle of whisky sitting where I had left it, on the kitchen dresser.

'Would you like one?' I asked; I could hardly march away without offering.

'Thank you, Leo, I won't say no.'

'I'm afraid I don't know your name; I can't call you "Da",' I said with an attempt at camaraderie.

'My name's Dai. "Dai", "Da", there's little difference. "Da" will do fine.'

He accepted his drink and settled himself on a chair, making my escape to my bedroom virtually impossible without appearing rude. He took a sip of whisky and came straight to the point.

'The shed,' he said thoughtfully. 'It's something of a shrine, see, boyo; a shrine to Claudia. That's why Josh keeps it locked.'

I thought I could detect a note of sarcasm in his voice.

'There's silly, to my mind,' he continued. 'A daft

notion: a potting-shed full of old junk and nobody allowed to go in and sort it out. Besides,' he looked at me out of shrewd eyes, black as currants, 'shrines are for saints.'

He raised his glass, still eying me over the rim. The whisky had brought my nerves under control, but all the same I shifted uncomfortably.

'I merely thought I'd find a few tools and tackle the garden tomorrow,' I said carelessly. 'But I expect Josh has his reasons.'

'Ah, there's hitting the nail on the head,' Da agreed, 'and he won't be letting on about them, look. Never known a boy like him for not letting on. Tight as a clam he can be, and always has been, even as a tiny brat.'

His thick mane of white hair, springing from a high, weathered forehead, gave him a biblical appearance. I was surprised to see his eyes glisten as if with tears.

'There's trouble in bottling things up,' he said, 'a strain on the system. It can only take so much before it blows a gasket. And there's Josh for you; I've seen it happen with him more than once and I know the signs.' He sighs. 'He's my favourite: well, the last one, see, and more bother than the rest of them put together.'

'What happens when he – er – blows a gasket?' I asked.

'Phew! Leo, there's temper for you,' he said, shaking his head. He took a small cigar from a packet and lit it with a gold lighter, drawing on it pensively. 'I don't know what he's got locked away inside his head ever since Claudia passed on, but it's more'n the contents of an old shed, there's for sure.'

Our conversation was interrupted at that point by

97

Josh and Sophie, leaving me with a sense of confidences left unaired.

'Josh has been showing me the studio,' Sophie said, 'and some of his paintings.'

She looked as serene as ever. There was a faint flush in her cheeks: where she had caught the sun, perhaps. Josh's expression seemed to me a little smug.

'Lucky old you,' I said sulkily. 'And did you approve, my little art expert?'

'They're different,' she said, sitting on a corner of the table and waggling an eyebrow at me comically, which presumably meant: ask no more!

'Hah!' Josh laughed, helping himself to a large measure of my whisky. 'They're certainly that, whatever else.'

'Anyway, he's going to show you after dinner,' Sophie announced. 'Aren't you, Josh?'

'If Leo would like to be shown,' said Josh politely, while his eyes held a challenge. 'Would you, Leo?'

So that was how it was left. God knows what I shall see on this conducted tour: obviously it is meant to shock, or is that just part of an elaborate plot to dismay and unnerve me? Possibly I am imagining the whole thing: the little innuendoes, the look in the eye, the hint of menace. That is what guilt does to you. We are all accustomed to Josh's moods; he is fairly close to being a genius, and geniuses are to be allowed their temperaments. He of all men would grow bitter through bereavement; it may well have nothing to do with me. Although I cannot help looking back with a certain nostalgia to those early days when Josh was new and green to success, and more than slightly in awe of me. There is a kind of shameful pleasure in being deferred to.

Downstairs I can hear the clatter of pots and pans: Sophie has volunteered to cook supper, which is a relief. It has to be an improvement on lunch. I have already tried to run a bath; rust-brown water gushed from the taps and swilled the spider down the drain, but remained tepid. The pipes in my bedroom are still clanking and grumbling from the onslaught, and a hot bath has become infinitely desirable, like everything that is denied one. The evenings are long and light; it is high summer. But I can anticipate the creepiness of this room when I am finally forced to sleep here for the night. Much of the vague menace springs from the house itself: even while Claudia was *alive* I felt it, and dismissed it casually, for there were other things that engrossed me.

I drink some of the whisky and get to my feet. The bandage on my left foot is starting to unravel. The smell of honeysuckle drifts through the window, stronger at the close of day, and with it a hopeless and overwhelming longing for Claudia that brings me childishly close to tears.

Chapter Five

I had known Claudia long enough to realize she had a many-sided personality. Whether these facets were moods, or merely poses which she chose to wear as other women choose a certain dress, I could not decide. Acting a part seemed to be so ingrained in her that one only noticed when she ceased to do so; like the time she pressed an unpainted cheek, wet from the rain, against mine in the Hornsey studio, without affectation or artifice. This was the Claudia with whom I fell in love and eventually the other rôle-models fell away from her, unwanted. But it was some time before we reached that stage, and on the day I had arranged to meet her I did not know what to expect. I could only hope for one of her less dramatic selves.

I remember the lunch clearly; I had booked a table at Overton's at the lower end of St James's Street, within walking distance of work. The tables were set wide enough apart for comfort, it was unpretentious and I could not be bothered to find anywhere more exciting. The day was still and damp, with the first depressing intimation of autumn passing into winter. There was none of the delirious anticipation induced by illicit meetings; for one reason, it was not a clandestine meeting and secondly, I felt nothing, numbed by Jane's death to the extent that I might have been living on another planet. As I walked downhill, oblivious of the gracious, bow-windowed shops and clubs, I could have been about to lunch with Josh in place of Claudia, for all that it mattered. It was someone with whom to communicate, and I was not sure I needed that either.

'I've worried about you,' she had told me on the telephone. 'We both have.'

Her call had not surprised me. People were incurably kind at that time.

'Do you feel like having a quiet supper? Just us, no-one else.'

'Sweet of you, Claudia. May I leave it awhile? I'm not quite ready. Give me a week or two, would you?'

'Of course.'

But we went on talking; I don't recall what was said, only that it grew easier after a few seconds. It occurred to me that, outside business, I had not talked to anyone but Sophie for countless days; I suggested lunch on an impulse and because I was grateful to Claudia for her gesture.

'I can manage a one-to-one conversation,' I explained feebly. 'Stupidly, two people at a time seems a crowd.'

'I'd love to have lunch,' she said.

Her dress-sense was haphazard; I had seen her look stunning and, equally, I had seen her look a mess. As she walked across the room to join me at a corner table, it was obvious this was not one of her glamour days. I helped her out of a drab fawn raincoat and watched her push up the sleeves of a black polo-neck sweater which, by its size, must have belonged to Josh, before she settled herself beside me. Despite the shape-lessness of these garments, she gave the impression of having lost weight; her face was thinner, or perhaps the framework of dark marmalade hair, unfettered by combs, made it seem so. And then I remembered she was pregnant, which probably accounted for these things.

'Leo.' She put a hand over mine. 'Are you managing?'

'Just. No, I'm all right; I don't feel anything now except a kind of merciful blankness.'

'And Sophie is—?'

'Being brave.'

Her eyes scanned my face with their usual attention, but none of the original suggestiveness.

'I'm not very good at this,' she said, meaning, I presumed, comforting the bereaved. 'I never know whether to talk about whoever's died or drivel on mindlessly about trivia. Which would you rather?'

'To talk about it. It's a relief and it doesn't hurt. People cross the road to avoid meeting you. They don't know what to say, but it makes one feel shunned.' I attempted a smile. 'Let's order first, shall we?'

'Grilled Dover sole, please,' she said, ignoring the menu: then took a quick look and added, 'Oh, Lord! What prices! I'll have fish cakes.'

'Two grilled Dover sole,' I ordered when the waiter arrived.

Our conversation was centred on myself for much of the time; I am sorry to say one becomes deplorably egotistical in this situation. Either one takes to drink or chooses to unburden oneself on a sympathetic stooge. Claudia was ideal for the purpose, poor darling; listening with her particular brand of wide-eyed intensity, so disconcerting when wielding her sexuality, so comforting when devoid of self-interest.

Today, as on that previous encounter at the studio, she was not bothering to act: perhaps in deference to the frailty of my feelings. I told her all about those: the gaping wound of aloneness, the guilt, the anger.

'The anger is the worst because you have no right to it.'

'Why not?' she said. 'I'd be livid with Josh if something happened to him.' She gave me a fleeting shadow of a smile. 'As for guilt, I believe everyone feels it, don't they? Even if there's no basis for it.'

I watched her slice a portion of fish carefully from the bone.

'Perhaps it's better when there is,' she suggested. 'Like having a genuine explanation for any sort of pain.'

It was only when I had finished unloading the last of my miserable psychological hang-ups and felt more peaceful for the catharsis that I began to notice Claudia as Claudia: the two little lines beside her mouth, for instance, which I could not recall having been there before. And the mouth itself, in repose, seemed to have tightened and lost some of its natural curl, as if suppressed by adversity. I realized I had talked exclusively about myself and her silences might not have been entirely taken up in listening. She had eaten one side of her sole and left the other: so had I, but that was another matter.

'That's enough about me,' I said. 'More than enough. Tell me about yourself, and Josh. When's the baby due?'

'It isn't,' she replied. 'I lost it.'

A simple statement delivered without emotion, which did not fool me.

'Oh, Claudia, I'm so very sorry. When did it happen?'

She put her knife and fork together. 'Four weeks ago, roughly.'

Two weeks after Jane's death: both of us living in our own private little hells and trying to scrabble our way out of them alone. I had been unaware of hers: a sudden impulse of tenderness made me want to take her in my arms, scruffy sweater and all, and hold her close without speaking.

'It's not the end of the world. Worse things have happened at sea, et cetera.' She shrugged. 'I honestly believe there's a purpose to such endings: the baby might have been handicapped in some way. Josh was right, I am too old for child-bearing.'

She said it without bitterness. I did not answer, merely asked stupidly, 'Would you like a pudding? Or just coffee?' – as if these were substitutes.

'What I'd like more than anything is a brandy. May I? And a cigarette; d'you have a cigarette, Leo?'

'I don't smoke, remember: and neither do you, do you?'

'Not for years. But right now I want one: and afterwards,' – she turned to me with a visible effort at her old vivacity – 'you could come and help me choose a tapestry. I'm into *gros point* at the moment and there's a shop in Jermyn Sreet. Unless you've got to get back to the Gallery?'

Whether or not I had to, I decided, did not come into the equation: her eyes held the shadowy fear of being alone that I could recognize well. I ordered a packet of cigarettes and the brandy, and watched her smoke with the careful gestures of one who has forgotten how.

'Anyway,' she said, 'I'm not a brilliant mother. I love them when they're older, but I'm not truly maternal; I never know what to do when they're ill. And I'm lucky; I've got Sam and Marcus.'

'How has Sam taken this?'

'I never told him,' she said. 'I don't know why; he is a very philosophical child, a practical person, thank heavens. God knows where he gets it from.' She thought for a while, then added, 'What I miss is being pregnant, people are so nice to you; you feel protected.'

I was startled by this revelation, Claudia being the last person I could imagine in need of a prop.

'Stupid, isn't it,' she said, 'the thought that an embryo can give you security? The child protecting the mother. But for me it does: and now that there's nothing left, I feel' – she lifted her hands helplessly – 'extraordinarily vulnerable.'

Where, I wondered, did Josh figure in this collapse of belief in self? It crossed my mind to ask, and I thought better of it, frightened that the answer would anger me.

'Not surprising, after all that's happened,' I reassured her. 'It will come back, the confidence; give it a little time.' I covered her hand with mine.

'Will it?' she asked sadly.

'Of course it will. You have every reason to possess it.'

'How do you mean?'

'You're beautiful, for a start.'

She did not deny it, but continued to look at me consideringly, as if judging the truth of the compliment.

'Thank you, Leo,' was all she said.

A watery sun had filtered its way through the greyness as we left the restaurant and turned towards Jermyn Street. A pram pushed vigorously by a nanny the shape and colour of a London pigeon divided us for a second.

'That's another thing I shall miss,' Claudia told me as we reunited. 'Bashing a push-chair along at a rate of knots: the power complex it gives you is enormous,' and she smiled properly for the first time that day.

A little further on she stopped and turned to me. 'Leo, I don't really feel like shopping; the tapestry can wait.'

'Do you want to go home?' I asked, feeling ridiculously disappointed.

She shook her head. 'Let's walk in St James's Park and watch the ducks.'

On our way there, she said suddenly, 'Do you realize we haven't mentioned Josh's work once?'

I had not realized: in fact, I had not given it a single thought.

Nothing is more evocative for me than certain locations in London's parks: evocative either of Claudia or of Jane, even of swiftly passing earlier passions. A bridge over the lake in St James's belongs to Claudia. Looking from west to east on a hazy October afternoon: that is where her ghost is likely to be found, wearing a fawn raincoat with the collar turned up, her hair dampened by Scotch mist.

In silence we leaned on the rail and studied the ducks circling and diving below us. Presently, because I supposed the subject had to be raised at some point, I told her I had managed to bring the date of Josh's exhibition forward a month, to the beginning of May.

'Oh Lord,' she said despondently.

Her reaction puzzled me. 'I thought you would be pleased.'

'I am. It's Josh who'll become frenetic about it.'

'Why, for God's sake?'

'Because he already feels under pressure to get the new paintings finished on time. Josh doesn't work well under pressure, he goes to pieces. You don't know him very well, Leo.'

There was a touch of reproach in her voice.

'If that's the trouble, it's unnecessary,' I said. 'I had no idea he felt that way. We have enough of his pictures for a decent exhibition as it is. The thing is, quite a lot of artists are apt to grow complacent before a show, so I encourage them to work, but I've obviously got it wrong with Josh.' I put my arm round her shoulders. 'Don't worry. I'll have a word with him, put his mind at rest.'

I thought she would thank me, but she did not speak. Her shoulders felt brittle with tension, giving an impression of tears held back: except she was not the crying sort. With a thumbnail she flicked a piece of lichen off the rail and into the water, causing a flurry of confusion amongst the ducks expecting a bonne-bouche.

'Actually, that isn't the whole story,' she said at last. 'I told you how he'd be in the build-up to the exhibition, d'you remember? Well, it's as I expected, only more so.' She straightened up, fumbled in her pocket for a tissue and blew her nose. 'My getting pregnant drove a wedge between us and it's become a chasm; we're out of reach of each other.'

I said sarcastically, 'I suppose he's overjoyed at the outcome?'

'No,' she said, 'no. He's feeling guilty, and that's ten times worse.'

'So he should be,' I told her, recalling his deplorable outburst the evening they had come to supper.

'He wanted me to have an abortion, you see,' she said as if she had not heard me.

I stared at her, appalled. 'Claudia, you didn't—'

'No, of course not,' she said, quietly furious. 'How can you even think it?'

I sank into shocked silence. The misty trees and islands of the lake blurred before my eyes with anger. I was aware my feelings were out of all proportion to my rôle in this matter, either as friend or professional adviser; I had no place in their lives, no right to an emotion of any sort. But it made no difference: despite my growing enthusiasm for Josh's talents, I could not envisage being reasonably controlled when we next met.

'Sorry I snapped,' she said. 'I really don't know why I'm telling you all this. It's our problem, and up to us to solve it: if we can.'

Her voice was suddenly remote as she distanced herself from me.

'A trouble shared,' I replied, matching my tone to hers, hurt by her reserve. 'But I dare say you're right.'

There followed one of those difficult silences generally confined to lovers, or those who wish to become so. The muffled noise of traffic could be heard, the hoarse cry of a sergeant from Wellington Barracks, the nervous clearing of my throat.

'I can't forgive him,' she admitted eventually, 'and he can't bring himself to apologize.'

I did not trust myself to speak, watching instead a dull brown duck trailing a distorted wing in the water as it approached the group by the bridge. It had a tentative look, as if unsure of its welcome: I knew how it felt. My own feelings were all over the place.

'It's like finding yourself married to a different man from the one you married,' she added. 'There's a part of him I never knew existed.'

'Are you saying,' I asked in a passably level voice, 'you no longer love him?'

'I don't know. I'm too hurt by him to work it out at the moment. I wish' – she swung round to face me – 'Oh, God! I wish I could get away somewhere just for a week or two to sort myself out.'

'Perhaps you should.'

'I can't. There's Sam and his schooling; and Josh is like yet another child. I still feel stupidly responsible for him.' She smiled, but all the unhappiness was in the eyes, as if she wept internally. 'Just as well about the baby,' she said. 'It would have been one too many, probably.' She put out a hand and touched me gently on the cheek. 'A fine day I've given you, Leo. I was supposed to be the comforter, remember?'

Moving abruptly, she leant against the rail, hands shoved deep inside her coat pockets.

'There's a duck down here with a broken wing, poor thing,' she murmured inconsequentially.

'I fully believe Josh's exhibition will be a success story, if that's any consolation.'

A smug statement: I could hear the pomposity in my voice as I made it. But that is how emotion affects me, and my head was full of wild and impossible dreams to which again I had no right. Besides, I could not think of an alternative to cheer her up. Whatever their finances, they could only be slender.

She nodded. 'I hope you're right; the money would help. He's got everything else, has Josh: the talent and now the opportunity. Whereas I'm good at practically nothing except a capacity for enjoying myself—'

'And gardens. I've seen your own garden.'

'Anyone can stick plants in the ground and wait for them to grow,' she said impatiently. 'Josh has a gift I'd give my eye-teeth for, and can't enjoy it. In fact, it makes him thoroughly nasty.'

'There go fifty per cent of all artists,' I told her.

'Then perhaps I shouldn't have married one,' she replied. 'Once upon a time he created, and I supplied the confidence he lacked. I can't do that any more – I've lost the will and the energy.'

I stared down at the opaque brown water, trying to conjure up some words of wisdom; avuncular advice which the situation undoubtedly demanded. Whatever else, I supposed I was counted as a friend, and it behoved friends to make an attempt at healing breaches. But my mind refused to work in an advisory capacity: it remained empty of everything except the fact that Claudia was beside me, disillusioned and therefore receptive to comfort. I am not sure my thoughts were as clear-cut as that, but they certainly were not altruistic, and I realized, with a terrible sense of shame, that Jane had not been part of them for half the day.

There seemed to be some sort of dissension going on amongst the duck community below us. They were making little rushes at each other with wide-open beaks and emitting raucous cries quite unlike their normal peaceful quacking. The water was churned to foam as wings and webbed feet beat furiously in semi-flight. I imagined a bystander had thrown them bread until Claudia grabbed my arm.

'Leo, look! They're attacking the one that's injured. Find something to throw at them!'

I started to search the ground for the odd stone or pebble, but she had already left my side, running towards the end of the bridge. I had no idea what I was meant to do as I followed her at a steady trot, unsuitably dressed in a dark-navy overcoat which caught at my knees. By the time I had reached her she had slid down the bank to the edge of the lake. From where I stood I could see that the birds were centred on one objective: the terrible systematic slaughter of the misfit, homing in on it repeatedly, biting and tearing with their faintly comical beaks as with lethal weapons. Claudia was scrabbling in the soil for stones and lobbing them into the furore. She yelled at me, her voice cracking on a sob: 'Stop them! Break them up! Do something, can't you?'

I found part of a dead branch and beat the lake with it ineffectually. The murderers remained impervious to her missiles and my thrashing alike: dedicated to completing their barbarism. The racket ceased as suddenly as it had begun: a flotilla of feathers floated on the surface, and eventually the pathetic brown-grey corpse could be seen, rocking half-submerged in the murky waters.

'Horrible,' Claudia whispered, unable to take her eyes away.

I took her arm. I am not nature-minded, but even I was shaken. 'There's nothing we can do.'

We climbed up the slope in silence and stood with our backs to the railings.

'Bloody birds,' she said, sniffing. 'I'll never feel the same about ducks again.'

'Neither shall I.'

'Fascists: slaughtering the outcasts. I always imagined animals to be nicer than humans, but they're exactly the same.'

She was crying, the tears coursing down her cheeks unchecked.

'Oh, Claudia.' I put my arms around her, wondering whether she saw the ritual killing we had witnessed as symbolic. I held her like that for several seconds, my cheek against her hair, until she lifted her head to look at me without speaking. I kissed her: gently and tenderly, the kiss you would give a child in trouble. That was how it was meant, I swear. Her lips, cool and tentative, tasted of salt; it lasted much longer than I had intended because I had waited to do this since we first met, and with its reality came the end to self-delusion.

When she finally drew back we stared at one another. Her expression said, 'Now look what we've done,' with resignation rather than accusation. Neither of us uttered a word about it as we walked away, arguing over her means of transport home. We were unwilling to admit that anything catalytic had happened; pretending it was of no account and would not upset the established tenor of our lives. But there was no doubt in my mind, nor in Claudia's, judging by her fleeting expression. I put her, protesting at the expense, into a taxi with enough money to cover the fare to

Hornsey. In any other circumstance I would have seen her home, but frankly I did not feel up to facing Josh; and this is how it would always be from now on, I thought, as the taxi sped away and disappeared along Constitution Hill.

'Did you enjoy your lunch?' Zelda asked sarcastically. The sarcasm sprang from concern but was none the less exasperating. Between three and half-past was the stated time of my return: it was now four-fifteen.

'Very much, thanks, Zelda. Any calls?'

'I've put a list of them on your desk. Joshua Jones telephoned,' her face softened, 'in something of a state, I felt.'

'Oh? What about, d'you know?'

'He didn't say, but I'd make him your first call. On second thoughts, perhaps a certain Paolo Rodriguez should be your priority,' she said flatly. 'Apparently you were due at his studio three-quarters of an hour ago.'

'God!' Poor wretch, left biting his nails. I turned towards the stairs.

'And how was Mrs Joshua?' Zelda adjusted the awful glasses on her nose and picked up a pen.

Had I mentioned lunching with Claudia?

'Joshua tells me she hasn't been well,' Zelda added. 'It probably accounts for his nerves.'

'Really?' I replied. 'She said nothing about it; we were discussing her husband's work, principally. She copes with the admin, you see.'

I could see Zelda thinking, *And that took all afternoon?*

I said abruptly, 'I'll be in my office for the next hour,' and disappeared.

113

I rang the anxious Rodriguez with profuse apologies and excuses, and an offer to arrive without fail the next morning. I had never missed an appointment in my life before: I was meticulous over such matters. My hand hesitated over the telephone: it was sod's law that I should be forced to ring Josh immediately, before I had had time to collect myself. Anger towards him warred uncomfortably with a desire to compensate, although it was not strictly necessary. As it happened, it was a question of framing which concerned him. I had the feeling he hadn't noticed Claudia's length of absence, or, if he had done so, it did not matter to him. This so infuriated me that I brought our conversation to a swift close without reassuring him about the pressure of work. Let him work his ass off, I decided.

I felt suddenly exhausted: by conflicting emotions, and the long day itself, and Zelda's snide remarks. These in particular had brought it home to me: the subterfuge and the explanations, the lies and excuses had already begun.

I think it is fair to say that, during this traumatic period of Sophie's life and mine, I did my best not to let her suffer as a result. I was terribly conscious of my rôle as single parent and of her vulnerability, teetering on the brink of womanhood. I stuck to a rigid rule of arriving home on time each evening; the preparing of a meal together gave us the chance to talk, to exchange details of our day. In this way I could gauge her mood, spot any troubles on her mind before she drove them underground. I worried about her constantly, wished sometimes for her sake she had been born a boy, whose need for a mother would not have been so great.

114

Sometimes we ate out to make a change, and to try to stimulate her appetite; she seemed to me alarmingly thin.

'I have to keep my weight down,' she said calmly on one of these occasions 'If I didn't, I wouldn't stand a chance.'

'You're begining to look anorexic,' I protested.

'Oh, do I? Good,' she said, as if I'd paid her a compliment.

'You're having a plain grilled steak,' I said firmly. 'It's full of iron; you can't dance on just salad.'

'I'd look pretty stupid dancing on a salad, Pa.' This was Jane's sense of the ridiculous; something I don't possess. But I like to hear it repeated in Sophie.

I watched her pick at her food, fragile neck bent over the plate, slanting eyes dominating the pale face. The excessive dedication to her work was her way of dealing with Jane's death: I knew that, and there were worse means of killing pain. But the routine of the ballet school was gruelling, let alone the normal school work and revision for exams. It left her little time for a social life; once in a while she brought girlfriends home, even less often visited them. Before long it would be boys, young men, and my present anxieties would be switched to other channels: they would never end, I saw that now. I sighed. She looked up swiftly, eying me with discernment.

'Pa?'

'Yes, kitten?'

'Why don't you take someone else out to supper sometimes? I mean, it's boring for you when it's always me.'

'You never bore me.'

It was her turn to sigh. 'You really worry me, you know that? You and Mum had a great time, masses of friends. Now you've given up seeing anybody,' she said, trying to sound severe. 'It's bad for you.'

I laughed.

'Why are you laughing?'

'I was thinking the same thing about you,' I said. 'No social life.'

'I'm too busy with other things at the moment,' she said. 'But one day I'll have a life of my own and there's miles of it ahead of me.'

Not so in my case, was her inference.

I told her, 'Give me time. I'm not quite ready for it yet.'

There was a pause while she tidied away a third of her steak to the side of the plate.

'Mum wouldn't mind, you know, your seeing people, going out with them,' she said quietly.

'No,' I said. 'I agree she wouldn't; if I wanted to.'

'Claudia and Josh, for instance,' she suggested.

'You approve of them, do you?'

'I like Josh; I'm not sure about her.' She frowned. 'She's different every time you meet her. I'd rather people stayed the same, so you know where you are.'

'We have an open invitation to stay a weekend with them. We might take them up on it in the spring; what do you think?'

'I think,' she said in this new mothering voice of hers, 'you should start accepting lots of invitations.'

Sophie was right, of course, in her assessment of Claudia. The next time we met, at a surprisingly-grand

116

dinner-party where the guests were seated at separate tables, she was wearing an arresting dress and projecting a new image. Instead of her habit of intense listening, she hardly drew breath aiming to amuse, or so it seemed. I suppose she succeeded, since the other five at her table peppered the air with bursts of laughter. But there was something frenetic about her behaviour and the laughter sounded slightly strained to me, from where I was sitting close by. Once I caught her eye, and she waggled her fingers at me and winked as if to say, 'Isn't this fun? See how well I'm managing.' I think she was a little drunk. Certainly she was unrecognizable as the Claudia I had seen sobbing over a dead bird three weeks previously. I was embarrassed for her; I left the party early, suddenly overcome by loneliness. It made it easier, however, to fight the good fight, which is roughly what I had been doing ever since the afternoon we had spent together. I still had some will-power left at the time, and I am not amoral by nature.

When I was touching sixteen, my mother gave me a short lecture on sex. I presume that was what she intended: she did not go into details. I was at the stage of dreaming erotic dreams and the evidence of these must have been discovered on the sheets of my bed.

'It's time we had a talk, Leo.'

We were being driven home from the Gallery. The fact that she employed a chauffeur was another source of shame to me. This was nineteen fifty-nine and none but the ostentatious had servants.

'I imagine you have been told the facts of life at school?' she asked, and I nodded dumbly, blushing to the roots of my hair.

'They won't have mentioned the woman's points of view,' she said. 'After all, it's principally a male establishment.'

Her lips curled sceptically whenever she talked of men: I watched this happen now.

'Think twice before you kiss a girl,' she continued. 'Kissing brings out the baser instincts in the man and expectations in the girl.'

'If you don't kiss someone, how do you know if you really like them?' I asked, bewildered.

'By their character, of course,' she said impatiently. 'The rest – love, if you like – will follow. And when you do marry,' she added, turning her autocratic gaze to the window, 'remember that women don't enjoy that side of married life as a rule; they merely put up with it because it's a necessity. The more understanding men are towards these differences, the more likely the marriage will be to succeed. If you *must* stray, do it discreetly.'

I could think of nothing to say and thanked God for the glass partition between myself and the chaffeur. My mother patted me on the hand in a rare gesture of affection. 'I'm glad we've had this little chat, Leo,' she said. 'It was no use leaving it up to your father.'

Thinking back on her monologue, I find it difficult to believe; it is a miracle I am not impotent as a result. Nature took its course and obliterated her extraordinarily outmoded attitudes, and Jane proved a fine exception to the rule about women's sexual appetites. I suppose I should feel sorry for my mother, since only a disastrous marriage could have warped her views in this way. Whose fault it was I have no idea; I never got to know my father well, he died when I was nineteen, but I remember him as a genial man with a loud voice and a proclivity towards country sports. How he came to marry a Jewish girl steeped in the rarefied atmosphere of the art world, God knows: a frigid Jewish girl at that, or so I suspect. It is difficult to sympathize with her, however: she is so unlikeable. There is none of the warmth normally inherent in her race, no gathering together on a Friday evening. To put it succinctly, she is a dominating, matriarchal old woman who has missed out on life. She loves Sophie: that is the one mitigating factor in my feelings for her. Sophie as a small child could get away with murder, calling her 'Gran'mops', playing with the priceless porcelain knick-knackery and dropping biscuit crumbs on the pale carpet. Now she confides startling revelations about her life, and 'Gran'mop's' fine dark eyes sparkle and the uncompromising stiffness gives way to relaxation. But then, Sophie is a girl and infinitely preferred.

Even at that tender age of fifteen-rising-sixteen, I was aware that however successful I became, I could never live down the fact that I was male. After that dreadful little talk, I stared at myself in the looking-glass and assessed my features: my mother's eyes, a mop of dark, curly hair, a wide, full mouth. The nose came from my father, which was a blessing. The hair has receded now. I see as little as possible of my mother; she has not mellowed with age. Gaunter, arthritic but upright as ever, she makes the occasional surprise foray on Siegler's, to pull rank and bully us shamelessly. My visits to her are even less frequent and undertaken purely when a sense of duty drives me.

Out of all her distorted views, the one about the kiss held a grain of truth; although my baser instincts were already roused where Claudia was concerned. At the same time, I still placed a hand on the side of the bed where Jane should have been, before falling asleep. The raw emptiness of life without her continued; to ache for two people simultaneously is difficult to comprehend unless one has experienced it. There seems nowhere the mind can turn for comfort.

It was on the last day of November that I caught sight of Claudia entering the house in Paradise Walk, and jumped to the most awful conclusions.

The lowest months of a low, mean year were upon us. The recession showed no signs of lifting, the whole country was couched in pre-election gloom and businesses continued to fold, an alarming number of art galleries amongst them. It was not as if one could rely on foreign trade, for this was a world-wide depression in which we were all trying to survive. We owed a lot to our reputation, as Zelda tediously kept reminding me. In the run-up to Christmas I made several satisfactory sales, including an enchanting small flower painting by a nineteenth-century French peasant, whose fifteen acknowledged pictures were sought after hungrily by serious collectors. I hankered after that painting myself and was sad to see it go, despite the sizeable recompense. Nevertheless, business was far from normal; the contemporary exhibition which we held in the autumn fell miserably short of expectations, and time hung heavily on my hands at a period when I badly needed to be occupied. I began to have misgivings about Josh's exhibition the following May. It was this nervousness that drove me to telephone him: I had to see his work again, convince myself that I had not imagined its extraordinary quality.

'Leo!' He sounded delighted. 'Come whenever: next week, any evening. I'll be on my own. We might go somewhere for a drink, I feel like getting pissed.'

We settled for the Monday. I found myself secretly relieved that Claudia would be absent; life was strain enough without adding to it. My anger at Josh's attitude towards her had not vanished, but it had abated somewhat; it is impossible to keep these feelings at boiling point, and I knew perfectly well he would manage to charm me once again. In the right mood, he was a difficult man to dislike.

I left work early on the Friday before I had arranged to see him, with the intention of finding a Christmas present for Sophie. It needed to be chosen with care; I wanted to give her something special without it seeming suspiciously like recompense for Jane's death. I had no clear idea in mind as I trawled round Peter Jones and down the King's Road, peering helplessly at displays of jewellery in shop windows. Jane had always coped with Christmas shopping, leaving me the sole and delightful task of choosing my present to her. A redundant pleasure now: I kept forgetting this, my eyes drawn to a particular antique ring or gold bracelet which would have suited her wonderfully. I faced Christmas with loathing; at the next crossing I turned my back on the tawdry coloured lights, artificial trees and pushy women shoppers, and headed towards home. Sophie's present would have to wait. Dull despair and raw cold attacked me equally.

Paradise Walk is a short cul-de-sac off Royal Hospital Road, consisting of a dozen or so doll's houses. I glanced down it as I passed; a man and a woman were standing by a blue Porsche. She was dressed in boots and jeans and a short coat, a long, striped muffler over her mouth and chin. The street lamp shone on her bare head. There was no mistaking the hair: it was Claudia.

I am ashamed to say I waited: lurked in the twilight shadows with my coat collar up and my hat pulled down over my eyes like a Damon Runyon character. I do not know what I expected to learn: it was simply a compulsion. Claudia opened the front door to one of the houses, her companion followed, and they both disappeared. Twenty minutes later no-one had re-emerged: that was all. It was enough. Did I really wait twenty minutes? I walked away stiffly, hands, feet and mind quite numbed, and ran a hot bath the moment I reached home.

Later, sitting before the fire nursing a whisky, I ran through the old spiel in my head. Claudia's life was no concern of mine; if she was cheating anyone, it was Josh; what kind of man was I, in any case, to feel the pain of loss and the pull of lust at the same time? Side by side with this familiar lecture, new lines of thought went unchecked. Claudia knew this man well: they had the air, the gestures, of friends. She had a key to his house. Was twenty minutes long enough to judge? Of course it bloody well was. Why, oh why, hadn't she warned me when she realized, as she must have done, how I felt about her? Because, Leo, she doesn't give a fuck: she's that sort of woman. I punished myself by all this and more; heaven knows how long I would have continued if Sophie had not arrived home.

I had to face it: I was suffering the jealousy of a wronged husband, or at very least a lover. No woman was worth it, I tried to persuade myself, and so very nearly succeeded. I remember reaching the lowest personal ebb of the long, low year that night.

'It's good to see you,' Josh repeated; he had already said so twice. 'Relieved, I was, when you rang.'

I had renewed my faith in his work, and we were sitting in the local pub discussing his two latest paintings and the sorry state of the economy. The subject was about to change: I could tell by the tone of his voice.

'I felt badly about not ringing you when Jane—' He hesitated, unable to be explicit. 'Well, you know. Not much cop at expressing myself, that's the problem.'

'I know,' I said. 'It isn't easy. Think nothing of it, Josh.'

'Lovely, she was.' He scowled into his glass. 'I miss her. For you it must be— Anyway, I just wanted you to know how sorry—'

He ground to an embarrassed halt and drank his whisky at a gulp.

'Yes. Thank you.'

'I'll get us another,' he said, obviously thankful to be through with commiseration.

'Do you realize,' he said when he returned with the drinks, 'I haven't seen you since we had supper at your place?'

I had realized, for various reasons.

'There's another thing.' It seemed to be his evening for confidences. 'I ought to apologize for making things awkward: having a set-to with Claudie and so on.' He grinned disarmingly. 'Behaved bloody badly, didn't I?'

'Yes,' I agreed calmly. 'I think you did.' There was a

coldness in my heart at the mention of Claudia.

'She lost the baby,' he said.

'She told me, when we had lunch.' I presumed he knew about the lunch, and if not, I no longer cared. 'I don't know whether to sympathize or not, Josh, since you clearly didn't want it.'

He was silent for a second or two, slowly rotating the glass on its stem. 'There *was* a reason,' he said eventually.

I had forgotten how swiftly his expression changed, like cloud chasing sun.

'I was frightened for her.' He looked at me, and I was inclined to believe him. 'She's over forty; too old to have children safely. Dangerous for her, it would have been, and for the baby.' He sighed. 'The fear of it made me angry,' he added, 'if it's any excuse.'

'You gave her a whole lot of other reasons besides. It seemed unnecessarily callous to me.'

'It's difficult to remind a woman she's getting older. I didn't want to rub it in.' He took a nervous swig of his drink. 'But I shouldn't have let fly in front of you and Jane.'

'It was the last thing that mattered,' I said, thinking of the suggested abortion.

The pub had become crowded, packed with young girls in weird and many-layered clothing and men in bomber jackets sporting either pony-tails or with their heads half-shaved. It was a miracle to me how the sexes remained attracted to each other, for they appeared supremely ugly in my view. I had spent a lot of time musing over the mysteries of attraction since the Claudia revelation and it had left a sour taste in my mouth. Another part of me, only half-acknowledged, envied this scruffy lot their youth and *joie de vivre*, both of which had passed me by.

Josh was saying something, lost in the vocal din.

'Sorry, I didn't quite catch—'

'I said,' he leaned towards me, 'I don't know what the hell I'd do if anything happened to her. Oh, Christ, sorry,' he groaned. 'I shouldn't have said that—'

'Forget it,' I said briefly.

I wondered what he would do if he found out she had a lover, and felt diabolically inclined to tell him.

'I love her,' he added, and his green eyes glistened with tears, to my shock. 'Trouble is, I'm no good at showing it.'

'Look,' I said bracingly, 'it'll take time for her to get over a miscarriage. By the spring everything will seem better; and the exhibition will be an unqualified success, if I have anything to do with it.'

I bought a third round because I felt sorry for the poor devil, having transferred my anger to his wife.

'You can relax now,' I told him, putting a glass in front of him, 'work at your own pace. I'm delighted with the new paintings.'

One in particular I coveted: a woman and a boy in a boat on the river, their heads bright against the subdued grey-green of the willow trees. And in the foreground a man, back view, watching; coins of sunlight falling on brown water. Marvellous!

'By the way,' I said on the way back to retrieve my car, 'I saw Claudia on Friday evening in my neck of the woods. In the distance.'

I hated myself the moment I spoke. He glanced at me and frowned. Josh frowning is quite fearsome.

'Paradise Walk?' I asked innocently.

His face cleared. 'Oh, right. Her ex lives there.'

'Ex?'

'Her ex-husband, Philip. He's gone on holiday to the Caribbean; Barbados or similar. Rich as Croesus, he is, lucky bugger; asked Claudie to keep an eye on the house once a week. She's only up on Fridays as a rule; no school for Sam the next day, see?'

'So they're – amicable, are they?' I said carelessly.

'She's kept it that way, because of the son, Marcus.' He laughed. 'And you know Claudie; she'll do anything for anyone.'

I laughed with him, agreeing that I knew her; light-headed with relief and the thought of my own stupidity.

The next Friday I shopped once more in the afternoon, starting in Knightsbridge and walking from there to Sloane Square. The fruits of this expedition consisted of a handbag for my mother and a scarf for Zelda; I failed again to find what I wanted for Sophie. The route home just happened to take me past Paradise Walk, or so I tried to delude myself. There was no chance attached to the decision; the intention had been lodged in my mind all along, hindering my concentration on the choice of presents. I despised myself for this lack of control, but it made no difference: my feet stopped automatically on the corner of Paradise Walk and I looked down it. No-one was about; neither could I see Claudia's car amongst those lining the street.

I waited, the two carrier bags dangling from my fingers. Unlike the first time, there was no shame involved in what I was doing. I had nothing more sinister in mind than asking her home for a cup of tea or a drink. The freezing snap continued: mist lay in pale strands over the nearby embankment, and the cold, sour smell of it stung my nostrils. After a while, I managed to frighten myself by the oddity of my behaviour. One had to be obsessed to risk frost-bite for a woman, I told myself as I stamped my feet and watched for a sight of her battered Metro. She would park behind her ex-husband's Porsche, and I would cross the end of the street nonchalantly and call out an amazed greeting: I had it all planned.

It did not work out like that. She came up behind me on foot while the foolishness of waiting indefinitely was at last persuading me to move on.

'Leo!'

I swung round to find her with two handfuls of bulky carrier bags.

'What *are* you doing?' she asked. 'I could see you from yards away, stomping on the spot like a guardsman.'

'Cramp,' I said promptly, massaging my leg and wincing. 'Absolute agony.'

She looked at me quizzically. 'It's better to walk than stand still,' she suggested.

'Probably. Amazing to see you, Claudia. What are you doing so far from home?'

She explained in much the same words as Josh.

'And I've been doing some of the wretched Christmas shopping, as you can see.'

She wore a big fur hood the colour of fox which framed her face and narrowed it to a heart-shape, and the tip of her nose was pink from the cold.

'Let me take those.' I relieved her of some of the parcels, grateful for an excuse to walk her as far as her Paradise Walk front door.

'Come in and look around,' she said. 'They've made it rather nice inside.'

'They?'

'There's a live-in girlfriend; she's gone abroad with Philip.'

Claudia had reached the end of the narrow hall, leaving the front door open, expecting me to follow. I put the carrier bags on a table.

'Where's Sam?' I asked.

'In the country being looked after by Mrs Morse, the cleaner. He would only have got bored with the shopping. Here's the living-room.'

She threw open a door; it was decorated in country style, printed linens against soft off-white carpet. The pictures were adequate but unexciting, apart from two good figure drawings, Augustus John possibly, either side of the fireplace. The effect was cosy and unpretentious. I duly admired it, wondering if I was to be shown more or whether I was now meant to take my leave.

'The kitchen's through here,' she said, opening another door.

'I was going to ask you back for tea,' I said.

'What do you mean, you were "going to"? You didn't know I was here.' She looked at me and her mouth curled into a smile. 'Or did you?' she said to herself rather than to me. 'Let's have tea here; I've bought crumpets. I can't resist them.'

She switched on the kettle, arranged the crumpets on a grill-pan. 'It's quite convenient having this place as a bolt-hole. Josh is working flat out at the moment,' she told me over her shoulder.

'How are things?' I asked tentatively.

'Oh, much the same as when I last saw you.'

I had the impression she did not want to talk about it. It was warm in the house. She had stripped off her jersey and was wearing a silk shirt belted into jeans. Her body moved under the liquid flow of the material as she regulated the grill, her hair falling forwards, soft and unmanageable. I started to shiver despite the warmth, standing close by her.

'What are you and Sophie doing for Christmas?' she asked with her back to me.

'Lunch with my mother is obligatory.' I tried to get a grip of myself. 'In the evening Sophie is going to a party and I have a choice of various friendly invitations.'

'Difficult to choose, I suppose,' she said cheerfully, peering at the crumpets.

'Not in the least. I shall go to bed with a book and a large whisky, and fall asleep knowing the whole bloody thing is behind me for this year.'

I tried to make my voice brisk and not self-pitying, but it could not have worked, because she swung round to look at me instantly.

'Oh, *Leo*.' She caught up both my hands in hers impulsively. 'God! You're cold,' she said.

I could not bear it, this close proximity.

'You should have come to us, we'd love it: you still could.'

She dropped my hands and, putting her own behind my head, she kissed me. Her eyes were blue and wide with concern. The last shreds of control deserted me. I pulled her close and took possession of her mouth, moving round it hungrily as if it were the last and only source of life. I swept the hair from her forehead, ran my fingers deeply into its softness, felt, where the other hand held her tightly, the giving warmth beneath slippery silk. Days and nights of denial and misery shrank and were lost in this searching oblivion. Somewhere, over the horizon of her shoulder, flames shot up to celebrate.

'Oh, God! The crumpets!'

She leaped for the oven cloth; a fiery pan was withdrawn and dumped in the sink to the hissing of the cold tap. I stood helpless, earthbound again, and too shattered to think coherently. The kitchen was full of black smoke.

'Open the back door, could you?'

I did as I was asked, and a freezing draught of foggy air coursed across the room forbiddingly. I shivered, unable to see a way back to the pursuit of glory as opposed to domesticity. I stared at Claudia; our eyes were streaming.

'Oh dear!' she said, and started to laugh. How infectious laughter is, and how therapeutic; I take myself too seriously. We rocked with it, clinging to each other, wiping wet cheeks on the backs of our hands. She closed the door eventually, emitting the last feeble giggle.

'Why are we standing here?' she asked, suddenly serious.

'I can't think. Perhaps I should leave—'

'Is that what you want?'

'You know I don't.'

We climbed the stairs in silence, and she led me to a room where the double bed took up most of the space. The shivers had turned to sweats, as if I was a callow youth once more, nerve-racked and inexperienced. I tried to undress her, but my fingers fumbled with the buttons and the jeans were an impossible hazard. Dealing with my own clothes was bad enough; I left them in a heap and waited for her, wishing to God we had not been interrupted by the bloody crumpets but had taken things on the flood on the kitchen floor.

The street lamp shone through a gap in the curtains and cut a swathe of light across her body, as the morning sun had done in Josh's painting: highlighting the tip of one breast. Facing me, she was as I had imagined her many times, going on to dream of her sinking backwards beneath me on the bed, smooth pliant arms pulling me on to her, her body curving up to meet mine. So long had I suppressed the images that the reality was explosive in its effect. I wanted desperately to show her that for me this was special, not just a careless act of copulation; to tell her by tenderness and expertise that I was falling in love. I wanted us to reach the point of no return together: I wanted it to be perfect. But you can want too much, wait too long; drunk on possession and her responses, restraint did not stand a chance; I felt her so near and yet so far before I capitulated and fell across her, groaning at my inadequacies and the wonder of it all.

'Sorry,' I mumbled, kissing her breasts. 'Sorry, darling Claudia.'

'What is there to be sorry for?' In the dim light she smiled up at me, dampened hair dark against the pillow.

'My timing.'

'Oh, that,' she said lazily. 'Too much fuss is made about that, don't you think?'

I kept silent, disagreeing with her.

'Anyway,' she added, 'we're not used to each other. It takes time, doesn't it?'

My heart leapt at the intimation that this was only a beginning: I couldn't bear the thought of a dead end. Neither did I want to think of the consequences just now, lying beside her; my conscience would doubtless catch up with me soon enough when I was alone.

The idea of Sophie returning to an empty house drove me to dress reluctantly, and afterwards I sat drinking an overdue cup of tea in the living-room, Claudia curled on the floor between my knees. She was wrapped in her discarded husband's towelling robe and the scene presented a marital cosiness; enjoyable but wildly out of keeping with our situation. She was quiet and it bothered me. I began to imagine the reasons why: regrets, guilt, my deficiencies as a lover. I longed to ask questions but sensed it wasn't the moment to voice them.

The telephone rang. I listened to her side of the conversation: 'I hadn't thought; tube, I suppose – oh, would you? – that would be an enormous help, I am a bit tired – thanks, darling – about three-quarters of an hour? – there are one or two things I still have to do – see you, 'bye.'

'That was Josh,' she told me unnecessarily. 'He's coming to fetch me in the car.' Two small furrows appeared between her eyebrows. 'It's so unlike him, he never thinks about things like that as a rule.'

'I'd better go,' I said.

Unwarranted jealousy welled up in me: jealousy for anyone who laid claim to her.

'Have you noticed, being wicked brings immediate repercussions?' she said lightly.

More likely the fact that she might not be home to cook supper had activated this one, I thought sourly, pulling on my coat and making sure I had left nothing incriminating behind. We stood by the front door, her hair flame-coloured and rampant still from its tumbling.

'Claudia, when—?'

'I don't know.' She pulled the robe more firmly round her, defensively, it seemed. 'Don't start tying me down, Leo darling. You can see it's difficult for me to plan ahead.' Her eyes held mine and in them I saw another, evasive and determined Claudia. 'There's Sam, and there's Josh,' she said, shrugging.

'Perhaps we should have thought of them before.'

'Don't *you* feel a certain responsibility towards Josh? You're somewhat involved now in his future, aren't you?'

'I am aware of that without being reminded,' I said coldly: cold at her bewildering mood change and desperate for reassurance. The warm and melting woman of the previous hour might never have existed and the unfairness of it hurt badly.

I opened the door a crack. 'Yes, well – I've got the message. We'll call it a day, shall we? Or rather an afternoon: one jolly afternoon's bonking, not to be repeated.'

Her face whitened, eyes glazed over.

'That,' she said quietly, 'is the remark of a shit.'

I closed the door. 'Then tell me, what *do* you want, Claudia?' She shook her head. I took her in my arms, seeing imminent tears, realizing I was miles from understanding her complexities. 'It was a dreadful remark and I'm sorry, darling. But you haven't said a word, and for all I know that's how you regard us. It unnerved me,' I murmured into her hair, 'not knowing whether I meant anything or nothing to you.'

She put her arms round my neck. 'I thought it was women who asked those sorts of questions,' she said with a hint of a smile.

I waited.

'You made me very happy,' she added. 'Didn't you realize? That's why I'm scared.'

And she kissed me, a gentle, unsexy kiss which would have to suffice for now and for an unknown length of time.

'See you soon,' she called after me softly as I left. Was that a promise or just a meaningless phrase? I walked home with a raw midwinter night adding to the bleakness of separation.

Sophie was in the kitchen when I arrived back, and she was not alone. A boy was there, leaning against the dresser.

'Hello, Pa, been working late?' she asked, hugging me. 'This is David, only he's known as Smog because he's a bit thick.'

There ensued one of those slap-and-tickle fights between adolescents to show there was no romantic attachment; that over, he shook my hand politely and I asked him what he did.

'He's one of our star dancers at the R.B.S.,' Sophie said proudly. 'You should see his leg muscles.'

I had harboured a misconceived notion that all male dancers looked like Nureyev and the majority of them were gay. Smog looked athletically masculine and more like a Rugby full-back. I would have preferred him effeminate on the whole, considering Sophie's tender age.

'You smell nice,' she told me, chattering on. 'What *have* you been doing, kissing Zelda?'

'Ha-ha. No, I've been trying out the scents in Harrods parfumerie, if you must know.'

The lie slipped as glibly from my tongue as if I had had a lifetime of practice.

'Ooh! Something for me?'

'Wait and see.'

'Smog and I are going to a film. Aren't we?'

'Yerse.' Smog was a man of few words, it seemed.

'You don't mind, Pa, do you?' She looked at me in a way she has when uncertain of my reaction: boyfriends had not existed until now.

'Of course not,' I said blandly. 'Have you eaten?'

'Not yet. We'll get Kentucky fried chicken or a hamburger, I expect.'

'I don't suppose you've got much cash on you. Better take this in case.' I handed her ten pounds, hoping I was not putting the escort's nose out of joint.

'Thank you, Pa.'

'Cheers,' said Smog, brightening up.

'You'll be all right on your own?' she said solicitously. 'You will cook something?'

'Off you go,' I told her. 'Have fun. Look after her, er – David.'

'Yerse,' he agreed amiably, ' 'bye, then.'

Their voices and laughter drifted back to me, the front door slammed and I was alone and at the mercy of a mare's-nest of confused emotions. It did not surprise me that happiness was not one of them; I am not made to take sexual adventures lightly, neither am I by nature a wife-stealer. The proper solution was to stop the affair before it had begun. Probably it would come as a relief to Claudia.

I ate a sandwich, drank a lot of wine and went to bed firmly resolved on this course of action, or non-action; knowing full well as I lay awake that I would find it impossible to carry out. She was in my blood now, a part of me; it was all a terrible mistake which I hadn't the strength to correct.

Someone is calling me. I have been standing at the open window of my bedroom in Josh's cottage, but in another time, another world, and Sophie is below me in the garden.

'Are you all right, Pa? I've been positively yelling at you.'

'Sorry, kitten.' I smile down at her upturned face. 'I was miles away.'

'Supper's nearly ready. I've worked wonders,' she hisses, 'considering the larder's practically bare. It's cheese soufflé, so hurry up, will you?'

And she scampers away in the direction of the kitchen.

Chapter Six

The garden lies beautifully empty of human life and
the morning, still and fresh and new-born, promises
heat later on. There was dew on the grass at five
o'clock: I saw it. God! What a night; I hardly slept: and
now I gaze balefully at all this rural perfection with
weary, half-open eyes, hating it. I cannot believe it is
only Saturday.

Sophie comes from behind my chair in the shade of
an apple tree and winds her arms round my neck
affectionately. 'Anything I can get you in Chichester?'
she asks.

She is going on a shopping expedition with Josh and
Sam.

'Just *The Times* and a litre bottle of whisky. My
original one lasted precisely one evening. You'll find
some money in my room, on the chest.'

'Is there anything wrong, Pa?' she asks anxiously.
'You're not *still* upset about the cat getting into your
bedroom, are you?'

'Nope. I'm a little tired, that's all.'

'Well, you can have a blissful hour or two on your
own. Try to unwind.' She kisses me on the top of my
head and dances away, all long legs and hot-pants.

How easy she makes it sound. Sweet innocent child,
she hasn't an inkling of the complications attached to
this misconceived visit. I have begun to think Josh is

definitely unhinged by the loss of Claudia; or by the other more sinister reason involving myself which I cannot face up to right now. I cannot believe he intends to do me actual physical injury. His wild mood changes could be due to alcohol: a bottle of wine to himself, topped up by several brandies, is no mean consumption. It is the atmosphere he creates that gets to me and makes me a mass of jangled nerves; the feeling that he is waiting for the right moment to produce a dénouement. I sensed it strongly when he was showing me the paintings last night.

Oh! The paintings! It is these travesties of his talent that convince me he is unbalanced. He cannot be serious: he must have painted them tongue-in-cheek, as a bad joke. But for what purpose? If it was with the sole aim of upsetting me, then he has succeeded. But in the end it is merely a form of self-abuse. If Sophie had only warned me, for she saw them first, then I might have avoided the studio and slept better as a result; even she can recognize a travesty when she sees one, surely? She was too busy, I suppose, catering for this weird household of males.

By the time I limped down to supper yesterday evening, Sophie was removing a dish from the oven and Josh was standing behind her, poised to pinch or slap her delectable bottom: or that was the distinct impression I had. Everybody else was standing expectantly at the table.

'What's with the foot?' Marcus asked. He was brown from the sun and looked more alive than at lunch-time.

'Blisters,' I said. 'Josh walked me up a mountain.'

'Salt and water,' Da said. 'Nothing like it for blisters.'

'You've taken off the bandage,' Sam observed acccusingly.

'Well, actually it fell off, Sam, and I'm not much good at putting it back again.'

'I'll fix it for you after supper,' he told me with no room for argument.

'Stand back!' Sophie bore a soufflé dish to the table, plonked it on to mats and returned for a second offering; both of them had risen high above the rim and were a golden brown on top. She taught herself the art and I was proud of her.

'That's my girl!' Josh said.

I tried not to take exception to this harmless remark. There was a scraping of chairs, an unwrapping of napkins – (dug out from some long-forgotten drawer by Sophie, presumably) – the chink of knives and forks on china and a popping of corks at Da's end of the table. This was the moment when I felt the evening might be ordinarily pleasant, a gathering of family and friends; my spirits rose a trifle.

'We saw you on the hill,' I told Marcus. 'In the distance, riding.'

I could not have chosen a more unfortunate opening gambit.

'Riding, was it?' Josh shot his stepson a wicked emerald-green stare. 'Sitting around is how it looked to me.' He lifted a forkful of soufflé from his plate. 'Delicious.' He beamed at Sophie. 'No wonder the horses are as fat as butter, if that's all the exercise Desmond gives them,' he said, swerving back to Marcus.

'Summer fat,' Marcus said. 'They're out to grass.'

'In that case, it's a pity they don't get stuck into our

lawn which hasn't been mown since God knows when: your job, if you remember.'

'Heard from that drama school of yours, boyo?' Da enquired, attempting a neat deflection of the conversation.

'Not yet.' Marcus looked haunted.

'What speeches did you do for your audition?' Sophie asked swiftly.

'A piece from *Look Back in Anger*; *Othello* for the Shakespeare,' he muttered.

'"It is the cause, it is the cause"?'

'Yes.' Marcus glanced up, eyeing her with a glimmer of interest. 'You know *Othello*, then?'

'Drama's included in our curriculum; it's an important part of ballet. I was Desdemona, smothered by a boy with halitosis.' She sighed. 'Not an inspiring part.'

It was the first time I had heard Marcus laugh. 'Put out the light,' he quoted.

'And then put out the light,' echoed Sophie.

Josh glowered.

'If-I-quench-thee-thou-flaming-minister-I-can-again-thy-former-light-restore,' gabbled Sam, joining in with his mouth full.

'When I have plucked the rose, I cannot give it vital growth again,' Marcus declaimed in tragic tones.

'Oh balmy breath, that dost almost persuade Justice to break her sword!' Sophie collapsed in giggles.

'One-more-one-more-be-thus-when-thou-art-dead-and-I-will-kill-thee,' Sam said loudly and triumphantly.

Josh shouted, 'What is this? A bloody talent contest?' – and banged his glass down on the table.

'It's the Immortal Bard,' Marcus said, grinning.

140

'I know it's the bloody Bard, and overrated at that.'

'Oh, dear,' Marcus sighed. 'Josh thinks it's tosh.'

This reduced Sophie and Sam to paroxysms of mirth. Josh lowered his head like an angry bull and glared at them.

Marcus said, 'As a matter of fact, you'd make a perfect Othello, Josh. A bit of blacking and the part is tailor-made for you; all that jealousy and fire and fury; you'd be terrific.' He looked thoughtfully at his stepfather. 'It's about an obsession,' he added. 'A man who imagines his wife has been unfaithful to him—'

Josh raised his head.

'—and so he kills her; mistakenly, in fact, because she's mad about him.'

'I know the story, thanks, boyo. I'm not entirely uneducated,' Josh retorted.

Sarcasm, it seemed, had taken over from irritation. He refilled his glass and added, 'The psychology's up the creek, though. He'd have killed the lover, not the wife.'

He pronounced it as 'lov–er', in two syllables, his Welshness increasing with argument.

'Wouldn't you agree, Leo?' He smiled blandly at me. 'Nine out of ten men would top the lover.'

I smiled back. The muscles round my mouth felt stiff. 'God knows, Josh,' I said lightly. 'A simple divorce sounds preferable to me.'

'In Spain,' Da said solemnly, 'the husband would murder them both. Very passionate, they are, the Spanish. It's the Latin temperament.'

'And how did you come to learn this stuff, Sam?' Josh asked, his voice deceptively gentle. 'Thinking of becoming a Thespian too, are you?'

'A *what*?' Sam eyed the nearest soufflé dish, his

141

mind obviously on food. 'I heard Marcus's lines for him so often I got to know them by heart. He's brilliant,' he added, his eyes round with admiration. 'I can't see why he has to go to drama school: he's good enough already.'

'Thanks, little bruv,' Marcus said.

'Well, so long as I don't have *you* catching the bug.' Josh leaned his massive arms on the table. 'I only hope you've thought it through,' he told Marcus. 'Madness, I call it, trying to make it in the most over-crowded profession there is.'

The atmosphere had become as tense as before a storm. Marcus's face whitened and his eyes snapped, his only sign of annoyance. It struck me he might make a good actor, given such control.

'No madder than becoming an artist,' he said, 'and then throwing it all up to paint weirdo stuff that no-one'll buy.'

Josh turned the colour of claret and brought his fists down with a crash that rocked the glasses.

'How dare you?' he shouted. 'What the hell d'you mean by sneaking into my studio?'

'If you must leave the door unlocked.' Marcus shrugged.

'That's it!' Josh was on his feet, jaw thrust forward, hair falling in black curls over his forehead: the bull on the point of charging. 'That settles it. You leave tomorrow. I'm not having a poncey little upstart teaching me my job, d'you hear?'

'No problem,' Marcus said in his most drawly voice. 'I was going anyway. And just for the record,' he added, 'I'm not actually gay, you know. Desmond is, but I'm not.'

142

'Get out! Get out now!' Josh roared, beside himself.

Marcus rose, picked up his glass of wine and with a funny little bow walked gracefully to the open french window and into the garden. Sophie, after a second's hesitation, slipped from her chair and followed him. Josh flung his napkin into the middle of the dinner debris, caught a bottle with his elbow and knocked it flat, where it lay pouring a steady stream of wine into my lap with great precision. It was a fortuitous accident in its way, breaking the stunned silence of those of us who were left. Da fetched a wet cloth from the sink, Sam a tin of salt; Josh said, 'Christ! Sorry, Leo,' and slumped back in his chair chewing a fingernail. An argument ensued between Da and Sam as to the best remedy for wine stains.

'Cold water, boyo. That's infallible.'

'No, Gran'da. Mum used salt, honestly.'

It kept them busy; I allowed them to mop and pour alternately, doubting the success of their efforts on my pale linen trousers, and enduring a nasty dampness round my private parts.

Sophie appeared in the doorway, ghost-like in her white dress against the darkness.

'Leave the clearing away,' she said. 'I'll do it later.'

'You'll do no such thing.' Josh rose heavily. 'Send that young bastard in to do something for his living.'

She smiled a secret smile that reminded me of Jane.

'Sophie, I'm sorry if I've upset you—' Josh said this almost pleadingly; though why he singled her out for apology, I failed to understand.

'Never complain, never explain,' she said cheerfully, and vanished.

'Sophie!'

'See you later,' she called from the garden.

Silence fell, interrupted by Sam. 'Anybody mind if I scrape the dishes?' he asked; and since nobody disagreed he proceeded to do so. 'The brown crispy bits are the best,' he confided to me, apparently unperturbed by the recent scene.

Da, on the other hand, had temporarily lost some of his jaunty humour.

'There's times when I reckon I should have taken my belt to you more often as a boy, Joshua,' he said, bright eyes fierce in his craggy face. 'It's tough you are on young Marcus with your bully-boy tactics.'

Josh had produced balloon glasses and a bottle of brandy.

'Oh, you belted me all right; you don't remember, that's all. Pissed as a newt, you'd be.' He drew the cork, poured three measures and raised his glass. 'In the face of disapproval,' he announced, 'there is nothing for it but to get drunk.'

The sound of Sam's spoon scraping the dish had ceased. I glanced at him. He was staring at the brandy bottle, his blue eyes no longer artless but shadowed by anxiety; and I felt a sudden spasm of anger that Josh should be the cause of it.

'Get drunk, and show Leo the studio,' he added. 'Like the old days, eh, Leo? Back to square one.' He pressed one of the glasses into my hand and flung his arm round my shoulders, guiding me forcibly towards the door. 'Bed, Sam,' he said: not a word to his father.

The garden was light as day as we walked from the

144

house to the studio, floodlit by a full moon. Josh hummed to himself as we went, clutching glass and brandy bottle in either hand, and marching along as if looking forward to a treat. I longed for bed and privacy, already full of foreboding over what was about to be displayed. On such a night as this – (my mind was still running on Shakespearean lines) – Claudia and I had sneaked off to the shelter of the willows, keeping a wary eye on the studio where a light burned, proclaiming Josh's occupation. The heady smell of roses brought her back to me vividly, painfully, so that I imagined her fingers touched mine while she kept in step beside me.

The studio lay at right-angles to the house; a barn conversion permitted, I supposed, because it was of no historic value. Across the lawn, through a small orchard of apple trees and we had arrived, Josh unlocking the door with a certain amount of fumbling. The whole of the upper floor provided a large studio. The north side of the room had been replaced by sky-lighting, leaving a clear wall for hanging space. The ground floor was used as a storage area; for paintings, unwanted articles from the house and, by the look of it, for supplies of drink and bottles of empties. The staircase was perilously steep and I followed after Josh clinging to the rope handrails. By the time I reached the top he had turned a switch and the pictures were illuminated to give me the immediate benefit of their shocking impact.

It took me several moments to realize they were all of Claudia: Claudia alone, Claudia in disguise, Claudia in weird groups. The style which Joshua had chosen to adopt was that of the grotesque; limbs and faces were bloated and caricatured, people rollicked in pubs, street-walkers leered lasciviously above feather boas, bulging men in dinner-jackets escorted elephantine women towards a dance floor. In each of these canvases he had placed Claudia as the focal point, distorted but distinct, only the dark flaming hair true to life. The paintings were not ill-executed; I doubt whether it is possible for Josh to paint badly. But they were overwhelmingly ugly and painted, I suspected, to satisfy some angry corner of his being rather than with a view to selling.

Of the three in which Claudia figured more or less alone, two portrayed her as a nun; one of them full-face, eyes blue and tranquil with piety, and the mouth a slash of scarlet. The other showed her full-length but in profile, her face barely visible behind a wimple. A grey shadow stretched from the hem of her robe to the feet of two anonymous males, their faces blanked out. The third presented her as a Madonna, holding a bunch of red roses in her lap in lieu of a child; her smile was not Claudia's smile, but a smug twitch of the lips in an almost direct crib of the Mona Lisa. Each one of these paintings, the groups included, were a symbolic and malicious insult to Claudia, and there was no doubt in my mind that it was deliberate.

I walked slowly by the nine pictures, playing for time. I did not know what to say. Phrases bounded and rebounded in and out of my mind, while my heart thudded and my mouth turned dry. Pent-up emotions strained to let rip at Josh, upbraid him, tell him what I thought of his black humour. Instinct warned me that humour it was not; more a cry of anguish, a violent catharsis of the soul by a man who knows himself to have been wronged and humiliated. He did not suspect; he *knew*. Whether or not that knowledge stretched far enough to include me was impossible to gauge; but the thought was enough to silence me as I walked snail-like down the room. He, too, was silent: waiting, presumably, for my reactions. The atmosphere was charged with waiting, like bated breath.

In front of the penultimate painting, I decided on the stance I should take: that of the aggrieved and saddened mentor who sees all his efforts gone to waste through one man's whim. It was not difficult to assume, for a part of me felt exactly that; the small part of me that was not dying to throttle him for desecrating Claudia's memory. Claudia must be left out of this; I would not give him the satisfaction of direct attack. Furious broadsides were his *métier*, not mine; and besides a trickle of fear, born of guilt, wormed its way persistently round my innards. My perfidy seemed to declare itself in every brushstroke of those macabre paintings.

I sighed regretfully, shook my head, turned to face him. He was leaning against the opposite wall, one eyebrow raised sardonically.

'I knew you wouldn't approve,' he said.

'It's not a matter of approval,' I answered with just the right tone of reproach. 'You've every right to paint as you wish. I'm simply puzzled by the style you happen to have adopted.' I glanced back to the canvases. 'You're not being true to yourself, Josh.'

'What crap!' he retorted. 'I paint as the spirit moves me. I've a different outlook on life to a year ago, you may have noticed. What do you expect? Artists should experiment, move forward, not remain static. Take

147

Picasso, if you want a clinchéd example.'

'Ah.' I looked at the unpleasing examples of Josh's 'experiment'. 'But Picasso in any of his periods was never a copyist.'

'Copyist?' He sounded genuinely indignant. 'That's a bloody offensive accusation, Leo. Do you mind explaining?'

'I mean they are not originals: in the broadest sense, of course.' I sighed again. 'This is old hat, it's all been done before; Paris in the 'twenties, Berlin in the early 'thirties, and so on. In fact,' I added truthfully, 'there was a retrospective of German artists held in London last year. Your paintings bear a marked resemblance to one or two included in the collection. At the Hayward, d'you remember?'

'No,' he said sulkily. 'Didn't get to see it.'

'But you must have seen the spread in the news-papers?'

'What if I did? What are you getting at?' He heaved himself away from a leaning position and began to pace irritably. 'Suggesting I made surreptitious sketches of this exhibition?' I had the impression this uncomfortable session was not going the way he had expected. 'Bloody hell! What you're looking at is all mine: it springs from here.' He rapped his head and his chest. 'And it's the outcome of how I feel right now, not a sodding crib.'

I thought this was most likely true, even if the result was a disaster. 'Calm down,' I said. 'Let's have some of that brandy.'

He poured two measures into glasses on the work-table. 'The trouble with you, Leo, is you're like all your breed. Galleries imagine they own their wretched

148

artists body and soul. Step out of line, dare to be a teeny bit adventurous and you start wagging fingers at us, like costive old nursemaids.'

I smiled annoyingly, as I might at a difficult child. 'Come, Josh, have a heart. Galleries don't run on air and altruism alone, and this is hardly the time to take chances.' I took a swig of the brandy and felt it pump a degree of confidence into my veins. 'You might grant us a little more altruism than your unkind words suggest, though,' I added.

He came to a halt, glass in hand, looking down at me. At moments like these he seems to tower, the breadth and height and darkness of him larger than life.

'So you're not going to offer me another exhibition on the strength of what I've done?'

I spread my hands in a hopeless gesture. 'On the strength of what I have seen tonight: no, Josh. I can't attempt to sell what I don't believe in.'

He shrugged. 'I never believed you would. There are other galleries.'

'Naturally,' I agreed.

His snub was juvenile and, as such, could not be seriously resented, for all that I was instrumental in building him a reputation. Besides, I knew these pictures had not been executed for the purpose of being shown: apart from this dreadful little private view between the two of us.

'What you had was magic, Josh,' I said. 'It can't have disappeared. I suspect it's buried beneath a pile of misery, which isn't surprising following a—'

'Don't mention that bloody word "bereavement",' he said softly, fiercely. 'I was bereaved before she died.'

My heart flew up into my throat and stuck there constrictingly. 'I know you had your problems before Claudia became ill—' The words hung feebly on the air and died away.

'You do, do you? And how would you know?' he asked, his voice on the same low note.

I wished he would shout; it was less unnerving. 'For God's sake, Josh,' I protested, 'how could anyone remain unaware? Your fights were phenomenal; they were the reason I stopped accepting invitations to stay here, if you remember. I was quite open about it.'

'Were you?' He gave me a piercing stare; then he swung away abruptly with a roar of laughter. 'Claudia wasn't; she was devious. But that's women for you. The whole bloody lot are devious.' He fetched the bottle and topped up our glasses. 'Or do you reckon Jane was an exception, Leo?'

'I certainly do,' I said, and at the same time wondered whether one could be certain of anyone. There was a trace of patronage about his smile which I didn't much like.

'In these paintings,' he said, waving a hand, 'I've tried to convey the different aspects of Claudia—'

'Yes, I can see that,' I said with sarcasm.

'The good, the bad, the loving—'

He broke off and I realized, suddenly and in amazed horror, that he was weeping.

There is nothing more disconcerting than feeling abject fear one moment and switching to compassion the next; particularly when the compassion concerns some crime you have committed. I pretended not to notice: the coward's way out, wandering over to the pictures and examining one of them.

'The colour's superb, as ever,' I remarked; the words of a kindergarten teacher to a promising four-year-old.

'Shit!' From the noises, I gathered Josh was mopping up and blowing his nose. 'You know something? I'm pissed.'

This was the moment, heaven-sent, to turn, pat him on the shoulder, render the sympathy I had no earthly right to offer. I did all this: 'So am I,' I said. 'Come on, time for bed.'

We negotiated the stairs with difficulty, Josh's bulk wavering above me dangerously. I took the keys from him, preparing to lock up and noticing as I did so the shotgun lodged behind the door.

'Burglars,' he said wisely, seeing me looking at it.

'You'd be in trouble if you shot one.'

'Be in trouble if you shot anyone,' he agreed, leaning heavily on me, 'more's the pity.'

The fresh air seemed to sober him somewhat, contrary to belief. As we made our way haphazardly back to the house, he said quite clearly, 'I'd like to paint Sophie. You don't mind, do you?'

'In the recent Jones period, or the original?'

'Don't know till I start.'

'I don't mind, Josh.' In fact, I felt a surge of optimism that this might mean the beginnings of his revival.

I walked to the window of my bedroom without switching on my light, to take a last look at the garden under moonlight: communing with the past. The figures of Sophie and Marcus were standing on the river bank, facing each other, as Claudia and I might once have stood. As I watched, they turned and started to walk slowly back across the blue-lit lawn, deep in conversation. I found a curious relief in their obvious compatibility for which I could not account. Then I groped my way to the door and snapped on the light, and there, curled up asleep on my bed, was one of the cats: a black and white creature, the same I had seen padding around the garden, keeping its distance.

Icy shivers ran up and down my spine. I remained stock still for at least thirty seconds, my hand glued to the door-handle in a paralysis of phobic terror. I turned it eventually, slowly and carefully opening the door, preparing to sidle out and plead for help: for if my life had depended on it, I would have been incapable of removing the animal myself. But there was a squeak from the hinges; the cat raised its head, summing me up with contemptuous feline eyes before dropping to the floor and starting to wind itself sinuously round my legs. I bounded like a hunted thing into the corridor and collided with Sophie: we staggered together for a moment in a kind of farcical dance before restoring our balance.

'For heaven's sake, Pa: drunk again?' she said, laughing.

The cat slid out of the bedroom, making towards me unerringly. I shrank against the wall.

'For God's sake, catch it!'

'Oh, I *see*. Here, pussikins.' Sophie picked it up and it nestled in her arms purring, while my skin crawled. 'How did it get in?' she asked, kind enough not to ridicule me.

'Lord knows,' I said grimly. 'The door was shut all evening.'

'Oh, then the window, I expect. It's no way from the ground.'

'Oh, yes?' Shame made me sarcastic. 'I suppose it sensed my antipathy and chose my window out of spite.'

She glanced at me seriously. 'You've gone awfully white; are you all right? I was coming to say good night, but I can get you a cup of tea, if you like.'

'No, just get rid of the bloody thing for me, put it under lock and key. All I want now is undisturbed sleep.' I blew her a kiss. 'Thank you, darling.'

When she had left, I searched the room thoroughly for further animal intrusions and found nothing but dust. Crawling cautiously between the bedclothes – (a sheet that inadequately covered my feet and a blanket that in my nervous state smelt to me of cat) – I attempted to relax. In no way did I believe the animal had entered of its own volition: someone had planted it there. Too tired to pursue the idea, I fell into an uneasy sleep broken by the groans of the plumbing system, and dreamt a series of tortuous dreams in which Josh's grotesque figures came horribly to life.

I must have dozed off in my chair under the tree. The shadow has moved and I am now in bright sunlight. Wandering to the driveway to see whether the shoppers have returned, I come across Da polishing his Jaguar lovingly. He is nattily dressed in beautifully-cut shorts out of which sprout a pair of bowed and hairy legs. He relays to me the plans for the day; a picnic lunch at a spot on the downs has been arranged, and there are people coming to dinner. He is to cook one of his famous paellas for which Sophie has promised to buy the ingredients. 'Josh has asked the vicar and his wife,' Da tells me with a grin. 'She's a well-built girl;'

and he draws a curvaceous figure in the air with his hands.

'There's tired you're looking this morning, Leo,' he remarks, eying me shrewdly. 'Late, were you, you and Josh?'

He does not ask about the paintings immediately, but I get the feeling he is waiting for me to say something.

'I'm going to make some coffee. Shall I bring you a cup?' I ask.

'Very kind, boyo; ta. I like to finish a job once I've started, see.'

The house is very quiet with the deep hush of summer. In the kitchen two flies sail lazily around in circles. There is a bowl of roses on the dresser; everything looks cleaner and tidier to my inexpert eye, and I suspect this to be Sophie's doing. I put the kettle on the hot plate of the Aga to boil and drift towards the sitting-room, where Claudia's bureau stands against the wall near the french windows. There will not be many chances to investigate; and although I don't expect to find my letters where one might imagine them to be, it is worth a quick look.

The sloping lid is locked and the key is missing: a disappointment from the start. I try the three drawers one by one; two are completely empty, the third has a single sheet of lined paper torn from a jotting pad. For a startled moment I expect to see written 'Foiled again' or 'Sucks to you', as if my searchings are merely a jolly treasure hunt played against a larky opponent. Picking it up I see it is a list made out neatly but in a juvenile hand; a list of drinks with the dates of purchase and the number of bottles bought and consumed within a week. The days of the week run meticulously down the side of the page with the entries opposite them. I am none the wiser; I replace it and push the drawer shut. Someone, Josh presumably, has made a clean sweep of Claudia's papers; it is as if he is trying to eradicate all traces of her living. Her memory must be more difficult to get rid of, and can only be distorted. I find the thought both miserable and disturbing.

Da is already in the kitchen when I return, pouring boiling water into two mugs of instant coffee. He must have seen me through the open door at Claudia's desk, but says nothing. I am beginning to have a lot of respect for this old man, whose motto has to be 'all things come to he who waits'. I feel an urge to talk to him, encourage him to continue where he left off yesterday, reflecting on his son.

'Came in for a let-up after all,' he says, mopping his forehead with a red silk handkerchief. 'Hot as Spain out there.'

We sit on the terrace where the sun has yet to reach us.

'Josh showed me his most recent work,' I tell him neutrally.

'Well?' He looks at me. 'Back on form, is he?'

I glance back at him, shaking my head. 'No, Da – that is, if you want my opinion.'

'It's the best opinion I've got, isn't it?' He shifts his thin shanks on the chair. 'There's no surprise. The boy's half out of his tree.'

'I agree.' I clear my throat, gather myself for the usual lies. 'Only to be expected, after the trauma of a death.'

'Nothing to do with it.' He bangs a fist down on the

155

garden table. There is a pause, then he looks sideways at me in a particularly cunning way he has.

'Claudia had a lover. Josh found out, don't ask me how. There's the crux of the trouble. Thought you'd have known.'

I deny it with surprised mendacity.

'Then she gets ill and dies,' Da continues. 'Easy it is to understand the torment; no time for him to have a bloody good row and get it out of his system, or to forgive her and start over again. No time to mourn, either. Left him a mass of frustration, it has.'

"Has he told you who it was – the other man?' I ask casually.

Da says succinctly, 'Josh is a clam; I told you, boyo. Not likely to tell who's been screwing his wife, is he? There's the shame of it, see, for one thing. Without excusing Claudia, he's not an easy man to live with and there's two sides to every question. Lively, she was, but not a whore by nature.' He makes a tut-tutting sound of regret. 'Well, you knew her, didn't you?'

I agree I knew her, while the biblical connotation of the phrasing strikes me uncomfortably.

'Is there nothing you can do to influence him, Leo?' he asks after a pause.

A moment of involuntary mirth, the same reversal of emotions that causes one to cry at weddings and laugh at funerals, dies within me: he sounds so helpless.

'I'm doing my best,' I assure him; recalling Josh's desire to paint Sophie, I add, 'I already have hopes.'

'It's young Sam who bothers me.' Da's brows draw together in an expression identical to that of Josh. 'He worries about his da's drinking; I've caught him marking the bottles.'

The list in Claudia's bureau makes instant sense.

'Josh,' he adds, 'is talking of selling up here and going to live in that poky little place of his in London; cash-flow problems, see. It's not right, though.' He stabs at me with a forefinger. 'The boy's security lies here, and that's important at his age.'

There is the distant crunch of wheels on gravel. The shoppers have returned.

'What Josh needs,' I remark, speaking my thoughts, 'is some sort of incentive to jolt him out of his self-destructive rut.'

Da snorts. 'Like a bloody good kick up the arse might do the trick,' he says derisively.

It is that indeterminate hour of half-past three in the afternoon. The picnic is over; Josh was restless and insisted on going home early. He has disappeared in the direction of the studio, which I take as an encouraging sign. Da is busy with his paella and pleasant smells waft from the kitchen. Marcus is declaiming to himself on the banks of the river; I can see him, mouthing and gesticulating, book in hand. Of Sophie there is no sign. My eyes open and shut spasmodically. I am somnolent from the heat and lack of sleep, would like to be stretched out on a bed rather than this long-chair, but the less I see of my bedroom the better. Sam's face swims suddenly into focus, close to mine; blue eyes wide and shockingly the same as his mother's. He is crouching by my chair.

'Leo?'

'Yes, Sam?'

'Have you seen my toad, by any chance?'

157

I am fully awake on the instant, with visions of stepping on the beastly creature.

'No, I haven't. Has it escaped?'

'Yes. Leo, would you come and help me search? I'd ask Sophie, only I can't find her, and everyone else is busy.'

About to make excuses, I change my mind. Heaving myself to my feet, I accompany him to the jungle territory which was once Claudia's 'little' garden.

'I can't understand it,' he says as we tread cautiously through the grass, parting it with sticks. 'The cage door was open. It's always latched; I never forget.'

'It can't have gone far, surely?'

'It can, actually. It's got an enormous leap.'

I peer nervously about me. We are close by the tree-house.

'As far as this?' I ask.

'Easily.' He pushes a hand through his hair so that it stands up in a flaming quiff. 'I think I'll climb up and see if I can spot him from above.'

From the depths of the foliage he calls, 'Like to come up, Leo?'

'Some other time, thanks, Sam.'

'That's what you said before,' he points out.

'Did I? Oh, well.' I grip the rope ladder with both hands. 'How do I climb this thing?' I enquire.

'Just sort of *pull* yourself up.'

The ladder has a sinuous life of its own; I arrive hot and breathless at the top and get myself hauled on to the wooden platform unceremoniously by Sam.

'I hope it doesn't collapse under my weight.'

'I don't suppose so,' he says cheerfully. 'You're quite thin, really.'

There is a surprising amount of space; I sit cross-legged in the verdant light beneath the heavy branches and imagine Claudia making up stories for her son, the two of them shut off from the world, weaving magic.

'Great up here, isn't it?' Sam says with pride.

I agree with genuine enthusiasm. I have no experience of tree-houses; they are just another missing element from my boyhood, and the secret fascination of this one stirs a dormant chord of childish glee in me; the thrill of a hiding place.

'If you had something private you wanted to hide, Sam, is this where you would choose?'

He hesitates, calculating, I suspect, whether or not I am to be trusted. Alert eyes give me a going-over; then he scrambles to the nether regions of his domain and brings back the kind of tin box used for petty cash.

'Promise you won't let on? To anyone?' he demands severely.

'I promise.'

'This is my savings box.' He rattles the tin. 'Whenever I get some money given to me, it goes in here.'

'Like pocket money and so on?'

'I don't get any of that at the moment: Josh can't afford it,' he says matter-of-factly. 'Birthdays and things like that. I usually get something for those. And Gran'da will give me a tenner when he leaves, which is terrific.'

'It sounds satisfactorily full, the box.'

'I don't spend much; only on things for my animals and chewing-gum for me. The rest,' he explains, 'is in case Josh goes bust.'

The Dickensian poignancy of the situation touches me; poor child, saving up to rescue his father. 'We must do our best to make sure he doesn't,' I say reassuringly.

'Yes, but suppose he does.' He scratches absent-mindedly at a mosquito bite on his arm. 'I've decided I'm not going to live in London. That's what the savings are for: it's my running-away money.'

I forget about his selflessness. 'Where would you run to?' I ask.

'I dunno. I expect Mrs Morse would let me live with her for a bit.'

'And get you to school every day? If you want to be a zoologist, exams are necessary.'

'There's the bus,' he says, staring at his feet.

'It's not running away you're planning on, it's running *out*,' I tell him. 'Have you thought how your mother would have felt about that?'

I am aware of not playing fair, but I consider it justified.

'Mum would have understood. She might have done it herself if she hadn't got ill,' he says with the air of one producing a trump card.

I can read from the expression in his eyes the naked disappointment at my attitude.

'It's none of my business,' I say with a placatory smile. 'Aren't we supposed to be looking for your toad?'

He grins back, not given to bearing grudges.

'No use,' he says. 'I forgot the field glasses; I'll never catch sight of him without them, he's too well camou-flaged.'

He leans backward and brings out a storage jar. 'Like a biscuit?' he asks as a peace-offering.

Accepting, I remember why I have allowed myself to

join the hunt for this animal and be dragged up a tree. Are we not all self-seeking in our way?

'That's quite a cache of goodies you have stashed away,' I remark through a mouthful of custard cream. 'Did your mother,' I ask as casually as possible, 'keep her own hoard of secrets up here as well?'

He shakes his head. 'Mum didn't have special places for anything, that's why she was always losing things.'

'So your cash-box is the only one?' I stare idly upwards through the canopy of green.

'Oh, yes.' He looks at me as if I am more than slightly wanting. 'Why shouldn't it be?'

'No reason at all,' I agree hurriedly.

'Of course,' he says, putting the lid on the biscuit jar, 'there was the time-capsule, but that's properly hidden—'

He stops abruptly.

'The what?'

'Sorry, I can't really tell you about it. I forgot it was a secret, Mum's and mine.' He is suddenly still. 'Listen!'

From the direction of the river, the harsh 'quark-quark' can be heard which even I know emanates from a frog.

'It *could* be my toad,' he says, and makes a scramble for the ladder.

'Hold it steady,' I shout to him. 'I don't want to be up here all night.'

He sees me safely to the ground with ill-concealed impatience, and I watch him scud away, darting between the trees like one of his creatures, the fox cub Troy maybe, with the same russet hair.

Had Claudia truly considered leaving Josh? If so, it was news to me. From the start she had made it plain that, despite the engrossment of our relationship, her commitment to Josh could never be broken. Walking back to the house, I thought about this and other revelations which family members had let slip unsolicited in the last twenty-four hours; Marcus, for instance, who had walked beside me to the picnic place up a chalk path on the downs, while the others had gone on ahead. We were both slow; my blisters were not quite healed, and Marcus was carrying two plastic bags containing bottles.

'Christ!' he said, halting halfway. 'Josh does have some bloody stupid ideas. Let's have a drink.'

We subsided on to the turf verge and he found the cider.

'We'll incur Josh's wrath,' I said warningly.

'So what's new? I incur it all the time; always have done.'

'I thought you were supposed to leave today.'

'Oh, that. He's forgotten he ever said it by now.'

'He's not easy,' I agreed, 'but he has his good points.'

'Such as?' He eased a squashed packet of cigarettes from his jeans pocket and offered it to me, a gesture as graceless as his words. Josh brought the worst out in him, apparently.

'He's amusing company, and he's brilliant in his own field: when he wants to be, of course,' I told him gently.

He drew on his cigarette and exhaled extravagantly. 'He's a bastard,' he said without emphasis, as if he had said it many times before.

I watched him in silence, since there was not an answer to this; dark eyes preoccupied, forearm propped on a raised knee, clear profile gazing unseeingly into the middle distance. A good-looking boy in whom I could see nothing of his mother; although, when he turned his head and spoke, I caught a flash of something – the angle of his head, perhaps – that recalled Claudia.

'Ma was thinking of leaving him,' he said out of the blue, 'before she got ill.'

'She told you?' I asked, privately amazed.

He nodded, plucking at the grass with long, thin fingers. 'There was someone else – another man. She didn't actually tell me so, but I guessed.'

My heartbeat doubled itself.

'I think Josh found out about it,' he continued. 'I overheard a monumental row about a message left on the answerphone: one of those rows they were having before Ma was diagnosed.' He wrenched the grass angrily, then looked at me and laughed. 'Can you imagine anyone being such a clot as to leave love messages on the answerphone?' he added.

I smiled weakly and agreed that I could not, while my mind went racing backwards in time, seeking to recall possible acts of emotional carelessness.

'Why do you come down here if you dislike him so much?' I enquired.

'I don't know,' he said. 'To get out of London, I suppose. It's wonderful country and I like the riding; and Desmond's fun. He used to act, you know.'

A yell echoed back to us; Josh stood some hundred yards away, gesticulating.

'We'd better get going,' I said.

'Yeah.' He unwound his limbs and climbed lethargically to his feet. 'I like to keep an eye on Sam, too, poor little bugger. It must be tough on him without Ma; she

163

was great.' He bent to pick up the carriers. 'Josh was foul to Ma when she was last pregnant, and that,' he said, 'I cannot forgive him for.'

We moved slowly towards the object of his anger, our shoes scuffling the chalk into little clouds. Words of comfort or at least wisdom would have been appropriate, but none sprang to mind. I wondered why he had chosen me as a recipient of his angst, and the answer was delivered in his next sentence.

'Ma was fond of you.'

'And I of her,' I replied with reasonable aplomb.

'I feel I can talk to you, Leo; you don't mind, do you?'

'Not at all; I'm pleased.'

We were drawing near the rest of the party, stationed on a plateau between gorse bushes; near enough to alarm me that Marcus's carrying voice could be heard.

'If Ma had some fun before she died, I'm glad,' he remarked. 'I'd like to meet the guy and tell him so, whoever he was.'

I wonder, stepping now from shade to sunlight through the luxuriant overgrown grass, whether Marcus would stand by his declaration if I gave him the truth. It is an odd situation, the villain being forced to play confidante, and I am not comfortable in the rôle. One does not know what may transpire next, and heaven knows I have been given enough food for thought for one day. It seems that everyone in this family is cognisant of Claudia's indiscretion to some extent; even Sam sensed a restlessness. It no longer seems extraordinary that she talked to Marcus; communication must have been thin on the ground with her marriage falling apart, and who else was there to listen?

There was, of course, myself: I think of this as I reach the drive and crunch to an abrupt halt on the gravel. Amongst the snippets of information imparted to me today, something grates at my mind like sand in an oyster shell. I have never, I am convinced, left a message on the Hornsey answerphone which did not concern Josh's work; caution is far too ingrained in me. Someone did so; someone spoke soft words of endearment, according to Marcus. If Claudia had planned to leave, whence and to whom would she have run? Not to me, so she led me to believe.

My gaze is on the open front door, the dark cave of hall beyond. Under the eaves, house martins dart to and from their solid little nests. My eyes watch, but it is Claudia I see: as I always see her, leaning against the lintel, the smile curving up her face in anticipation and welcome. I shake my head, clear my eyes of the vision, walk forward briskly. I do not want my love for her desecrated by suspicion; I wish it to remain quietly sleeping with me, intact.

In the cool of the hall, depression descends momentarily. I walk through to the kitchen, but for once Da is not in the mood for a chat. He is wrapped in a butcher's apron, busily stirring a couple of cauldrons like one of the witches from *Macbeth*. I do not like to make a cup of tea for fear of disturbing things. Jane springs to mind because she used to wear the same type of apron. I long suddenly for her presence and her calm appraisal of problems, imagine her raising a sceptical eyebrow in my direction; although I know in reality she would not have taken infidelity lightly. The two women who coloured my life are both dead, yet their influence lives on, causing me to query my every move.

I have Sophie, I remind myself before I give way to self-pity; a very special bonus whom I have not seen, by the way, since returning from the picnic. In answer to my question Da waves a spoon abstractedly and says, 'The studio,' as he adds a sprinkling of saffron to the rice. I leave by the french windows and strike off through the orchard, buoyed up by sudden optimism. It may well be, if Sophie is sitting for Josh, that I shall not be welcome, but I am willing to risk it. A mere glimpse of him standing by his easel intent on some serious work is worth his irritation. Also, it gives me something to do, fills in that torpid hour before the legitimate time for a drink.

The door to the studio is closed but not locked. The mustiness of the lower floor, reminiscent of old and mildewing trunks, is topped by the unmistakable smells of turpentine and oil paint. Above me the murmur of voices can be heard while I climb the stairs, calling out, 'Hi, there!' softly as my head appears at the top. Josh is how I pictured him, legs wide apart, broad back towards me, palette and brush in either hand, alternately bending forwards and back in concentration. There is a large canvas on the easel, and no rancour to his tone at all.

'Come to see how things are going, Leo?' he says jovially, without turning.

'I—' I start to say, and get no further.

Sophie is lying on a *chaise-longue* on which is draped a black and gold fringed shawl. She waggles a little finger at me.

'Don't disturb her,' Josh warns. 'She's been a very good girl up till now; held the pose like a pro.'

Sophie continues to hold it through my silence. The light from the setting sun falls on her long, beautiful limbs and her dark head, and on the hand tapering over her spread of pubic hair. She smiles at me unperturbed, Jane's secret smile: she is as naked as the day she was born.

Chapter Seven

I had chosen the most fortuitous month in which to hold Josh's exhibition. The general air of optimism following a popular election result had given a welcome, if temporary, boost to the business world, and the bleakness of winter was forgotten. It was the best May I could remember, day after day blessed with the perfection of early summer. It was also a month of precarious happiness for Claudia and myself, and the month in which Josh knew success for the first time: before he lost his peace of mind and threw it all away.

I went to a great deal of trouble over the private view: hand-picking from the guest lists, spending hours on publicity, checking and re-checking that the smallest detail had been attended to. That which was normally left to an efficient team headed by Zelda received my personal attention, and Zelda did not like it. She was always edgy on such occasions, and more so than usual over this one since Josh had touched her heart-strings. She took it out on the two girls currently employed as her assistants, and on the day before the private view she balked at my interference. We both lost our tempers.

'It is obvious,' she said, 'that you no longer regard me as competent.'

'Heaven forbid,' I apologized, pinching my eyes

between thumb and forefinger. 'Truth is, I am over-wrought and I've got a stinking headache.'

'That,' she said, 'makes two of us. But I think you are the more deserving of it.' And she gave me a keen glance that seemed to absorb all my misdemeanours, real and imaginary.

Later I suggested I take her for a drink; to my surprise she agreed, and we went round the corner to a pub and took the edge off our nerves with dry sherry in her case and whisky in mine. Later still, when the last employee had left, I wandered round the Gallery and sank down at last on the leather seat in the far room. Josh's art came to life on the dove-grey walls and sprang to meet me, filling me with the reassurance of its extraordinary quality and the fact that I was not, after all, making a dreadful mistake. The thought of going home, even to my beloved Sophie, seemed suddenly unbearable: for there was no Jane on the receiving end, and in the context of home there never was, and never would be, Claudia.

For once, my love for them both had come close to overlapping. Confusion had set in, and although Claudia was now my lover and had the advantage of being alive, I lived continuously with the ghost of Jane. I found myself making comparisons, trying to solve the enigmas of their different temperaments. For all her outward signals of a passionate need for giving and receiving love, there was a part of Claudia that was missing, something withheld; I could not help but recall Jane's whole-hearted accessibility. Common sense told me that this was the difference between a marriage and an illicit affair; the relaxation of one compared to the secretive uncertainty of the other.

Instinct spoke otherwise. I needed to straighten out my thoughts and this was not the time to do so; slightly drunk, and more than a little weary, Josh's exhibition appeared to me as a watershed, the point where the three of us must divide or eventually destroy each other. The effect his painting had on me, and my desperate desire for Claudia in her entirety, melded together into one emotion and threatened to overwhelm me.

By the time I had made sure of the elaborate alarm system and left for home, it was ten-thirty. Sophie had gone to bed; she had an early rehearsal the following morning, but she had left me a note and a fish pie in the warming oven. She was becoming quite a practised cook. I was glad to be left alone; I would have made lousy company that night.

That foggy evening of the previous December was the one and only occasion Claudia and I met at the house in Paradise Walk. Her ex-husband returned from Barbados. At the time it made no odds; I had lost hope of seeing her again except in chance social circumstances.

I do not know how I got through the Christmas of that year: it passed in a sea of conflicting pain and numbness. Sophie bore it with her usual stoicism, showing her sadness only in lack of appetite. And then came January, when gale-force winds lashed at the window with sleet in the air; day after long day in which I waited for a call from Claudia and prevented myself from ringing her number by a superhuman effort. Josh telephoned to suggest we all meet for supper: I pleaded a cold, persuading myself that if I could merely survive the month, the intensity of longing must ease.

She rang me from the country late one night when I was more or less certain to be on my own. I wasn't; Sophie was sitting on the end of my bed.

'Claudia! Lovely to hear from you. Josh rang the other day. How are things?'

I heard my voice echo in my ears, stiltedly hearty with the guilt of deception, while Sophie, devoid of her normal tact, continued to lounge at my feet. Claudia left the talking to me: left me to prattle on about details of Josh's exhibition unnecessarily, and to arrange a lunch – ('Both of you, if possible') – the following Friday, while my heart grew wings and January became all of a sudden spring.

Sophie asked, yawning, 'Was that Josh's wife?'

'Yes, kitten. Off you go, it's time we got some sleep.' I wondered why she bothered to ask: Claudia is not a usual name.

The arranged lunch never transpired, as I knew it would not. Claudia came alone, meeting me at the Ritz where I had not even bothered to book a table; guessing, quite rightly, that neither of us would feel like eating. We sat amongst well-lined, respectable people and drank our drinks until our hands steadied and we were able to look at each other properly; and that wonderful smile of hers curved slowly up her face until it reached her eyes.

'What are we going to do about us?' she asked simply.

I took a deep breath. 'I know what I *should* do. Walk away. Is that what you'd prefer?'

'No.' She stared at her drink. 'I've tried doing that myself and it hasn't worked.'

We were silent for a moment. 'There is nowhere for us to go,' she said eventually, as if a decision had been reached. 'We can't meet at Paradise Walk; Philip's back.'

I felt light-headed, full of a nervous anticipation at what she was suggesting.

'I'll rent a flat. It'll take a little time, I'm afraid,' I said, grabbing at the first idea that entered my head.

The question of my own home was tacitly avoided: for a dozen reasons.

'Is this really what you want?' she asked seriously.

'Do you really have to ask?' I watched her light a cigarette, wondered whether this had become habitual or was merely a sign of nervousness. 'You have more to lose than I.'

There was an almost imperceptible change in her expression.

'If I lose Josh, I lose Sam,' she said, 'so I don't mean to lose either.'

I felt the slightest chill of reproval.

She added gently, 'It's rather a dead-end for us, you see. That's why I asked.'

I whispered, hurt, 'Are you sure you want me at all, in the circumstances?'

'Oh, Leo,' she sighed, smiled again. 'Not here; not now. Later.'

The idea of the flat had occurred to me on the spur of the moment, born of a desperation to hold on to her at all costs. Reckless actions were the antithesis of my normal behaviour; but it was too late to query behaviour of any sort, or where it would lead us. I found the flat within a week, in a large, anonymous block off Sloane Avenue which had a constantly changing population disinterested in its neighbours. We would arrive and leave separately; no risks would be taken, discretion must be absolute. As I left the box-like rooms after my preliminary visit, I wanted to run down the street whooping like a boy out of school. It was not until I reached home that I sobered up a little, discomfited by a picture of Jane in my mind's eye, her expression one of resigned scepticism.

Claudia's first reaction to the flat, on the other hand, was involuntary mirth. I have to say I was slightly wounded. I was proud of myself for having acquired somewhere so rapidly, and already I had a pro-prietorial fondness for the place.

'The décor,' she giggled. 'Faded actress circa nineteen-fifty, I'd say, wouldn't you?'

This was ridiculously apposite. There was spotted muslin everywhere, at the windows, round the bed, billowing out from the kidney-shaped dressing-table. Satin bows proliferated and a white poodle-dog covered the old-fashioned telephone. In fact, the flat belonged to an elderly woman who was taking an extended holiday with her daughter in Canada.

'It's clean; and it has everything,' I pointed out in the manner of an offended estate agent.

'It's lovely, darling,' she said consolingly, throwing herself lengthways on the bed. 'Come and join me.' She held out her arms.

Light from the street lamps shining through the window, striping the sheet in fluorescent bands; Claudia kissing me. 'Wonderful,' she murmured, fall-ing asleep with her head on my chest.

I lay awake, uncertain of a word so often used to make the other person feel good. I had behaved in a more adult fashion this time and waited for her, which had not been easy considering the strength of the effect she had on me. I could feel the need in her to be loved; but now, despite her enthusiasm, I was convinced the end was a brilliant mime of rapture on her part, and felt for a brief moment cheated.

I did not worry for long; I told myself it did not matter, it was to be expected. We were under the strain of acting unethically, and knew nothing of each other; and besides, too much fuss was made about orgasms, it was the fault of the media. Little by little we would learn more; I already knew she had a mole behind her right knee. By the time I found out where the rest were situated, we would have forgotten the trepidations of these opening chapters. As for unethical behaviour, I am afraid my delight in Claudia far outweighed the deceit we practised. Everything and everyone, even Sophie, dwindled to a diffused blur in the face of this abstraction.

Nemesis has a way of catching up with forbidden happiness and of delivering a warning. There is not a lot with which one can get away, in my experience.

The hours we spent at the flat were pathetically few: snatched ones which highlighted weeks of commitment on both sides. As a general rule she would come up from Sussex on a Friday, leaving Sam in the care of Mrs Morse, and flee from me in the evening to Hornsey, shopping for Josh's supper on the way. This hectic and poignant arrangement was not conducive to peace of mind, and I suppose I was particularly affected because I had not indulged in such a thing before. But what was the alternative? After a week or two, the thought of ending it filled me with misery. I was fast on the way to becoming obsessed. From time to time Sam would stay the night with a school-friend in the middle of the week, and Claudia would escape in the morning, giving us longer together. Those bonus hours were rare and special; I would desert the Gallery and we would play at keeping house, eating lunch at the flat, if we bothered to eat at all.

On one such occasion I returned to the Gallery to keep a four o'clock appointment and to be met by a sombre-faced Zelda.

'You'd better ring the house,' she said. 'Sophie's been sent home ill, in a taxi.'

My heart turned over in guilt-ridden panic. 'How ill?'

Zelda did not spare me. 'Apparently she fainted in a practice class. She's got a high temperature and a very sore throat.' She added coldly, 'She telephoned you here, but of course I had no idea how to contact you, did I?'

'You wouldn't have been able to: I was moving around,' I dissembled, reaching for the phone.

'You should have given me some sort of itinerary,' she said, turning away, 'as you normally do. I felt sick with worry about the child.'

Sophie, answering eventually, was barely able to speak. I left Zelda to either cancel my appointment or deal with a disgruntled client, while I battled my way across London in the rush-hour traffic. At the red crossing-lights in Sloane Square, Claudia stepped across my path without seeing me, her hair aflame above the dark coat and a carrier bag in each hand. Her face wore the abstracted expression of any woman shopper. Desire for her was cancelled out by my anxiety over Sophie: for a shocking moment I felt it was all Claudia's fault.

I found Sophie in my bed, her face flushed against the pillows. 'Sorry, Pa. I expect I'll give you my germs,' she croaked.

I kissed her burning forehead. 'It doesn't matter. I'm going to ring the doctor and get you something soothing to drink, in that order.'

'Can't swallow.' Her eyes were huge and glassy.

'Disprin will help,' I said, trying to remember what Jane would have done in similar circumstances, my alarm increasing by the minute.

She was in bed for four days. I nursed her through two feverish nights while the cleaner stayed with her for most of the day. Suffering from loss of sleep when the worst was over, I thought how many times Jane had done the same without my appreciating the strain.

During Sophie's convalescence, I came home to find her in tears, curled pale and listless in front of the television. She so seldom cried, all my panic was rekindled.

'Darling girl, what is it?' I put my arms round her and gave her my handkerchief. 'You're not worse, are you?'

She shook her head, gulping. 'Dr Casey thinks it may be glandular fever; he's taken a blood test.'

'Well,' I said comfortingly, knowing nothing about it, 'if it is, it's not the end of the world. You'll just have to take it easy for a bit.'

My words merely brought on a fresh flood.

'You don't understand,' she wailed. 'This is *the* important year for me, the exams are in October. If I don't pass, they'll throw me out.'

I soothed and consoled her to the best of my ability, and made her an egg-nog to build up her resistance. Her excessive commitment to dancing worried me; I began to wonder whether she was strong enough physically for such an arduous career. Eventually she blew her nose and said, 'Sorry, Pa. It's not fair of me to take it out on you, especially when you're terribly busy.'

'I'm not; well, no more so than usual.'

'Oh. You've been so late home sometimes before I was ill, I thought you must be. I don't think you'll want this back,' she said of the handkerchief, stuffing it in a pocket. 'Oh, by the way, Claudia rang up. She suggested we go down to that house in Sussex for a weekend when I'm better,' she added.

'Would you like to?'

She shrugged. 'I don't mind,' she said without enthusiasm, 'You decide.'

This attitude was unlike my easy-going Sophie. I wondered whether post-viral depression or mistrust of Claudia was to blame, and in time I had my answer.

Sophie did not have glandular fever, as it turned out, but a vicious attack of tonsilitis, and in early April she had the offending objects removed. Towards the end of her stay in hospital Claudia visited her, bringing a bowl of real primroses and a bunch of grapes. She had a fresh, unmade-up appearance which I felt was deliberate: the simple country wife up in London for the day. She tried too hard. Sophie, pale from incarceration, watched her from her position against banked-up pillows; I watched them both and knew that Sophie's mistrust was still there, had grown, if anything, into near dislike. I could see it in the dark, slanting eyes: the wariness of a young animal sensing danger. She was not rude: I have never known Sophie to be impolite. But the flatness of tone was there when she thanked Claudia and asked after Josh and Sam; and Claudia was at her most intense, fixing Sophie with a concerned gaze.

'Poor little thing,' she said sympathetically. 'You must bring her to us for Easter, Leo. Get some colour into those cheeks.'

When she left she pressed her own cheek against Sophie's unreceptive one. 'I'll leave you two together. Visitors who stay too long are anathema.'

I saw her to the lift, Sophie saying from her bed, 'You're coming back, aren't you, Pa?' in the demanding voice of an invalid.

'I wasn't a wild success, was I?' Claudia said with a little laugh that betrayed hurt, before the lift doors closed and she was whisked away.

I had a feeling of being torn in half. It seemed important to me that they should like each other and it was patently obvious, certainly in Sophie's case, that this was not to be. With the intuition that children have about their parents, I think she sensed a connection between myself and Claudia, unapparent to the outside observer; perhaps she feared a desecration of Jane's memory. If this was so, then her motive was understandable and she was all the things that I was not; and still I found myself powerless to alter the double life I had begun to lead.

*　　*　　*

Josh's country studio was to be ready at Easter and an inspection of the finished conversion made an excellent excuse to take Claudia up on her invitation.

'You don't have to come if you don't want to,' I told Sophie. She was almost recovered and, at rising seventeen, quite adult enough to be left.

'I'll come,' she said, adding, 'I'd like to see Josh again. He's fun.'

This would have struck me as pointed if it had not been Sophie speaking, as she was not given to making snide remarks.

Sam took to her and she to Sam; Josh and I watched from the south-facing window of the studio as they embarked in a dinghy on the river.

'I hope she doesn't fall in,' I said.

'Sam'll look after her.' Sam was all of nine or ten. 'He's got a practical disposition,' Josh said, and turned the conversation to his work and the exhibition which was barely a month away.

His nervousness was increasing palpably by the day, and I devoted most of my time that weekend to trying to instil more confidence in him. This entailed frequent visits to the village pub, just the two of us, since it was my company he demanded at that moment and no-one else's. Easter was abnormally warm and we sat outside on a bench and drank light ale, which gives me wind and no uplift. He was Josh at his most endearing, with the bombast and flamboyance knocked out of him by uncertainty, and gratefully ready to accept any words of encouragement. Sitting there with the spring sunshine on our faces, I felt a great rush of affection for him and wished to God I had not fallen in love with his wife.

'Claudie's looking well, don't you think?' he said out of the blue.

'Very.' I stared at the froth on my beer. 'How are things between you now?' I asked.

I could not help it; I wanted to know.

'Never been better.' He glanced at me and grinned; the grin might have been a wink or a leer for all it implied, and I felt in that instant an appalling stab of unjustified jealousy. 'And I reckon I have you to thank for that,' he said.

I stared at him in horror, probably with my mouth open. 'Oh?' I queried weakly.

He put his head back and roared with laughter, white teeth gleaming. 'Could have put it better, couldn't I? I meant,' he said, 'all you've done for me has made a difference. She's able to see a future for us now; security, which has always been thin on the ground before. I only hope to hell I can live up to her expectations.'

'Now don't start that again,' I said. 'I thought I'd put you in a more optimistic frame of mind.' And I picked up our glasses and retired to the bar for a second round, taking the opportunity of buying myself a whisky which I swallowed at a gulp, quelling the sensation I had of balancing on a tightrope.

There was no hope of being alone with Claudia. I watched her from a distance, working in the garden against a sea of daffodils. Sophie joined her on the Monday and helped to plant herbs. Claudia's untidy hair showed up as a brilliant blot of colour against the green background; she had the added attraction of a woman totally absorbed in what she was doing. I turned away, frustrated, unable to watch for long, and allowed Sam to show me his guinea pigs which had multiplied alarmingly.

It seemed Claudia was occupied the entire four days, either in the garden or the kitchen where she dished up surprisingly good meals at haphazard intervals. I realize there was a purpose to this busyness because she told me so later; but at the time I felt abandoned. Sitting round the table at mealtimes, the five of us, I might have been any old close friend of the family included in the conversation and the in-jokes. The grittiness of her communication with Josh, which used to be uncomfortably apparent, was non-existent; she treated him with affection, her attitude so utterly carefree and relaxed I could not believe it was an act. I left them waving to us from the front door, the complete and happy couple, while I shouted my enthusiastic thanks through the car window. Inside, I was a mass of churning irritability and chagrin.

'You're frowning,' Sophie remarked. 'Didn't you enjoy it?'

'In parts,' I replied, 'like the curate's egg. Did you?'

'Yes, I did.' She said thoughtfully, 'Claudia's nicer in the country. Funny: people often are in their own homes. Have you noticed?'

Despite her words, she never came with me again to visit them: until the present. I think the monosyllabic Smog made a comeback around this time, and she was happy to remain in London. I could hardly disapprove since I had, months ago, urged her to leave space in her life for amusement.

It was after the Easter break that my weekends at Lower Pelling became an item; although, when

Claudia suggested the next one on an afternoon at the flat, I was reluctant.

'I'm not sure I can stand the strain,' I told her.

'If I can, surely you can?' She was being purposely obtuse.

'Yes, I noticed you didn't seem in the least disturbed by the situation,' I replied, 'and frankly I couldn't understand how.'

'Are you saying I'm plain insensitive,' she said coldly, 'or insensitive *and* amoral?'

'Neither. At least,' I added, 'we are both being amoral, if we're honest with ourselves.'

She swung her legs over the side of the bed. 'Why should we be honest with ourselves when we aren't with others?' Wrapping herself in a dressing-gown, she said, 'You're merely upset because I acted normally over Easter. That's how I am with Josh and Sam; I love them. What did you expect: to take me into the shrubbery and get down to it?'

'That's a bitchy thing to say.'

What is it with women that they know exactly where to put the knife in and twist it?

'I'm going to have a shower,' I said distantly. It's amazingly difficult to appear dignified with nothing on; even a towel makes a difference.

I thought when I returned we could leave it at that, put it down to frayed nerves or whatever. It was a pity we had already made love, the universal remedy for healing rifts. It occurred to me as I showered that there was a reason for this snappish aftermath. Time had run into months since I rented the flat, and I had yet to make her happy. I could not believe that a woman as warm and sensuous as Claudia was frigid. The fault must lie with myself or the circumstances in which we had landed ourselves; perhaps both. I stared at myself in the bathroom mirror, unable to judge my own desirability, seeing only a dark-haired, pale-faced middle-aged man who had failed where he probably deserved to fail.

She was sitting where I had left her, at the dressing-table; but her head was turned towards the window.

'I feel claustrophobic,' she said. 'I think I'll go for a walk.' No mention of my going as well.

'I don't make you happy, do I?' I had not meant to say anything of the sort.

She swung to face me. 'What makes you say that?'

'Instinct.' Too late to retract; I tucked the towel more firmly round my middle and sat on the end of the bed. 'What made you become involved with me?' I asked.

'Because you wanted it.' She started to brush her hair with hard, swinging strokes: it seemed somehow a defensive gesture. 'It was your idea, this flat, remember.'

'You agreed to the decision,' I pointed out. 'You must have had a motive. If it isn't love,' I added, 'then what is it?'

'I never said I didn't love you,' she said, dropping the brush with a clatter on the dressing-table.

I saw her reflected in the triple mirror, three angles of her. Her eyes had turned a dark blue, which I had grown to realize meant temper.

'But you've never said you did.'

'I don't know whether I do or I don't. I'm trying hard not to. Have you seen my shoes?' She started to search by the bed.

I was silent, knowing that in this contrary mood I would get nothing out of her.

'I thought we'd have trouble,' she said, kneeling on the floor as she searched. 'I told you how it would be – a dead-end. But you didn't believe me, did you?'

She got to her feet, a shoe in each hand. 'I can't afford to fall in love with you, can I?' she asked.

'You still haven't answered my question,' I insisted, maddened by her calculated argument, unable to be logical in my feelings for her.

'All right,' she said, sounding defiant. 'I went to bed with you in the beginning because I found you attractive. I was having a bad time with Josh and you were kind to me. I did it selfishly because I thought it would be therapeutic and comforting; and it was. There.'

'But it hasn't made you happy?'

'Not exactly.' She looked at me, and there was confusion in her eyes. 'It's not your fault,' she said more gently.

'No?' I turned away and started to dress, bitter with sadness. 'Perhaps we'd better end it.'

'Perhaps we better had,' she agreed. I could feel her anger without watching her.

She walked to the bathroom and stopped by the door. 'I'm the one with problems. If you don't feel able to help me with them, like propping up Josh's morale by coming down occasionally, well, then—'

She disappeared and slammed the door behind her, leaving her sentence unfinished.

I had blown it. I completed my dressing in solitude and went to stare out of the window between the drapes of muslin. The April skies hung low and grey, and there was an east wind that competed with my own bitterness. The future looked unbearably bleak.

She left the flat before me and I watched her, wrapped in a red wool jacket against the cold, walking quickly away from me in the street below. We had hardly spoken again, made no mention of a next time. She had been crying; make-up did not entirely hide the tear stains. I was furious, but only with myself; a supposedly mature man who could not handle the simplest emotional problem and had no right to claim a woman like Claudia for a lover. I took Sophie to *La Bohème* that night, and found relief in weeping through the death of Mimi. Sophie saw nothing odd in it: I have never had much control in that direction.

I sent her flowers to the cottage; twenty-pounds' worth of yellow and white spring flowers, all of which were most likely growing in her garden. It was a gesture, a begging for forgiveness, and she accepted it, and our rapprochement was almost worth the original agony. Yet there remained that part of her which was elusive. Whether it was withheld by design or from inhibition, it was impossible to tell; but I settled for the fact since there was no alternative. I did not want another confrontation, could not bear to lose her.

Shortly afterwards I drove down to Sussex for the first of the visits that were to become habitual. It was not the ordeal I expected; in those days both of them needed me. Josh was putting the finishing touches to paintings destined for the exhibition and Claudia and I went for walks, discovering the delights of the beech wood close to the village. The three of us were strangely in harmony: by the very nature of things, it was too good to last. But for a short while we seemed protected by a false presumption of security, as if there was no malignancy within the magic circle and nothing could break it.

An hour and a quarter after the opening of the private view I began to relax, cautiously optimistic of success. Serious interest was being shown in Josh's pictures; there was a comforting sprinkling of red stickers to be seen and inquiries were being made of Zelda about deposits. Only now, as I felt a load lifted tangibly from my shoulders, did I realize the weight of my anxiety. I had dreaded the evening ending without a single sale, seeing the haggard disappointment growing on Josh's face as the last guest drifted away. There is the same hazard attached to the exhibiting of any comparatively-unknown artist; but in this case my concern was doubled, had become a personal issue. I dried my palms with a handkerchief and drank a glass of champagne, allowing myself a brief respite from my duties as host.

Amongst the shifting crowd Josh and Claudia could be seen, their faces animated. Josh, I was glad to note, was still deep in conversation with the dealer of repute to whom I had introduced him; while two middle-aged, designer-clad women waited impatiently to claim his attention. Claudia was talking to a group comprising several men and one female, and concentrating with tact on the latter, working hard at the newly-acquired rôle of professional wife. She was wearing a white, softly-draped dress and her hair was drawn back in a coil at the nape of the neck. She looked unfamiliar and unapproachable; I had a swift longing to pull the pins from the hair, see it tumble free in one flaming mass, before an old friend from Sotheby's drew me aside, full of praise, and the urge was suppressed.

Moving steadily from group to group, introducing, exchanging a few sentences here, receiving congratulations there, smiling, charming my way around and all the time noting the comments, the number of people seriously viewing, the ones stopping by the front desk manned by Zelda and her team; for two hours there was no let-up. Two Japanese dealers conversed rapidly and incomprehensibly in front of one of Josh's priciest paintings, 'Deck-chairs', attempting solemnly to pronounce the title. A bulky man with a Texan accent and a high colour, whose name I should have known and which escaped me, was being dominated in his artistic judgement by a blonde and brittle wife. And there were, of course, the regulars: the elderly Polish Countess Zarkovska, for example, who had never to my knowledge missed a private view of Siegler's. Her auburn wig sitting perilously on her head like a curly toque, she sailed imperiously back and forth, a small following of androgynous courtiers in her wake. Two of the art critics I could almost certainly rely upon to turn in favourable reviews were in no hurry to leave; a good sign and not entirely due to the quality of the champagne, I dared to surmise.

My mother chose to make her entrance at the very end, when the guests had dwindled to a scattered few determined to make the most of a free drink. I did not expect her: she seldom attended contemporary private views, considering such exhibitions a wrong move on my part, a waste of time and money. As she walked through the doors towards me, leaning heavily on her stick, I wondered what quirk of temperament had persuaded her to come. I led her on a tour of the pictures, during which she made no comment apart from the odd grunt; introducing her to Josh and Claudia only as she was about to leave. Apprehensive about Josh's intake of liquor, I glanced at him anxiously. But he stood as solid as a rock, kissed her hand and smiled into her eyes without fear. Either the smile or the lack of trepidation impressed her; her lips twitched upwards slightly in response, vastly improving her expression.

'You have a talented husband,' she remarked to Claudia, while her eyes did not miss a trick, taking in Claudia's looks and the enhancing dress in one sweeping glance. Only I knew the rarity of my mother's compliments.

I walked her slowly to her car, aware of a deterioration in her agility.

'You aren't such a fool, Leo,' she said succinctly as I helped her on to the back seat. 'You've chosen well this time.' With another twitch of her lips she added, 'He's an attractive man. Powerful.'

The inference being that I was neither of these things. I had the instant sense of physical inferiority that came over me occasionally, as if I had shrunk to half my size.

'Where's Sophie, by the way?' she asked.

'She's got a performance tonight, I'm afraid.'

'You should think of remarrying,' she said out of the blue.

'Mother,' I protested, 'it's too soon even to contemplate.'

'Bear it in mind.' She wound down the window. 'I'd

like some more grandchildren: someone to carry on all this.' She waved a hand towards the frontage of Siegler's. 'Sophie clearly isn't cut out for it.'

'I must get back, see to things,' I said firmly. 'Good night, Mother. Good of you to come.'

I retraced my steps, wondering what had triggered off this sudden interest in my personal life. Claudia's presence crossed my mind, but I ruled it out immediately. On this occasion of all occasions any vibes between us were strictly under control; we had scarcely looked at each other throughout the evening.

The last guests were being shepherded out when I returned, and Josh and Claudia were with Zelda. I had expected him to be jubilant, but instead I found him in a mood of restrained excitement.

'How have I done?' he asked nervously, searching for approval.

'It's gone marvellously well,' I told him. 'I'd say we've sold twenty-five to thirty per cent. We have another five weeks to run. We should reach fifty per cent on the strength of this excellent beginning.'

Over his shoulder I saw Claudia leaning against the desk, smiling, her eyes shining with happiness.

'So you see, all your worry was for nought,' I added, patting him on the shoulder.

He sighed in relief. 'It's not bad, is it?' he said modestly. 'Thanks, Leo. It's been a wonderful opening. What happens now?' He looked at his empty glass. 'I could do with a Scotch.'

'What happens now is I'm carting you off for dinner. You can have your whisky at the restaurant.'

I remember that evening as clearly as if it were last week. I remember walking in the still, warm night to claim our table, and warning Josh on the way not to get hopelessly drunk before the end of the meal. Three people who mattered were to meet us at the restaurant: Martin Fortescue of Sotheby's and his wife, and the dealer to whom I had already introduced Josh. It was important for us all to talk sense for a while longer. Claudia was humming a tune under her breath and holding Josh's arm firmly, as if making a statement of their closeness. I felt her disassociation from myself, but it did not worry me; on an evening such as this it was actually desirable.

There was an air of celebration at dinner: thank God it was a celebration and not an attempt, as is often the way, to salvage an artist's battered ego. Josh, gaining confidence, received congratulations from the rest of the party gracefully.

'A very satisfactory result,' Martin Fortescue remarked. 'You should feel extremely gratified, Josh.'

'Pole-axed,' Josh said with a grin. 'That's how I feel right now.'

A warm glow of affection and a deep satisfaction at the success I had wrought for him welled up in me, dispelling tiredness. Further discussion about which paintings had been bought by whom, and what advantages he might expect in the future, carried us halfway through dinner. Claudia was keeping a low profile, talking without assertion; this modest demeanour was new to me. This is Josh's day, she seemed to be saying, and I shall do nothing to detract from his triumph. The part she had chosen to play irritated me unreasonably.

'Do you ever sit for Josh?' Sarah Fortescue enquired of her across the table.

'Once only.' Claudia's smile curved upwards, returning her momentarily to normal. 'I made him furious; apparently I fidget. Leo has that painting, haven't you, Leo?'

She looked at me blandly and I nodded.

'Claudia's back view,' I said, pouring the claret calmly. 'I wouldn't part with it for the world,' and I returned her look in kind.

It was not until our three dinner guests eventually left that Josh asked for brandy and threw away his best behaviour like a restricting garment. At one o'clock in the morning Claudia and I hauled him from an impromptu vocal chorus with the Italian waiters and bundled him, unresisting, into a taxi. I pressed a note into Claudia's palm, gave the tolerant driver directions and asked him to lend the lady any assistance needed on arrival. Josh had his head stuck out of the window.

'Dear old Leo,' he sang. 'I love you, Leo.'

Claudia pushed him aside. 'I love you, too,' she said seriously.

The taxi drew away and I watched its tail lights disappear from view. I kept the sound of her last words in my ears as long as possible. Josh would remember none of this in the morning.

There ensued, after the private view, another dreadful hiatus in which Claudia was lost to me. I realized the inevitability of these barren stretches, but I never became reconciled to them.

Josh wrote me a letter of thanks and apologies for his behaviour, followed by an invitation to dinner. 'At a posh restaurant,' he announced proudly over the telephone.

But it was not to be; his mother died in the next day or so from her prolonged illness.

'Poor Josh, he's terribly upset,' Claudia said when she rang to let me know.

I said inadequately, 'I'm so sorry. Please give him all my sympathy.'

'I shall, thanks, Leo. We'll be in Wales until Friday for the funeral. Perhaps we could all meet the following week?'

'Yes, of course.' I cleared my throat, adding more positively, 'Let's do that, Claudia. Ring me when you return.'

The formality of this conversation left me flattened; no 'darling' this or that, just plain, down-to-earth 'Claudia' and 'Leo'. Where I should have been feeling genuine sadness for Josh, there was a hollowness born of a selfish longing for something that was forever out of reach. At that moment I believed there to be no future for myself and Claudia, and that there was no point in continuing to rent an unused flat. I had been going there once or twice a week to air it and give it a perfunctory dusting; also to reveal myself to one or other of the porters in case they imagined someone had died behind the locked doors. I went once more, wandered about its doll-like confines where traces of her scent still lingered, and found myself quite unable to let it go. Not just yet, I told myself, wait for a week or two. The porter barely lifted his head from the *Evening Standard* when I entered and departed; the block's inhabitants were all one to him, alive or dead.

Josh was subdued when they gave me dinner; but I brought good news. His sales figures had already risen to forty per cent, a New York gallery was taking a positive interest in his work and one of the reviews was as enthusiastic as I had hoped it would be. In the face of such encouraging facts, it was difficult for him to continue mourning and his old ebullience gradually came back during the evening.

'I plan to use the studio at the cottage much more in the summer,' he announced; 'spend long weekends there. Better for Claudia, too. She won't feel pushed to come up on a Friday and give me one square meal a week.'

Claudia raised her eyes to mine and dropped them swiftly. 'Oh, I don't know,' she said. 'I quite like London for a change. Come and stay next weekend, Leo. Marcus will be there; bring Sophie if she'd like it.'

But Sophie had other plans, and in fact I found myself reluctant to go. I wanted Claudia on her own, not surrounded by family; increasingly the possibility of this seemed more and more remote. The depression into which I had fallen was quite removed from resentment of her other life; it was basic despair. I went in the end because I could not think of a reasonable excuse; it poured with rain and I spent the time there imbued with restlessness. Marcus, in those days, was working in a Battersea restaurant and hankering after the stage. The hair was already in a pony-tail and the dissension between himself and Josh in evidence. Perhaps that was why he attached himself to me; I taught him backgammon, and in return he amused me by trying out his various dialects.

'Accents are important for the theatre,' he told me. 'Scots is difficult for me, Irish easy, and Welsh even easier because of Josh being around.'

'His speech isn't *that* Welsh.'

'Haven't you heard him in a temper?' Marcus grinned and proceeded to do a surprisingly accurate imitation of his stepfather.

'You're good,' I said. 'Perhaps you should become an impersonator.'

'Do you know who this is?' he asked. I listened to the deeply accentuated upper-crust sentences and shook my head. 'Donald Sinden?' I suggested.

'No. You.' He laughed.

'Oh, God,' I said, 'I can't believe I sound like that.'

'Well,' he admitted, 'it's a bit over the top. Actually, your sort of voice is awkward to get right. You don't mind, do you?'

'I don't,' I said, 'but Josh might object to being mimicked.'

'Oh, what the hell,' he said carelessly, lounging in a chair. He was at an ungainly age, all large hands and feet, had yet to grow into his own body. A year has made a difference; we did not meet again until the present.

The rain stopped on the day I left and I walked with Claudia in the sodden garden. The beginning of June, and the roses were starting to flower.

'I'm thinking of giving up the flat,' I remarked, miserably hoping for a heart-broken reaction.

She was silent.

'There doesn't seem much point in keeping it if we no longer use it,' I added.

She bent over a rose, running a thumb along the bud. 'Greenfly,' she murmured inconsequentially; then, straightening up, gave me a smile. 'We can't let it go just like that, without saying goodbye to it.'

Away to the left, Sam was climbing the ladder to his tree-house. 'You are quite content,' I said, and it sounded like an accusation, 'and I am merely a complication in your life.'

'Not a complication.' She looked at me, shaking her head as if I were Sam having committed a minor error. 'Just complicated.'

She put her arm through mine and turned me towards the house. 'I shall be at the flat next Friday,' she said, 'quite early. That's where you'll find me if you want to.'

If I *wanted* to; if I lived to be a hundred, I decided, I would never understand the woman.

A light breeze stirred the muslin curtains; from the street below came the unwavering hum of distant traffic. I pictured an endless procession of taxis carrying women to Peter Jones to buy bed-linen; following their mundane pursuits while we, far above them, had spent the day in a less worthy but far more valuable quest.

I raised myself on one elbow and watched Claudia, her arms flung sideways like a baby's in sleep. The line of her body curved softly as far as the hip bone's clean angle, where the sheet lay carelessly pushed back across her legs. Uninhibited, I had the chance to notice little things about her: the lashes on the closed lids were tawny near the base and dark at the ends; I could see the mole beneath her right breast and leant over to kiss it, stopping myself because I did not want to wake her. I needed time to myself to relive the previous moments and hold on to them in contemplation.

She had been early in arriving at the flat, but I had

been earlier; I felt suddenly on edge, as if I had never made love to her before. She put a small wrapped parcel on the dressing-table.

'I've brought you a present,' she said, her eyes full of a calmness that was seldom there. I made to open it but she held me back. 'Later,' she said.

She was indefinably changed; scent and touch were the same, her reactions different, so that for a while I still had the sensation of loving someone strange to me and uncharted. I was tensed up with the remembrance of all the times past when I had thought myself to be inadequate, aware of the importance of here and now, as if the whole of our future depended on the moment. And then my nervousness evaporated in delighted acceptance of what was happening. She was no longer pretending. I had time to wonder what the hell I had done to sweep the barriers away and release the new Claudia before she arched beneath me; all the hours of doubting were carried away on a tidal wave of climax and lost in her shout of triumph. Afterwards she lay damply in the crook of my arm and the street sounds drifted through our silence, and I put the other arm round her as though she needed protection.

She said at last, 'That never happens to me.'

'Never?' I pushed the hair gently away from her face to see her expression. 'Do you really mean it?'

'Oh, a long time ago, perhaps. Not any more.' She sighed a great sigh of contentment. 'I do love you, Leo,' she said before she fell asleep.

We ate toast and paté for lunch and drank white wine, telling each other things about ourselves that we had not managed to divulge before; freed for the present from anxiety and preoccupation with our lives.

We talked of childhood and children, our favourite music, books and places, of pet likes and dislikes and of fears.

'Would Jane have minded about us?' she asked at one point. 'You always seemed so – well, married in the real sense; close, you know? I was envious of you,' she added.

I wondered a great deal about Jane's opinion, but I would not have dreamt of admitting it.

'It's supposed to be a sign of a happy marriage if you remarry soon after being bereaved,' I said. 'Since that's impossible, perhaps what we have counts as well.'

'Perhaps,' she said thoughtfully. 'You haven't opened your present.'

She handed it to me. Inside I found a gold St Christopher medallion on a link chain.

'To keep you safe,' she told me.

'I'm too cautious to be accident-prone.'

'No-one's immune to accidents,' she said. 'I know you're not a medallion man, but promise me you'll wear it under your shirt.'

'Thank you, darling Claudia.' I kissed her.

'Shall we go back to bed now?' she asked, as though this were a new and exciting game she had just discovered.

Later, she fell asleep once more. I did not feel like sleeping, content to let my thoughts roam backwards, and then forwards to some hazy and wishful goal. I wondered if the difference in her stemmed from gratitude for Josh's success; or whether the security it promised had brought its own relief from tension. I was too much at peace, too happily tired to pursue the question of cause and effect.

It was late when she left and the sun was low in the sky. I took the unprecedented step of going with her to shop for food, following her past the indifferent porter at his desk. We trundled a trolley up and down the aisles of Europa, pulling things off shelves and out of freezers, laughing like children. An inability to leave her had seized me; each minute I spent with her was a bonus, even in a crowded supermarket. There was no time for her to take the tube; as we waited for a taxi she said suddenly: 'Nothing will be the same from now on. You realize that?'

For a dreadful moment I misunderstood her, thought that she was hinting at a finale.

'It will be more difficult for me after today,' she added.

An empty taxi drew to the kerb. I handed the carrier bags to Claudia and closed the door, not knowing how to answer.

'I tried so hard not to fall in love with you,' she said through the window, smiling at me as the taxi shot away.

I stared after her, my mind battling with confused emotions of joy, elation, conceit and the eternal element of guilt. It was too late for guilt-ridden feelings. I saw the taxi reach the end of Sloane Avenue and a small hand wave from the open window. I turned and started to walk home, resenting the fact that she was always to be whisked away from me for unspecified aeons of time.

Chapter Eight

I stand in the doorway of my bedroom, dressed only in a pair of boxer pants, and survey the shambles. The picture which hung over the bed has fallen, a corner of its unnecessarily heavy frame bursting the pillow where it landed. Clouds of feathers flutter diversely to join those already settled on the floor and counterpane. With a haunted feeling I subside on to the foot of the bed and put my head in my hands, my worst fears of persecution confirmed.

There is no hot water. At the best of times it is tepid; tonight, not a single drip appears from the hot tap. Nothing is more demoralizing when one is low than being unable to lie in a warm bath and soothe away the aggro. With the going-down of the sun, this mean little room grows meaner still, the walls drawing closer around one as darkness approaches. I recall a short story in which a four-poster bed, built for the purpose, slowly concertinas together and crushes the unsuspecting occupants as they sleep. You could not get a four-poster into this room but the atmosphere created is similar, of being encroached upon by a nameless malignancy.

I cast my mind over what might be explained as trivial incidents and decide that, trivial or not, they are also contrived. The cat was shut inside my room on purpose; the picture fell because the wire was fixed.

The washing facilities, the close proximity of the raucous water-pipes, the very room itself to which even an Edwardian 'tweeny' would have objected: all these, I am convinced, are designed to lower morale and unnerve me. The instigator is of course Josh. The boys are out of the question. Sam is too engrossed in his own interests to bother and is not by nature a practical joker; and Marcus is more likely to play silly buggers against his stepfather. In any case, they would have no say in the sleeping arrangements of the household. This is Josh's doing, each futile discomfort echoing the sense of humour of an overgrown school-boy; except there is not much humour in having your head smashed in by a picture frame, now I come to think of it. I glance automatically over my shoulder at the desecrated pillow.

Way out in front of these happenings, however, is a far greater threat to my tranquillity; the sight of Sophie posing in the nude. That was the moment, coming upon them unawares, when I had my first intimation of what Josh has in mind; retribution of a far more subtle nature than I would have thought possible. I hope I am proved wrong, because if not, I won't be held responsible for my actions.

I had waited transfixed on the threshold of the studio, unable to utter.

'Don't disturb her; she's been a very good girl up till now: held the position like a pro.' Those were Josh's words. Sophie merely smiled, intent on not moving a muscle.

'Ah, well,' I said with considerable aplomb, I felt, 'I'll leave you to it,' and I stumbled down the staircase and out into the evening sun, drawing in deep breaths of fresh air.

I wandered aimlessly in the direction of the garden, trying to pull myself together and calm the pounding of my heart. I attempted to rationalize my feelings. I have no hang-ups about nudity: surveying the depiction of it forms a large part of my working life, and it would be ridiculously squeamish of me to mind my own daughter sitting naked to oblige a friend. But I did mind: I minded like hell. Pausing feverishly by Claudia's rose-bed, I tried to pin-point the exact cause of my aggravation. Josh, if he did not actually lie to me, was economical with the truth when he asked to paint Sophie. I would have appreciated it had I been told what it entailed. The scent of roses was having a tranquillizing effect; gradually my pulse slowed and my thoughts fell into some kind of order.

It dawned on me that Sophie's nudity had nothing to do with the equation, nor yet Josh's underhand way of persuading her. It was the implications that lay behind these actions that had triggered off my mental anguish. Their mutual attitude had been one of total unconcern, and while this in Josh was unsurprising, I would have expected a certain amount of confusion from Sophie at my entrance: but no, not a blush, not a stammer. She might have been stripping off every day of the week for months. It would have puzzled me less if she was totally without inhibitions; but she covers up quickly enough if I walk into her room unannounced. It was as if Josh were no stranger to her body, for how else could she have found such composure? If I was correct, there was only one way in which he could have gained that experience, and it was not through her use as a model.

I thought of their adjacent rooms and the opportunities of the previous night, and understood with sudden bitter clarity Josh's diabolical intentions.

Small incidents crowded back to me: his arm so frequently round her shoulders, the meaningful looks, the making sure of her place at the table next to him, the little jokes; things which I had taken to be merely a middle-aged man's flirtation with a young girl, fool that I was. Sophie is that dangerous combination, green as the grass and outstandingly beautiful, and Josh can lay on the charm with the best of them. But his machinations went much deeper than the simple securing of Sophie's attractions, of that I was convinced. I had searched for a reason for being invited back into his fold, and I needed to look no further. He had planned all this, weeks ago in all probability; my daughter in exchange for his wife: an eye for an eye. The dirty bastard, how could anyone's mind work that way? Sophie was seventeen; there was no comparison between the wrong I had done him and the devious seduction of my child. The dark red rose I had been absently stroking snapped between my fingers and I was left holding its perfection, wishing the severed stem was Josh's neck.

A sudden whoop of sheer exuberance broke the stillness of the evening and my brooding, and Marcus charged from the kitchen doorway, punching the air in a victory salute.

'I've made it!' he was yelling. Catching sight of me he bounded forward, delighted to find someone in the otherwise deserted garden. 'I've got in!' he said, grinning from ear to ear. 'They've accepted me, isn't it great?'

'Wonderful!' I told him, making a huge effort to appear normal, for after all I liked this boy whose whole life was just beginning. 'Congratulations. Which drama school?'

'Central,' he said, flushed with success.

'That's supposed to be the best, isn't it?'

'The tops. God! I couldn't believe it when Father rang to let me know. I must tell Sophie. Have you seen her?'

'I'm afraid not,' I said, disowning her entirely. 'I'm delighted for you, Marcus.'

'Thanks. I'll go and look for her. See you.'

He started towards the river bank, trotting in his eagerness; a character transformed from the lethargic youth of yesterday. A sudden idea struck me: I called after him.

'Marcus.'

He stopped, turned. 'Yeah?'

I hesitated. 'Doesn't matter; just something I wanted to ask you. It can wait.'

He was gone with a wave of the hand. I looked towards the house, and thought with distaste of the evening that lay before me, helping to entertain the vicar and his wife. Only God knew what flight of fancy had inspired Josh to invite the clergy for dinner: it was not his usual scene. In that moment I would have given a great deal to pack up and leave there and then; but it would have been playing into Josh's hands, making me appear a fool and a coward. This situation had to be seen through to its unforeseeable conclusion.

Da had his feet up on a long-chair outside the kitchen, and was reading the *Financial Times*. He glanced up at me.

'Hope you've got an appetite, boyo,' he said amiably. 'There's perfection, my paella.' His shrewd eyes scanned my face. 'Something wrong, is there?'

'I wish you'd tell me, Da,' I answered shortly, and swept past him without bothering to explain. Climbing the stairs, I regretted my rudeness; he had done nothing to warrant my biting his head off. I was merely unfit for human company.

The picture wire has been tampered with; strands are frayed, but not from wear and tear. Sawn with a file of some sort, I imagine; the rest of it is quite new and in good order. I straighten up from examining it and try not to visualize my crushed and lifeless head beneath the frame. Luckily anger is now my chief emotion, a powerful antidote to fear. Josh has a lot to answer for; he would be in deep trouble had he succeeded in murdering me. Pulling on a dressing-gown, I go in search of whisky, which has become an overriding priority all of a sudden; and the wherewithal to clear up the dishevelled room, a job my bloody host should be tackling by rights. Da is back in the kitchen, tasting his efforts from a vast open cauldron on top of the stove.

'Smells good,' I say with forced cheerfulness, taking the opportunity to add, 'Sorry I snapped you up, Da. It was unforgivable and I apologize.'

'Think nothing of it, Leo.' He blows on the spoon he is holding. 'Got something on your mind, have you?' he asks without turning.

'You could say that.' I pour a generous measure of whisky into a tumbler, and wonder whether to mention such items as attempted homicide and seduction of a minor. But Sophie is a grown woman by law, I remember with a shock, and Josh is Da's son, and I cannot prove either accusation. 'There's been a slight accident in my bedroom,' I explain weakly, asking for a dustpan and brush and a new pillow. Da is ignorant on both counts.

'Better wait till Josh comes in,' he advises, 'and Sophie. She'll clear up the room for you; proper little housewife – lovely, she is.'

At present I can think of other descriptions for her, torn as I am between love and fury.

'She's going to do the table for me,' Da says fondly, sipping at his drink. 'Flowers, candles; the works.'

'Then she's going to be kept very busy, isn't she?' I comment nastily; and at that moment Sophie and Josh appear in the kitchen, laughing at one of his unfunny quips.

'A very satisfactory afternoon's work,' he announces, at his most ebullient. 'Everything is going splendidly, you'll be pleased to hear, Leo. Isn't it, poppet?' he adds, patting her bottom.

'I don't doubt it.' My tone is sheer ice but he ignores it.

'And what have you been up to while we slave?' he asks.

Sophie is standing beside Da, sticking a finger in the paella. 'Mmm. Lovely.' Is it my imagination that she looks fulfilled?

'Doing a lot of thinking,' I tell him sarcastically, 'about accidents in the home and the fact that I could have been decapitated by your fucking picture falling on me. As it happens,' I say with a shrug, 'it has only ruined a pillow and the place is a mess of feathers.'

'My dear boy!' (I wince inwardly at the condescension). 'My God! That's terrible.' He frowns. 'I *can't* have wired it myself; I must come and look.'

In an instant they are streaming up to my bedroom; only Da wisely stays behind, deciding another body in that cell would be too many. Josh scrutinizes the broken wire, tut-tuts and pronounces it to be faulty, which I am convinced it is not.

'One of Claudia's paintings; I suppose she hung it.' He shakes his head sadly and lifts the picture gently to the floor, silent for a moment as if remembering things best forgotten. Then he shouts, 'Sam!'

Sam appears eventually in the doorway.

'Cor!' is his only comment before fetching a brush and a garbage bag. While he and Sophie get to work, Josh gives my arm an apologetic squeeze.

'Really sorry about that, Leo,' he says, looking into my eyes with deep sincerity. 'It's never happened before and it won't happen again,' he assures me before making himself absent.

Of course it won't; but something else will.

Sophie and I are at last alone, and I do not know what to say to her. She, it seems, has no worries on that score.

'There,' she says, glancing round the room. 'Back to normal. Poor Pa, it's really upset you, hasn't it?' She gives me a kiss on the cheek. 'I'll bring you a couple of pillows from my room; I shan't be using them, anyway.'

'What do you mean, you won't be using them?'

'I sleep without them,' she smiles at me, 'to keep my back straight.'

My blood subsides. I look at her. Can anyone who has been bedded by a man old enough to be her father, retain that clear, untroubled innocence of expression?

She returns my stare quizzically.

'Anything wrong? Have I come out in spots or something?'

'Nothing's wrong,' I say unconvincingly.

'You can't fool me,' she says in the maternal voice she adopts every so often. 'Let me think. Ooh –' a long drawn-out syllable of enlightenment '– I know. You don't like me posing for Josh in the nude, do you? I could tell when you walked into the studio.'

'I don't object. I was taken aback, that's all,' I reply austerely.

'I can't think why.' She drops to her knees to retrieve a scatter of overlooked feathers. 'You, of all people; you've always taught me to be laid back about nudity. In fact,' she puts the feathers in the garbage bag, 'I used to think you made too much of a point of it; it embarrassed me a bit when I was about twelve.'

One cannot get it right with children, I think resentfully. Besides, how little she knows of my true agony of mind.

She sits back on her heels. 'I thought you'd be terribly pleased Josh was starting to paint again seriously.' Laughing, she adds, 'The ones he did of Claudia are pretty weird, aren't they? Crap, really, even if I don't know much about it.'

'My attitude to nakedness hasn't changed. Your modelling for Josh doesn't worry me.'

I stop, painfully aware I should be issuing some kind of warning: a homily on promiscuity, safe sex and the perils of falling for unscrupulous older men. I cannot do so; the words stick in my throat. Her gender is the barrier; Jane would have no difficulty. I feel a familiar stab of anger at the loss of her, without which we would not be trapped together in this cramped little room. 'So long as he doesn't want you for other purposes,' I say as lightly as possible. It is the best I can manage.

'But it's nice to be wanted,' she protests happily. 'Oh, Pa, what an old worry-guts you are. I'm not a child any longer: I can take care of myself.' She puts her arms round my neck and looks me in the eyes with her dark, slanting ones. 'Why don't you drink up your whisky and I'll get you another one, and some pillows? I love you.'

And she kisses me on the forehead and prances away with the garbage bag and the empty glass in either hand. Nothing she has said diminishes my fears one iota; on the contrary, I am left feeling singularly helpless. A part of me would like to put her over my knee and spank her, the other half longs to whisk her away to safety. It is not until the second drink she brings me has succeeded in calming my raw nerve-ends that I am capable of collected thought.

At least I now have the measure of Josh. I cannot anticipate his every move, but it helps to know where I stand. It is a curious relief to realize his awareness of my affair with Claudia. I am tempted to declare my guilt openly and put an end to this charade; held back only by the fear of pushing him over the edge of reason. A normal man would have accused me long ago rather than play a series of tortuous games. I am still at a loss to know the means of his discovery; and I have no real proof of that apart from his behaviour. But each sip of whisky facilitates the ideas forming in my mind. I dress, run the razor over my chin and go in search of Sam.

The guests have arrived, and Josh has herded them to the river-bank. I cross the lawn to join them and to be introduced, and to stand amongst a vicious cloud of gnats while he extols the virtues of country life. The vicar and his wife are in their early thirties and dressed casually; they are both blond, round-faced, bursting with eagerness and might be mistaken for brother and sister. She is on the plump side: certainly curvaceous, which probably accounts for Josh having invited them. While her husband's head nods rhythmically in answer to Josh's discourse, she asks me polite questions about the Gallery; her eyes on my face but her mind elsewhere; perhaps on the two small children she has left in the care of a baby-sitter.

'Goodness!' she says. 'Really? You learn something every day, don't you?'

She is happier on her own subject, which is music; it turns out that she leads the choir and plays the violin, while her husband Nigel has formed a pop group of the local lads. Her conversation is interspersed with a nervous, rippling giggle; every so often she waves a hand in front of her face to scatter the insects.

When the ice no longer clinks in our glasses we turn and walk slowly back, bitten to blazes. The muscles of her bottom work visibly beneath tight-clinging trousers chopped off above the ankles, which Sophie has informed me are called leggings. I see Josh's eyes on this object of dubious attraction, and feel a mild uplifting of the spirits.

*   *   *

Outside the widespread french windows, sky and landscape are melding in the dusk, the willow trees etched finely under a creamy half-moon. Candles cast a warm glow over the big pine table, the bowl of roses in the centre and the ruby-red of filled wine glasses. The flames burn straight without a flicker, for the air is still, and moths dance perilously in their perimeter.

Some of us are having second helpings of the paella, which tastes surprisingly good. I take covert glances at the faces in the candlelight; expressions vary from the animated to the solemnly attentive.

'The stock market is always bullish at this time of year,' Da informs his neighbour Lucy Rathbone, the vicar's wife. 'Come August it'll drop a hundred points. Happens every time,' he assures her.

She, her fair skin flushed from the wine and gleaming from the warmth, nods enthusiastically.

'You learn something every day, don't you?' she says without the least idea of what he is talking about. Perhaps, with the mention of stock and bulls, she vaguely imagines Smithfield.

Josh has placed himself between the only two women amongst us. So far he has behaved in exemplary fashion, passing the pepper-mill and the salad, remembering to top up people's glasses and being altogether pleasantly attentive. But it cannot last; he has been refilling his own glass at frequent and surreptitious intervals, a recipe for disaster. With Lucy on one side of him and Sophie in virginal white on the other, he is like a satanic Bacchus surrounded by nymphs.

Sam is looking unusually well-scrubbed and in a clean shirt; I remark on the fact.

'Sophie got at me,' he says in disgust, 'said how nice I'd look in blue, yuk! She went through all the drawers till she found this poncey thing.' He makes a face.

'Well, so you do look nice.' Sophie, not meant to hear, grins at him.

'You look yuppie, not poncey,' Marcus tells him. He is amiable and relaxed, a friend of all the world, for it is going his way. He has been questioning Nigel Rathbone on the art of the guitar.

'One of my boys is playing in church tomorrow during Matins,' Nigel says, anxious for converts. 'Perhaps you'd like to come along and hear him?'

'Right.' Marcus searches visibly for a polite excuse. 'I may be leaving before lunch, but I'd love to if I'm here.'

'How about you, Josh?' Nigel suggests hopefully. 'We could do with a good Welsh voice to lead the congregation in song.'

'What's the attendance like?' I ask.

'Poor, I'm afraid.'

'We thought jollying the service up would appeal to young people,' Lucy says, 'but all it's done is drive the old ladies away.'

'They take exception to the Te Deum being sung to a modern tune,' admits Nigel sadly.

'And to shaking hands with their neighbours during the service,' Lucy adds.

Josh is collecting a bottle of Grand Marnier and one of brandy from the dresser. 'I'm not surprised: they probably all loathe each other. I'll come if you preach a thundering good sermon,' he announces, putting the bottles on the table in front of him. 'Full of hellfire and damnation, like we had in chapel when I was a boy. You remember, Da?'

'Seldom went,' Da replies. 'Your mam took you. In love with preacher Owen, she was.' His eyes gleam wickedly.

'Adultery: now there's a fine theme for you,' Josh tells Nigel. 'Full of possibilities, and much neglected these days, I'll bet.'

'My parishioners are rather a conservative bunch, well-behaved as a rule,' Nigel says with a touch of regret. 'I think they'd be highly indignant. There isn't much hanky-panky in Lower Pelling.'

'Ah, but how do you know what goes on behind closed doors?' Josh draws a cork with a pop. 'I'll lay a hundred-to-one you don't. Take this household: it might be a seething den of iniquity for all you can tell.'

His voice is jocular, his gaze on me.

'Ha-ha-ha!' Nigel gives a braying laugh at the very idea.

'There's iniquity, you sitting with those bottles by you and doing nothing about them,' Da interrupts.

'You're a greedy old bugger.' Josh heaves himself upright and starts round the table, a bottle in each hand. 'But you're not a bad cook, for all that.'

He is already not quite steady on his feet, leaning against Lucy's chair as he offers her a choice of drink. She giggles, declines and puts a plump hand over her glass. Sophie is clearing plates with the help of Marcus; Josh spreads his arms wide as she comes within reach.

'And what may I give you, my lovely? I can think of better libations for you than these pathetic offerings,' he says with awful clarity.

Nigel's pale eyebrows shoot into his fluffy blond hairline. Sophie sighs tolerantly and side-steps, balancing a stack of dirty plates. Several forks fall to the floor with a ringing clatter; Marcus dives to rescue them. Lucy Rathbone gives another nervous giggle; then everyone starts talking at once. The evening is well on its precarious and ill-founded way.

Half an hour later finds us on the terrace, coffee cups and glasses clustered on the rickety table. In the awkward hiatus engendered by Josh's licentious little speech, Nigel has shown unexpected presence of mind in fetching his own guitar which, he tells us modestly, he just happened to have strapped to his bicycle. He now sits slightly apart from us and outside the beam of light thrown from the kitchen, thrumming softly. Sam is cross-legged at his feet and Marcus standing beside him, both watching his fingers on the strings. Throughout this gentle serenade, Josh has not ceased his talking. His arm is flung round Lucy's shoulders as he emphasizes a point with his free hand.

'The state of the art,' he is saying. 'I'll tell you what the state of the art is right here. I am a mere artist, while Leo –' he waves vaguely in my direction '– Leo is a prestigious art dealer.'

The word 'prestigious' emerges slightly slurred.

'He thought highly of me once, did Leo, but not now. I have dared to paint the way I choose, the way I feel, and –' he prods Lucy '– I have fallen from grace. I-am-a-figurist,' he explains, his face close to hers, 'and Leo doesn't like my figures.' He frowns, then roars with laughter. 'That sounds bloody funny to me.'

I listen with a half-smile: these are drunken ramblings and do not matter as such.

'Well, I do think free expression is terribly important,' Lucy says solemnly, 'in all forms of art.'

Out of the corner of my eye I see Da move from his chair to whisper in the strumming Nigel's ear. He nods, tries one or two chords and breaks into passable flamenco. Sam has joined us at the table, drawn by some unknown instinct, and sits silently peeling the wax drips from the single candle. His eyes go from Josh's replenished brandy glass to his father's face, without expression.

'Leo,' continues Josh, like the rumbling of an imminently active volcano, 'is a hard man to please. Today,' he says, trying to get me into focus, 'I have started to paint again in the approved manner – approved by Leo, that is. And even that doesn't satisfy him, does it, Leo?' His eyes burn into me.

'It's too soon to say: early stages yet,' I tell him calmly, while the fury of remembrance grips me.

'Admit it.' He leans heavily on the table towards me. 'You didn't like the subject-matter one little bit, did you?'

The words stab at me mockingly; I avert my face, hands clenched through tension in my lap. Da is tapping his feet to the music, his face rapt like an old war-horse scenting gunpowder.

'Oh hell, what's the use?' Josh tosses his drink back in one, suddenly tired of baiting me. 'What the hell's the use? It's a mug's game. I'll sell up and emigrate to Australia, where they don't give a shit for culture. Do something manual and mindless like rounding up sheep. Sam can have a pet wallaby.'

Sam slips from his chair, blue eyes blazing in a chalk-white face. 'I don't want a pet wallaby,' he says in a strangled voice, and bursts into tears. Turning, stumbling in his haste, he disappears into the night.

'Oh dear, poor little boy,' Lucy says, her face pinker than ever from anxiety. I feel sorry for her; the strain of pretending that supper-parties such as this are normal practice in Lower Pelling is beginning to show. 'Should we go after him, do you think?' she asks, half-rising from her seat.

'I'll go. Later,' Josh growls.

I can tell, where others could not, that he is ashamed.

Conversation is drowned suddenly in the rapid staccato stamping of feet. Da, unable to resist the rhythm of the guitar, is dancing flamenco on the terrace; one hand behind his arched back, the other across his chest, in fair imitation of the real thing. He knows the steps – heel, toe, toe heel toe: bowed legs shuddering, he taps with increasing speed to Nigel's hectic strumming. I wonder where he finds the energy and whether indeed he should be indulging in such strenuous activities at his age. Sophie appears from the house and joins him, making a graceful charade in her ignorance, dancing because she cannot help but do so. We start to clap in accompaniment, caught up in the careless enjoyment; all of us, that is, except Josh, who rises precipitately, rocking the table and barging against the wretched Lucy, and strides haphazardly towards his father.

'You stupid old bugger,' he shouts. 'You're making an exhibition of yourself, d'you know that?'

The music ceases abruptly and Nigel sits motionless, his mouth ajar in disbelief. Sophie's face is a blank. Da says nothing: drawing himself up to his full height, he considers his son, takes one step forward and gives Josh a powerful shove in the chest. The effect is startling. He staggers backwards across the lawn as if pulled by invisible forces, arms flailing like windmills, and vanishes into the darkness. There is a cry or a grunt, a noise of rustling in some bush or other, and then silence. We wait for his reappearance amongst us: and nothing happens. We peer into the shadows searching for a moving figure, but only the vague shapes of the trees are discernible. It is as if he has been swallowed up by the night itself.

'Well, now, boyo,' Da says cheerfully to Nigel, quite unrepentant of his actions, 'how about an encore, then?'

'I'm afraid we must go,' Lucy says, darting to Nigel's side. 'It's getting late, and the baby-sitter— Come along, pet.'

She shows a definite firmness, her mouth compressed in a thin line of disapproval.

'It's been an awfully pleasant evening,' Nigel says. In the absence of a host, he does not know whom to thank. 'Good night, and perhaps we shall see some of you in church tomorrow.'

There is a polite and non-committal murmur in reply.

'Come along,' Lucy says impatiently, making it obvious she hopes never to set eyes on any of us again.

'Goodbye,' Nigel says as he is yanked away by the arm. 'Nice meeting you.'

'Thank you for playing for us,' Sophie calls after them.

Out of politeness I feel someone should make the gesture of seeing them on their way. But by the time I turn the corner of the house, they are already astride their bicycles, lamps ablaze. Lucy's voice carries back to me on a note of hysteria as they wobble off along the drive.

'The man's insane! Call me a prude if you like, but there's a limit. And what about that wretched child in floods of tears – nobody doing a thing about him—'

I watch their rear lights glow in the distance and disappear. Inwardly I sigh; am I wholly responsible for the mess that Josh had become? Is this the outcome of, and the retribution for, my helplessly loving Claudia and all that is left of that love? It is a poor sort of legacy. Sam weighs on my conscience heavily, a hostage to fortune. The least I can do is to find him and provide some sort of comfort and advice: unless Josh has vanished on the same errand. But I catch sight of a glimmer of Sophie's white dress down by the river-bank, and hear voices and the splash of water. The moon comes out from behind a cloud as I walk across the lawn, defining her gesticulating figure.

'What's going on?'

She turns, a sylphide in the moonlight. 'It's Josh. He's in the punt and he insists on taking it downriver. Josh! *Please* get out!'

Standing beside her, I can see him the other side of the rushes, wobbling perilously as he shifts position, pole in hand.

'Come on, Sophe. Come with me!'

'Don't you dare,' I order her. 'The punt's rotten.'

She looks at me in horror. 'It isn't, is it?'

'It won't go fifty yards without sinking.' I turn away.

'Don't go, Pa!' She grabs my arm. 'We must do something. He'll drown.'

217

'I doubt it. The water will sober him up; just what he needs.'

'Oh, God! Where are you going?'

'To find Sam. It's rather more important.' Halfway to the house I call back to her: 'And I should get to bed if I were you,' as if she was eleven. For the first time in my life, I am fed up to the teeth with my beloved daughter.

Sitting on the side of my bed, I balance the shed key in the palm of my hand. I had to search for it myself; Sam refused to be involved to the extent of handing it over, although he told me where to look: hanging on a hook on the side of the dresser. It will be up to me to return it to its proper place. The door to my room is ajar: I am waiting until the last sounds of preparation for bed have died away.

To some extent the original purpose of discovering the letters no longer applies; if Josh has them, they have already incriminated me. But this is by no means certain. There is the answerphone theory produced by Marcus: inexplicable though it may seem, for I swear it is not my voice on the tape, it stays obstinately at the back of my mind as a possibility. One could say that none of this matters now, since Josh gives every sign of being cognizant of my treachery. However, there are other reasons for wanting the letters in my keeping. I cannot bear the thought of prurient eyes devouring the expressions of my love: they are intensely private, a link in the chain that bound me to Claudia. And I have a longing to re-read them, and to remember the occasions on which I wrote them. Nostalgic, maybe, but it is a way of bringing her closer to me, of keeping her memory alive. Strangely, it is Jane who stays so clearly delineated in my memory, while Claudia is summoned back by touch and smell and sight.

I have no idea what the potting-shed conceals other than old flowerpots and rusty tools. I only know it was Claudia's haunt where she raised plants and pursued her latest transitory interest. Sam did not need persuading to tell me the whereabouts of the key; his loyalty towards Josh had taken a hard knock during the evening. After leaving Sophie by the river, I looked for him in his room to no avail, and neither Da nor Marcus had seen him since his disappearance. Marcus offered to search, but I made the excuse of wanting some fresh air, and set out with a torch for the neglected garden. I guessed that Sam would turn to his animals for solace, and I was right; I found him in the zoo, stroking the slumbering form of Troy. He glanced up briefly and away again, saying nothing. His tears had dried, leaving black smudges on his cheeks where he had wiped them away with a hand. The pristine shirt chosen by Sophie had suffered the same fate; he was the old Sam, back to normal.

I did not know how to begin. We stood side by side in silence, the colour sapped from our clothes and faces by the light of the moon. The rank animal smell seemed more noticeable than ever.

'Are any of your animals nocturnal?' I said in a low voice.

He shook his head. 'The baby owl was, but he's gone now.' The fox cub was curled nose to tail in its sleep. 'There's no need to whisper,' he said. 'He won't wake up.'

'Did you find the toad?' I asked.

'No. But he was ready to go. He was dehydrated

when I first found him, but he'll be all right now near the river.'

The furry ball of a cub had a certain appeal. 'I can understand your not wanting to lose them,' I said.

He did not answer, but from the thrust of his jaw I could see that tears were being held back.

'I don't suppose for a moment Josh meant what he said; all that nonsense about Australia,' I added.

'It wasn't just that,' Sam said explosively. 'It was the bit about the pet wallaby. I don't *have* pets: I'm an animal doctor and a zoologist, and he won't take me seriously. He treats me like a stupid kid.'

It was true that Josh's behaviour at present was rather more fourth-form than his son's.

'Perhaps,' I suggested, 'you shouldn't take *him* too seriously just for the moment, at least when he makes wild statements.' I paused, searching for the right words. 'He's going through a difficult patch. Even adults lose confidence,' I told him, wondering why I bothered to defend a man who was doing his best to humiliate me.

'I don't see why,' he answered stubbornly, fiddling with the latch to Troy's cage. 'He sold lots of paintings at that exhibition, didn't he? If you're good at something, you don't suddenly stop being good at it.'

'No,' I agreed, 'but you can lose the creative urge.'

'What's that?'

'It's the driving force inside people that enables them to produce works of art.'

He glanced at me. 'Has Josh lost it?' he asked.

'To a certain extent, I believe.'

'Will he get it back, d'you think?'

'Oh, yes.' I thought of the canvas which undoubtedly

220

bore the sketched outline of Sophie, although I had been too upset at the time to take note of it. 'Quite soon, I wouldn't be surprised,' I said, hoping my voice did not betray the bitterness of my feelings.

'He doesn't drink so much when he's painting,' he remarked, showing a welcome return to practicality. 'I suppose you can't do anything well if you're drunk.'

'No.'

He closed the cub's cage and leant his back against it, gazing past me at the garden where moonlight and shadows combined to soften the unkempt grass.

'It was different with Mum here,' he said, 'in spite of the rows. It felt safe, like nothing would ever change. But it *has* changed now; I never know what will happen next. I have awful dreams, ones where I wake up and find everything gone, the house and my animals and everything, and there's just a kind of empty field where they used to be.' He hugged himself as if he were cold. 'It's frightening,' he said in a whisper.

The transition from well-balanced and contented child to one demoralized and vulnerable struck at me painfully. It had all become too much for him, this precarious existence with a rudderless father. I felt his vulnerability as if it were my own, compounded by a sense of guilt over my part in the scenario. His square, freckled face looked bleak and drawn and much older, like someone who has been asked to grow up too soon. I longed to hug him, but guessed he would be shocked by such an unmasculine gesture. A more practical form of comfort was needed.

'Sam, would you like to come and stay with Sophie and me sometime? She'd love to have you.'

He turned his head quickly to look at me, eyes wide with consideration of the pros and cons of this offer. 'When?' he asked cautiously.

'Any time you want to. I know London isn't your favourite place, but I don't think you've seen the best of it. We could go to Whipsnade, where the animals roam around in the open.'

His face lit up with interest. 'I'd like that. Thank you,' he remembered to add.

'Good. Then we'll arrange a weekend when Sophie and I will both be available to take you to places.'

'I'd have to get someone to look after the animals; feed them and so on.'

'Would Josh do it?'

He stared at me as if I were mad.

'Or Mrs Morse?' I suggested quickly.

'She's frightened of them,' he said, grinning for the first time. 'But Roy might do it for me; he's the gardener at the Hall. I'd have to pay him something. It could come out of my running-away money.'

'I'll happily foot the bill,' I told him.

'Oh, thanks, Leo.' He seemed a great deal happier once that problem was solved.

'I think we'd both better get some sleep now, don't you?'

In trying to provide consolation, the letters had been completely driven from my mind; as we shut the door to the zoo, the potting-shed close by reminded me. I asked for the key on our way back to the house, feeling uncomfortably as if I were demanding a favour in return for mine, and fully expecting a flat refusal. Sam, however, had far from forgiven his father: his mood was defiant.

'He'll shoot me if he finds out, but I don't care. It's only an old shed, anyway. All his empties are stacked in there, that's why he doesn't want anyone snooping around.'

'Empties?' I said, puzzled.

'Yes. He doesn't put them out for the dustmen at one go because of what they'd say, so he keeps them in garbage bags at the back of the shed, and throws them away in twos and threes.'

I could say nothing; what was there to say?

'I'll tell you where the key is,' Sam decided. 'That's not quite the same as giving it to you, is it?'

Personally, I saw little difference. 'If Josh discovers, I'll take full blame.'

'What do you want it for?' he asked me curiously.

I had anticipated this question and stuck as close to the truth as I dared. 'Your mother used to make pottery at one time,' I said. 'There might be one or two bits lying around. I was very fond of her and I'd like to have something that belonged to her.'

He thought about this for a moment before saying, 'I don't think there's much of her stuff left in there, but I'm not certain. She put her best bit in our time-capsule, a little saucer with leaves painted on.' He added warningly, 'You won't find the time-capsule in there if you're thinking of looking.'

'I wouldn't dream of it.'

Lights in the bedroom windows were still shining as we crept round the house. I wondered whether Josh had got the wetting he deserved, callously unbothered as he appeared to be about his son's distress. Sam caught hold of my arm before I could open the kitchen door.

'Leo.'

'Yes?'

'If anything really went wrong here, like Josh selling the house, could I come and live with you?'

I looked into his earnest, upturned face and wondered how on earth to answer. 'It would make your father miserable, Sam, if you wanted to leave him.'

'He wouldn't mind; he doesn't care.'

'Wrong, on both counts,' I said firmly. 'He has a funny way of showing he cares, that's all.'

'You're telling me.' He scuffed his shoe at a pebble, sending it shooting across the terrace, and sighed. 'Oh, well,' he said, 'I suppose I couldn't, then. He'd be all alone, wouldn't he?'

Before he disappeared to bed, I said, 'But if ever you're seriously worried, you can always telephone me,' and I scribbled the two numbers on a kitchen pad and gave them to him. His back view as he left seemed to me intensely lonely.

I have grown attached to the boy. Sitting here, waiting for the household sounds to die away, I find myself hoping that he is not lying awake in the darkness but has dropped asleep from sheer tiredness. Involving myself in his life is, of course, only part of a promise I made to Claudia. Circumstances have rendered such a thing impossible up until this time; I have been banned from all connections with Josh. But the attachment I feel for Sam goes deeper than promises; he is another link with the past, binding me to her memory, reminding me of her in the likeness of his hair and eyes and smile.

I listen: all noise seems to have died away. Leaning out of the window, I can see no beams of light from other windows. The desire for sleep has left me. Slipping the key in my pocket, I negotiate the stairs which squawk at every step, and go out through the front door, leaving it on the latch.

The shed door opens smoothly, as if it has been recently oiled. An owl screeches from the trees down by the river. I peer into the dimness of the shed's recesses, flash my torch over the shapes of its contents, and enter with an absurd sense of *Boy's Own* adventure.

My first impression is one of accumulated rubbish which no-one has bothered to sort out or throw away; as Da informed me. A wooden work-bench runs the length of the wall opposite the door and carries on at right-angles along the shorter wall at the far end. Underneath it are some half-dozen black garbage sacks bulging with what I now know to be empty bottles. A cluster of spades, forks and rakes lean neglected in a corner, the mud still adhering to their rust-ingrained blades and prongs; a pathetic monument to Claudia, untouched since her death.

Placing the torch on the work-bench, I begin to take stock of the objects cluttering its length. Pyramids of flowerpots of every size are stacked inside each other, some broken or toppled over to lie among balls of garden string, half-used packets of fertilizer, an assortment of old gloves, a coil of thin wire, canes and a trowel tossed down carelessly. There are other things as I work my way along, all connected with the garden until I reach the end and find, in the cobweb-strewn debris, a small cluster of her pottery, rejects of her efforts judging by their appearance. I pick up a jug, glazed but touchingly misshapen, and hold it in my hands, imagining her own hands attempting to mould it evenly.

My eyes have become accustomed to the gloom; I can see into all the corners and crevices and it is hopelessly apparent there is nothing here for me except an excess of nostalgia. There are no containers of any kind beneath the work-bench; only a pair of her mud-caked gumboots. It is not the place to store letters other than in an airtight box or tin: the atmosphere reeks with damp and mildew. I realize it is a wasted endeavour, and I am cold without a sweater; and still I am loath to drag myself away from somewhere that was entirely hers. I do not know what lies behind the garbage bags, but my guess is that if there was anything of interest Josh would have found it a long time ago. Nevertheless, reluctance to leave makes me bend and half-heartedly drag out the foremost bag, which causes the others to shift with an agonizing rattle and clatter that could be heard as far as the house.

I hold my breath and listen. Once again there is silence, apart from the minute sounds of the country at night; vague rustlings in the undergrowth and the squeakings of nocturnal creatures. I dare not try to replace the bottle-heavy sacks. I feel all of a sudden enormously weary. Retrieving the torch, I have a last look round and take Claudia's little jug on impulse; not solely as a memento, but also to prove my explanation to Sam. I turn to go and find the open doorway darkened, the light of the moon blocked out by a bulky figure standing there, silently waiting. My heart goes out of control, racing wildly in shock: I want to run. I take a step forward as he does the same, and find myself checked by the hard, cold steel of Josh's shotgun, while his eyes hold mine in an equally implacable glare.

Chapter Nine

On a Saturday morning towards the end of June, I drove down to spend the weekend at Lower Pelling and found that Claudia was not at the front entrance to greet me. Her absence, trivial enough in itself, nevertheless left me with a hollow feeling in the pit of my stomach. It was not a misplaced foreboding; for that weekend denoted the beginning of the end, although nothing could have been further from my mind at the time.

The reason for no-one being around became apparent when I wandered through the house in the direction of the kitchen, where people were apt to congregate. The door was open and the sound of Claudia and Josh, their voices raised in flinging insults at each other, drove me swiftly and silently back the way I had come, to lean against the car while I worked out what to do. I had been a witness to one or two of their milder disagreements, but this bore the signs of something more serious. I could have disappeared to the pub for half an hour but there was no guarantee their tempers would have cooled by my return. I decided eventually to take a walk across the lawn to the river, where my figure was bound to be seen from the windows.

The noise of their row reached me easily on the river-bank; I remember hoping young Sam was out of earshot: and then, to my embarrassment, they burst from the french windows to continue on the terrace, where fragments of sentences could be clearly heard. I kept my back studiously turned and watched a moorhen hustling her brood into the rushes. An uneasy suspicion crossed my mind that, somewhere within the acrimony going on behind me, I was involved.

'Ssh! For God's sake, Josh, Leo's just arrived, so shut up—'

'Why? Part of the family, isn't he? Practically lives here, so to hell with that—'

'That's right, take it out on Leo. Don't expect lunch, I'm not sitting there with you in a flaming temper—'

'I don't want any sodding lunch,' I heard him shout; and then, silence. Out of the corner of my eye I could see him striding through the orchard towards his studio. I knew instinctively she was walking towards me, although her feet made no sound on the grass.

'Leo?' she asked tentatively, joining me and slipping her arm through mine. 'I'm so sorry,' she murmured.

We stared at the idly-flowing water together. 'I turned up at the wrong moment,' I ventured after a minute or two.

'No moment would have been the right one,' she said, 'as he is now.'

'What started it, or shouldn't I ask?'

'This particular slanging match?' She seemed evasive, bending to pick up a twig and started to peel it. 'He's been impossible for the past two weeks. Ever since I – we were last in London.'

I cast my mind back. That Friday had been one of the lucky ones; we had spent half the day at the flat. Josh

229

had been at the Hornsey studio. The last time I had seen them together, the atmosphere had been normal.

'Is it to do with me?' I asked.

She shook her head, shrugged as if uncertain. 'I've been accused of just about everything recently: I'm never around, he hardly ever sees me – well, whose fault is that? I'm a lousy mother who spoils *and* neglects her child, and I allow Marcus to be rude to him. I've become cold and unapproachable, and I don't give him the slightest bit of support or encouragement.'

She flung the stick into the river to be carried away on the current.

'I only do his tax, pay the bills – eventually – answer the telephone and run the diary for him, besides cook and garden and massage his ego.' She raised her hands in a gesture of frustration and ran them through the untidy mass of hair. 'I could *kill* him when he's like this,' she said hoarsely, as if it were an effort not to scream.

The hands fell to her sides; I took one of them and held it in mine, uncomfortably aware that Josh's accusations were bluster, and his serious cause for complaint lay elsewhere.

'The trouble is,' she said, 'there are grains of truth in what he says. I am not the same person he married. But even so, these listed sins of mine are only a cover-up for the real thing that's bugging him,' she added, echoing my thoughts.

'You'd better tell me.'

'It came out in the course of this morning's row. He accused me of having an affair; nothing else would explain the change in me, so he claims.' She looked at me with a faint smile. 'And that, of course, is the truth, not just a grain of it.'

'You think he has evidence?'

She sighed. 'I really don't know.'

'Something must have sparked off this sudden mood change of his,' I said uneasily.

'It's probably as he says, dissatisfaction with the married state. I've been feeling rather tired lately; perhaps he takes that as lack of enthusiasm. Come on, let's have a drink.'

As we walked back to the house, I said, 'I think I'd better not come down here so often. He may well feel I am abusing your hospitality.' I glanced at her. 'Am I?'

'Don't be silly.' She squeezed my arm. 'Josh'll be all right by this evening, you'll see. He will have worked off his aggro.'

I did not share her confidence. Something in what she had said worried me. I, of all people, knew she could feign enthusiasm when it was necessary. The hollowness had returned to my stomach, and the windows of the house seemed to wink slyly in the sun as if sniggering at my endangered double life.

It was a relief to return to work on the following Monday. The morning unfolded in a familiar pattern, consisting of an hour or so spent at Sotheby's and my reaching the Gallery soon after eleven-thirty, where Zelda brought me coffee while I made telephone calls and answered faxes. The first commitment in the book was at three o'clock; a dealer scheduled for a private viewing of Impressionists on behalf of a Greek shipping magnate. I planned to slip in one of Josh's paintings in order to keep his name and talent to the fore.

Siegler's had done well for him. Twenty-five per cent of his pictures had been sold through the private view, and a further twenty-five per cent in single sales thereafter. Fifty per cent could be considered a major triumph in the middle of a recession. Negotiations with the New York gallery were hanging fire: they were suffering from a similar political crisis and unwilling to commit themselves. I had not lost hope, however. The business side of my conscience, as far as Josh was concerned, was clear: not so the moral aspect of it. It had begun to prick, and for the shameful reason that I was afraid of being discovered.

I did not feel like going out to lunch that day; I was not hungry and had an urge for solitude. Zelda left with her assistant to find their own sustenance and to bring me back a sandwich. Alone, I made fresh coffee and sat down to drink it on the leather seat in the far gallery. It is where I inevitably go in search of peace: a great place for contemplation. Surrounded by cool walls and the pictures of my choice, I am as much at home there as in my own house; the very smell of Siegler's has the power to calm me. I needed to think, to retrace the events of the past weekend in the hopes of dispelling a growing sense of anxiety.

Josh did not reappear until the evening of that Saturday. As Claudia predicted, he had recovered his humour to the point of geniality.

'Leo, I've neglected you,' he said, clasping my hand. 'Forgive me, but it's been in a good cause. Wanted to put the finishing touches to something and time ran away with me. Now let me get you a drink.'

'I already have one, thanks, Josh.'

Judging by the aroma of whisky on his breath, it was not the first of the day he poured for himself. I was not taken in by his warmth, recalling the phrase, 'He practically lives here'. But I was too relieved to question the change in him. The temptation that morning had been for me to turn tail and drive back to London, leaving them both to sort out their differences; until I reminded myself sharply that Claudia's problem might well be mine also.

'Are you going to show me around?' I asked: by which I meant his current work.

'Of course, of course. Now, if you like. Claudie'll be busy in the kitchen, won't you, sweetheart?'

'No,' she replied shortly. 'Supper's cold. But take Leo, I can see your paintings any time.'

It was plain that the rancour of the morning lingered and she was not ready for a rapprochement.

The canvas on the easel was finished: a reclining nude, her back half-turned to catch the sharp angle of the hip bone; a shaft of sunlight, Josh's trademark, falling on the folded thighs. I admired this and two or three others that were hung or stacked against the walls; reminded afresh of his talent. We talked a little of sales and future possibilities, but I could see his mind was elsewhere. A restlessness drove him to fiddle with things, rearranging tubes of paint and clusters of brushes on his work-bench.

'How do you think Claudia is?' he asked out of the blue.

'Fine.' What else could one say? 'Why do you ask?'

'You don't notice a difference in her?' he said obliquely.

'Frankly, no. Should I? Look, what is all this, Josh? Are you worried about her?'

I wanted to draw him out, get him to reveal his misgivings. But I was disappointed. He merely said, 'Yes. No. Oh, shit! I only hope she's not pregnant again. Forget it, Leo. Let's go back to the whisky.'

The same thought had crossed my mind during the afternoon spent with Claudia. I had indeed noticed a difference in her, but it was physical rather than psychological. We had a picnic lunch in the garden with Sam; after we had finished and were lounging in chairs on the lawn, he asked for help in moving an overflow of guinea pigs from one cage to another.

'Can't it wait, darling?' she said. 'I don't feel very energetic at the moment.'

This was so uncharacteristic of Claudia that I glanced at her sharply. Her face was drained of colour, and there were dark smudges under her eyes.

'Shall I give you a hand?' I offered Sam.

He gave my clothes an appraising look. 'It's a bit tricky, handling guinea pigs: they run all over the place. I think I'll wait till later, thank you, Leo.'

I cannot say I was sorry to be turned down. Claudia and I did little that afternoon, apart from a stroll by the river. She was quiet and kept her arm tucked in mine as if it gave her security. I could sense the lack of eagerness for any other contact.

'Are you feeling all right?' I asked at some point, and she turned her head and smiled; but it was not the curving smile I knew.

'I've had an upset stomach; nothing serious,' she said. 'Nerves, I expect. Too many rows.'

Guilt of a different kind to that of cheating on Josh

234

attacked me as we moved slowly through the filtered shade of the willows; guilt, and worry that the strain of our meetings was getting all too much for her. I could not now imagine life without them, and the idea of giving her up made me feel literally ill. I shied away from it, relegating it determinedly to the subconscious.

At dinner that evening she ate the minimum possible without arousing attention, and in the shadowy light of the candles her cheeks seemed more hollowed than usual; but I persuaded myself it was an illusion. I saw Josh's eyes on her, speculative and baffled, and wondered down which avenue his mind was racing. Only Sam appeared entirely carefree, having success-fully transferred his guinea pigs by himself.

'Two ran into the long grass and one hid in a flowerpot. It took me ages to find it. You haven't eaten your treacle tart, Mum.'

'I've had enough.'

'Shall I eat it for you, then?'

I left them soon after lunch on Sunday; Sophie and I had been asked out to supper and I wanted time alone with her. There were few enough opportunities for me to catch up on what was happening in her life.

I drove home steadily, pondering the double quan-dary of Claudia's health and Josh's suspicions; unable to decide whether or not they were two separate issues. I suspected that his accusation over Claudia's lover was a shot in the dark; but it was uncomfortably accurate, and my mind wrestled with the possibilities of some indiscretion which might have caused it. I could think of none but the letters I had written her since the early spring. She had got up late on the

Sunday morning, looking pale but less heavy-eyed. We had barely an hour alone, while Sam was busy with his own ploys, and Josh had gone to buy cans of lager at the pub. Helping her to dead-head the roses, I asked her whether she had the letters in a safe place.

'What a worrier you are, darling,' she said. 'They are perfectly safe.'

I knew her idea of security did not tally with mine: the bread-bin was likely to be as good a hiding-place as any other, in her view.

'You don't believe me, do you?' she said with a little more of her old spirit. 'I can promise you, I've put them where no-one can find them.'

'You've burnt them?' I looked at her, feeling relieved and hurt in one.

'I have *not*,' she said indignantly, then sighed. 'I do miss getting your letters, you know.'

We had agreed I should stop writing during the summer months while Josh was spending more time at the cottage; the off-chance of his opening the envelope could not be risked. The originals were a potential time-bomb: I was left with no choice but to believe her promise, although I would have felt happier to be told where they were.

In the same way, I could not stop myself wondering whether she was pregnant. The idea played havoc with my emotions. Appalled by the danger it would entail, I nevertheless felt an exhilaration that I might be the father. Claudia's child, *my* child: it would have to be a son, for no girl could compete for beauty and my affections against Sophie. For a full minute as I drove home I let my imagination run riot, down to the features of the mythical baby and the brilliance of its brain. And then the fact that Josh might well be the father, and the sudden movement of a traffic jam, brought me to earth with a crash. Depression and a vague headache accompanied me in the slow procession into London. Going over the events the next day by myself in the Gallery did nothing to reassure me. Claudia's face, a study in black and white, hovered before my eyes. In contrast, the reasons for Josh's distemper shrank to insignificance; it was she who worried me, and had the power to make life worth living or not, depending on circumstance. At two o'clock I shut myself in the office and telephoned her, desperate suddenly for the sound of her voice. Her cheerfulness when she answered, breathless from running across the garden, drove away any fears I had for her. She sounded back to normal. Somewhere in the background I heard Josh call her from a distance.

'Friday?' she said briefly.

'Friday,' I agreed with a lightened heart.

When I arrived home on the Sunday, I had found Sophie in her room, bent over the sewing machine.

'Hi, Pa,' she said, frowning in concentration. 'Good weekend?'

I kissed the top of her head. 'So-so, thanks.'

'Only so-so?' She glanced at me. 'Hang on just a sec, I've got this beastly thing in a tangle. There. You look really tired,' she added accusingly, as if suspecting me of debauchery.

'The traffic was hell.'

'Poor old Pa. I'll make you some tea, shall I? Then we can sit and swop gossip while you recover.'

'Good idea,' I said wearily; I find her mothering instinct a little too much at times.

In the kitchen I watched her pouring hot water into the teapot, her hair the way I liked it, in a ballerina knot. Long legs sprouted from one of her absurd little skirts, no more than a frilly pelmet. She grew more exquisite every day, and with it grew my sense of responsibility, the pangs of which attacked me occasionally.

'It's half-term at the end of next week,' she said as we drank our tea.

'I know.' But I didn't; I had forgotten. 'What have you got planned?' I asked.

She fiddled with a teaspoon. 'Would you mind very much if I was away for the ten days?'

'Where, exactly?'

'Smog's asked me to stay with his parents near Whitby. It's lovely country round there,' she said, as if this perfectly innocent invitation needed an explanation. 'Do you mind, Pa? After all, you'll be working most of the time, so I really wouldn't see much of you.'

'True,' I agreed, nevertheless managing to feel neglected. 'It's an excellent idea, kitten. Smog is still first in the boyfriend league, is he?'

'I've told you, Pa, I don't have time for boyfriends,' she said sternly. 'He's a mate, that's all.'

This I knew to be modern parlance for 'just good friends', which was reassuring. Besides, Smog's parents were probably strict Yorkshire stock who would not hold with the young sharing a bedroom. 'What are you making with that machine? I thought you hated sewing,' I asked, changing the subject.

'Oh, I do, but I need a new bikini.'

'You could have bought one; we can just about afford it.'

'I know, but I saw this great material in leopard-skin spots, so I decided to have a go.'

'You're an optimist if you're thinking of wearing it in Yorkshire.'

'You never know.' She blushed, for no reason that I could think of, and moved to refill the teapot. 'So, what was wrong with the weekend?'

'Nothing specific,' I said lamely. 'Claudia was unwell and Josh had a mood; no more than that.'

I had a sudden longing to tell her the real story, of the way I felt about these two people who in many ways dominated my life. But I knew she would not understand and, worse, would never forgive me.

'By the way,' she said, 'you haven't forgotten it's the half-term production on Saturday?'

'How could I when you're dancing the lead?' I smiled. *La Fille Mal Gardée.* I hope that doesn't apply to you.'

She gave a whoop of laughter. 'You must be joking; I can hardly move without your fussing. Mum wouldn't have been nearly so bad about it.'

I was not joking. There were things I should be doing for her; subjects like contraception that I shied away from discussing because the very idea she might require it filled me with distaste. I had no notion of how much or how little she knew of life. A woman friend was needed, someone who could talk to her without embarrassment. Claudia would have offered her advice willingly, but Sophie would probably decline it. I sighed.

'There you are, you see,' Sophie said, pouring

second cups of tea. 'You're worrying right now about something, aren't you?'

Later that evening she appeared in one of Jane's dresses, a pale aquamarine sheath with a tantalizing slit up one side. 'You don't mind, do you, my wearing this?' she asked tentatively in the car.

'Darling, I wanted you to have it, remember? That's why we didn't give it away.'

After a pause, she said, 'We don't talk much about her now, do we?'

'No, but I think about her. Do you?'

'Yes.' She smiled, refusing to let sentimentality creep in. 'She wouldn't have approved, Pa.'

My heart stopped beating at the words, then thudded forwards. I jammed my foot on the brake as the lights turned red. 'What do you mean?'

'Your not having anyone in your life; Mum wouldn't have thought it a good thing, you know.'

'It's a small matter,' I said, 'of finding the right one. Isn't it?'

'You don't have to *marry* them,' she told me, peering at her face in the sun-shield mirror. 'You could just find a mate. Take it from me, they're good news.'

I tried to recall, and failed, whether life had ever seemed so simple as that.

Claudia telephoned me very early one morning after the weekend, to say that something had cropped up which prevented her from meeting me. We postponed it until the following Friday, and I spent a week of speculation as to the reason: a week that dragged by interminably.

There were no more calls, but she was late on the

day we had arranged. I stood by the window waiting for her, full of a vague unease. I had kept the day clear of commitments, putting in a cursory appearance only at the Gallery. Zelda had begun silently to question such transgressions, giving keen looks incorporating a mixture of disapproval and curiosity; no director of Siegler's should behave in such an irresponsible fashion, her expression inferred.

'You should leave me at least one number where you can be reached,' she stipulated, pushing the spectacles into place on her nose. 'Remember the crisis over Sophie; we don't want a similar episode.'

But I was reluctant to do so; the fewer people who knew the number of the flat, the greater the security. 'I shall be moving around, visiting studios; I'll ring you after lunch,' I said firmly.

I was at the door of the flat when the lift stopped at our floor with a clunk. Claudia was wearing a blue cotton dress cinched in at the waist with a wide belt, accentuating a thinness I did not recognize. Her face was carefully made up, as if she had taken trouble to cover imperfections she did not want me to see. She gave me a full, curving smile, but I had the feeling that even this was part of the camouflage; beneath it all I noticed a weariness and the pallor of a fortnight ago. She was carrying flowers wrapped in tinfoil.

'Roses from the garden,' she said, kissing me. 'Mad of me to bring them, they'll only last a day. I thought we could enjoy them while we're here,' she added from the kitchen, bringing them through in a water-jug and putting them on the sofa table.

'They're wonderful,' I said, bending to smell them.

'Would you like some lunch? I've brought smoked salmon and brown bread.'

'I'm not really hungry,' she said brightly. 'Later, shall we?'

'A drink, then.'

The day was sullen and humid with thunder in the air. She sat with her shoeless feet curled under her on the sofa while I asked her about the way things were at home.

'Much the same. Josh is in an extraordinary mood, disagreeable one moment and all sweetness and light the next.' She ran a finger round the rim of her glass; I watched the dark spread of her lashes against her cheek, and thought quite suddenly how much I loved her. 'I've decided none of it really matters any longer,' she said, yawning hugely and leaning her head on my shoulder. 'If we go to bed, I warn you I'll probably fall asleep, I'm so tired. Must be the weather.'

I did not understand her words about it not mattering any longer, although they increased my anxiety. I decided that once we were making love it would vanish, everything would swing back to normal and I would find my imagination had been playing tricks. It was wishful thinking. Before very long I realized her body was damp with sweat and there was a kind of desperation in the way she was clinging to me. I could feel the thudding of her heart; frightened, I drew back and held her still with two hands, staring down at her face on the pillow. It was the colour of putty.

'Darling, you're not well. What is it?'

She looked at me as if I were invisible, mumbled, 'Sorry,' then swung her legs out of bed in one convulsive movement and staggered to the bathroom.

I lay where I was, helpless. Through my mind trooped an assortment of horrors, pregnancy and miscarriage uppermost. Behind the closed door I could hear the terrible sound of retching. It seemed to last forever; and then the spasms stopped, and there was silence. She did not appear; unable to bear it a second longer, I knocked on the door, but there was no answer. I found her sitting on the bathroom floor, leaning her head against the rim of the bath, exhausted. Half-carrying her, I guided her back to bed and covered her with the duvet, where she lay, shivering now, her face turned away from me. She lifted an arm and fumbled for my hand.

'Sorry,' she murmured again.

'Look, darling, you're obviously quite ill. I think I should call a doctor.'

The complications and embarrassing explanations this would entail shrank to insignificance beside my worry.

'No, don't do that.' She looked up at me out of tired eyes. 'Later,' she said, 'I'll explain everything. I'd like to sleep for a bit, please.'

The nightmarish quality of the afternoon lives with me to this day; it is unforgettable. She slept, and then she talked; while my mind rejected the things she told me, as minds will reject the unacceptable. I made her weak tea and dry toast, and at half-past five I drove her home to Hornsey. I parked as near to the studio as she would let me, and watched her walk the fifty yards to her house feeling as if the whole of me would disintegrate with misery, in company with the part of her being consumed by illness.

She had sat huddled in a dressing-gown, giving me the facts in an unemotional voice, while my own quavered over my questions.

'So you see,' she said, 'why there is no point in getting a doctor. I have already seen one of the best there is, apparently.'

'They can make mistakes. Tests can be unreliable, or even get confused with another person's; it happens.' Clutching at straws, I fought my panic.

She looked at me in pity. 'No, Leo. I know what I've got; instinctively you know.'

'But it's happened so suddenly.'

'These things do. You feel a lack of energy, then there's a stomach upset or two, and there you are: suddenly.'

I got up and walked to the window, dangerously near to tears. That was all she needed, a crumbling wimp of a lover.

'We must be positive about this. There are treatments.' I swallowed hard. 'People do recover; they know so much more about it these days.'

'Yes, people do.' She spread her hands fan-wise in her lap, as if looking at them for the first time. 'But I'm not going to accept the orthodox treatment.'

'For God's sake, Claudia —' I swung round on her, and realized that it was no time for anger — 'Surely it's worth trying everything?' I said with as much control as possible.

'Not for this one; nothing works for this one. You go through a second hell and, in the end, you haven't won. I don't want to lose my hair for nothing. I'm vain.' She smiled in a resigned way that made me want to scream.

'Don't you want to – to get well?' I asked; I could not bring myself to say 'live'. *For my sake*, I cried out silently, selfishly, *if not your own*.

'Of course.' She leant her head against the back of the sofa as if tired of discussing it. 'I'll fight it my way. I'll try will-power; I'm a great believer in that. There are people who help you to use it; special places where you can go. It would help, I suppose,' she added, 'if I believed in something stronger. A faith would come in handy.'

Unable to bear the thought of losing her to vague theories, I reiterated what I felt stubbornly, knowing it was no use.

'I really don't want to talk any more,' she said. 'I think I'll sleep a little.'

Minute by minute the endless afternoon inched forward. I lay beside her, wanting to hold her and not daring to wake her, stranded on an island of loneliness. There was too much time to think, to imagine, to envisage a short, capsulated future in which Claudia would exist: just; and I would be on the periphery, an onlooker cut off from her by tubes and drips. There were many things I wanted to know and could not make myself ask her.

'Am I able to talk to your specialist?' I put the question to her without much hope. She sat on the sofa sipping the tea I had brought her, looking almost normal. Some colour had returned to her cheeks, and with it a rush of optimism on my part. I was not to know how often this would happen; a sudden uplift of the spirits only to have them dashed again.

She shook her head. 'They're very busy people; they'll only see relatives. Josh, in other words.

245

Besides,' she said with a stab at humour, 'you might run into him in the waiting-room.'

'As you say, does that matter?'

'I've been thinking,' she said seriously, 'and I believe it does. I'd like you and Josh to remain friends; he's going to need them, and he hasn't many. And there's his work. Without you, he'll go off the rails.'

'Those are your wishes; they may not be his,' I pointed out.

'I think they will be.'

'Try and eat a little,' I urged.

Nibbling a piece of toast, she said without looking at me, 'I'll understand if you want to end this now, darling. It won't be much fun for you.'

'End it?' I said, appalled. 'End what, for God's sake?'

'Us. Being together as lovers. I have an idea I'm going to be difficult to love.'

'Is that all the confidence you have in me?' Sitting beside her, I took her free hand and kissed the palm. 'So what's new? You've always been difficult.' Beneath the joking, I felt stricken. 'Unless, of course, you want to get rid of me.'

'You know the answer to that,' she said mildly.

'You're going to get well. You're so calm about it, you're probably halfway there.'

'It won't always be like that,' she said. 'There'll be days when I rant and rave and weep at the unfairness of it happening to me. And I'll be frightened. I'm frightened now.'

I pulled her to me and held her close for some time without speaking. After a while she said, 'Oh, hell! I haven't bought anything for supper.'

'Why can't Josh do the bloody shopping?' I looked at

her. 'You have told him what's wrong, haven't you?'

'No.' She sighed, straightened up. 'I'll tell him tonight. I'd hoped to put it off as long as possible.'

I felt absurdly touched that I was the first to know.

I would not allow her to shop; she made me a list and I went to Europa for her. So it was that I found myself putting tins and frozen food into a wire basket for the man I had cheated; wondering as I did so how he was going to take the news that was about to hit him. The rows, I very much hoped, would stop, for Claudia was in no state to bear them. His temperament was so unpredictable, I did not dare attempt to read their immediate future together: I merely prayed that, from time to time, I would be allowed to be a part of it.

Before she left me in the car, she said, 'Come down to the cottage soon, please.'

'Whenever you want me.'

Her face was bathed by the setting sun through the windscreen, giving it a deceptively healthy glow. I kissed her long and hard on the lips to show her she was still a desirable being, and because the number of times I would be able to do so from now on could not be calculated.

I immersed myself in work during the weeks that followed, finding a measure of solace in wearing myself out. Zelda, having shown her suspicions over my absences, now raised her eyebrows at this new-found zeal. Luckily it was a busy time, in any case, with a retrospective exhibition coming up in four weeks, and a dozen matters which I should have attended to days ago. The absentee Fridays had left their mark in unfinished business, although in no way did I regret them. Unable to face the fact that shortly they might come to an end, I metaphorically buried my head.

Soon after the day I had dropped Claudia a few yards from his studio, Josh paid the Gallery an unannounced visit. I happened to be talking to Zelda as he walked in, and watched her greet him with marked enthusiasm. But he was not in the mood for flirting, giving her only a ghost of a smile before saying, 'Can we talk somewhere, Leo?'

Taking one look at his haunted expression, I wheeled him out of the door and down the street to the pub.

Pretending I knew nothing of Claudia's illness was the worst part of the next hour; feigning horror-struck surprise and, after a while, offering sympathy and advice without appearing involved beyond the call of friendship. I felt pity for Josh, but as we sat there over our drinks I longed to demand recognition of my own despair. At least you are married to her, I wanted to say; at least you can spend twenty-four hours of every day and night with her, whilst I can merely skulk in the shadows and wait.

'It's the waiting,' he said, breaking into my thoughts with a jolt, 'not knowing what will happen next, or how long—' His voice trailed away.

'You mustn't think like that,' I told him. 'There's always hope, and you must encourage her to believe it, too. I'm sure will-power helps and Claudia's got a lot of that—'

I stopped myself in mid-sentence, realizing how easy it was to give myself away. 'When are you seeing her doctor?' I asked hurriedly.

'This afternoon.'

'He will be able to tell you much of what you want to know.' And a lot of what you'd rather not hear, I decided miserably.

'I'm bloody scared,' Josh said, his eyes a brilliant green with unshed tears. 'Come with me, won't you, Leo?'

I envisaged being relegated to the waiting-room, a friend of the family with no status, no right to ask questions.

'He'll want to see you alone. I wouldn't be much help,' I pointed out.

'Just for me, Leo: for when I come out of the damned place.'

How could I refuse? His hair was a mess from agitated finger-combing; the unaccustomed tie had wriggled itself to one side. He looked like a man who might fall to pieces at the least rejection.

'Suppose I come and fetch you? Would that do?'

He gripped my arm in a wordless gesture of acknowledgement.

'I've been pretty bloody to her lately,' he said at some point. 'There've been rows and I've made them. I have an awful feeling,' he added, 'it may be one of the reasons she got ill. D'you think that's possible?'

'No,' I said firmly. 'It may have made her feel worse; no more than that.'

'Do you realize, I accused her of having a lover?' He leant dangerously on the small pub table and put his head in his hands. 'D'you realize that, Leo? And all the time she was suffering, and didn't tell me.'

I felt a complete shit: his words brought home to me exactly how much I had to answer for.

249

'Recriminations are useless, Josh. It was quite understandable.' I picked up the empty glasses, preparatory to buying a second round. 'Listen,' I said, 'what we must do is persuade her it's possible to recover; it's that belief that will keep her going.'

'She's refusing all treatment.'

'I believe lots of people do. Maybe she'll change her mind.'

'I don't know what to tell Sam,' he said.

'Don't tell him anything unless it gets impossible to keep it from him.'

'You're a tower of strength, Leo,' he said gratefully, doubling my load of guilt.

We drank our drinks and then I made my excuses, which were genuine since I was meeting someone for lunch. I advised him to have a sandwich, and make a round of the art galleries in the vicinity to fill in time. I did not like leaving him in a state of depression, but as I walked away through the dusty July streets it was with a feeling of deep relief that this hurdle was behind me.

It was as well I collected him from the specialist's consulting-rooms. I could read from his face, when he joined me in the waiting-room, the outcome of the interview. Six months to a year, he had been told, with a gentle finality that left little room for doubt.

Three more weekends were to be spent at the cottage before the sudden and dramatic change in Josh took place, and I was no longer welcome. Claudia and I decided between us that it would only make for an impossible atmosphere if I attempted another visit.

In the meantime Sophie returned from her ten days at Whitby, looking remarkably sun-tanned and healthy for a northern holiday. I did not know how to hide my pain over Claudia, and to explain was out of the question. I invented a load of mythical problems at work to account for my lack of exuberance: adding a strained back for good measure, unwisely as it turned out. Sophie knows all about strains: I found myself having to lie on my stomach and have a pungent ointment rubbed into the dorsal muscles.

'You're terribly tense,' she noted professionally as she massaged. 'The muscles are like a knotted-up old bicycle chain.'

'Tell me some more about the holiday,' I said. 'Where you went, what you did.'

'Oh. Well, we didn't *do* very much in the end. The weather was good, so we were on the beach a lot of the time. A place called Robin Hood Bay.'

'Did you swim?'

'Yes.'

'Must have been cold.'

'Freezing.'

'And you christened the bikini?'

'Yes.'

It struck me this was all rather monosyllabic. 'You haven't fallen out with Smog, have you?' I asked.

She laughed: I thought she sounded relieved. 'No. Why should I? I expect we'll always be mates.' She added, 'We walked in the Dales. It's wonderful country, Pa; you should see it.'

'You might have been in the South of France by the look of you.'

'Goodness, is that the time?' She finished my treatment abruptly, and flung a towel across my back. 'Don't get a chill,' she warned.

'No, Nanny. What's the rush?'

'I've got an early rehearsal and I must get to bed. 'Night, Pa.'

It was unlike Sophie to clam up on me, but that was how it seemed. It was only a fleeting thought: my mind was seldom away from Claudia in those tortuous days. I told Sophie about her illness over supper one night, as casually as one can be imparting such news.

'How dreadful,' she said. 'Poor Josh, whatever will he do now?'

I thought then, as I think now, that Sophie is strangely old-fashioned. There is not an ounce of feminism in her; she is entirely geared to the comforts of the men in her life. Endearing in some respects, it nevertheless makes her vulnerable to any self-seeking male.

During those last days at the cottage, I saw a transformation in Josh. He had grown fiercely possessive of Claudia, resenting any outside intrusion in caring for her. He would do the shopping, coming home with fillets of plaice or sole for her, and oven-ready food for the rest of us. He was anxious to take the cooking off her hands, but Claudia was obstinate, determined not to become an invalid before it was necessary. I watched her prepare a meal and sit while we ate it, toying with her steamed fish. Sometimes the smell of the food would prove too much for her and Josh would take over while she disappeared for half an hour. I wondered how long this could continue before alternative arrangements would have to be made; how long also before Sam must be told the truth. His eyes, wide and deceptively dreamy, rested on her face from time to time.

Josh's work was suffering as a result of the new routine. I tried to persuade him to let me help in ways not directly connected with Claudia.

'It would do you good to get your fingers round a paintbrush for an hour or two,' I told him. 'At least let me do the shopping since I'm down here.'

'I know what she likes.' They were as stubborn as each other.

'Any fool can follow a list. I could take Sam with me if he'd like to come.'

Josh shot me a look of reluctant gratitude. 'It might be a good idea.' He ruffled a hand through his hair. 'I haven't given him much time lately.'

'Why not ask one of his friends over?'

He shrugged. 'He hasn't got many. Oh, he gets on all right at school; but he's basically a loner.'

The self-sufficient Sam leapt at the chance, mainly, I suspect, because he needed things from the pet shop. We drove to Chichester on a morning full of bright, intermittent sun with clouds scudding before the breeze, leaving mauve shadows on the hillsides as they passed.

'Josh gets impatient when I ask him to get things from the pet shop,' he explained, 'and it's worse now Mum's not well.'

Out of the corner of my eye I was aware of him giving me a straight stare.

'What's wrong with her, d'you think, Leo? She's never, ever ill as a rule.'

'I don't think anyone quite knows,' I lied helplessly. 'I expect she'll have some more tests, and that may solve it.'

'I think vets are better than doctors,' he said,

squinting into the sun. 'They always seem to know what's wrong with animals. Do they have condition powders for humans?' he asked. 'Because that's what she needs, if you ask me.'

Laughter rose in my throat hysterically. 'I imagine they have the equivalent,' I told him gravely. 'I'll suggest it to your mother, and she can ask the doctor.'

I wanted to buy a present for Claudia, something that would express how I felt without catching the guardian eye of Josh. After we had bought the provisions and dumped half a dozen plastic carriers in the boot of the car, I left Sam at the pet shop with instructions not to move until I returned. I found a second-hand bookshop and, within it, a volume of Yeats' poems bound in red leather. I could not have been there more than fifteen minutes, but when I went back to fetch Sam he was gone. Wild panic seized me: I ran into the street, searching in all directions for a give-away head of flame-coloured hair. There was no sign of him. I started to ask passers-by impatient to finish their Saturday morning shopping; and then there was a tug at my sleeve, and Sam's freckled face at my elbow.

'Where the hell have you been?' I demanded, ready to strangle him.

'Sorry, Leo'

'I said not to move, didn't I?'

'I hardly did.' He looked up at me, warily gauging the extent of my wrath. 'I only went next door to the vet. I was in the doorway waiting for you.'

We started the homeward journey in silence; gradually my fear and my temper subsided. It was my turn to apologize.

'I'm sorry, Sam, but you gave me a fright, you see.'

'It's all right,' he said cheerfully.

'What were you doing at the vet's, anyway? One of the guinea pigs poorly?'

He hesitated. 'No. I wanted to ask him about condition powders for humans.'

'And what did he say?' I asked, keeping my eyes firmly on the road.

'He said what you said: ask a doctor. The trouble is, our doctor isn't very helpful; he's always in a hurry.'

'Your mother is seeing one in London now,' I explained, 'and he'll have more time, I expect.'

'Oh.' Sam stared down at the paper bag of pet requisites in his lap. After a pause, he said, 'That must mean she's quite bad, then.'

I could have bitten my tongue out at my carelessness.

In the late afternoon Claudia and I had an hour alone together. Josh had withdrawn grudgingly to his studio, having first made sure she had taken the pills to control the nausea. I read to her while she lay on a chair in the shade: sun made her feel worse. She wanted me to read from Yeats' poems, but when I started: *Had I the Heaven's embroidered cloths*, its poignancy brought me to a standstill. I moved to safer ground with a Nigel Williams novel, which made her giggle. Stretched out on the chair, it was more noticeable how thin she was becoming, the bones of her hands and feet closer to the surface. There was a tinge of yellow in her face and the whites of her eyes, and when she laughed the skin grew taut across her cheekbones. She seemed very nearly out of reach, slipping away from me before my eyes. It was August.

* * *

255

In the middle of her illness there was a remission, when my hopes were rekindled. For the first time for weeks she was able to meet me at the flat. It broke a long period of desolation, for I had been cut off from her by every form of communication apart from the telephone.

She had telephoned early one morning to tell me Josh had refused to have me to stay, for reasons unknown.

'Something has happened to him.' Her voice sounded as if she had been crying. 'He says he can't cope with having people in the house while I'm unwell.'

'People! For God's sake! I'll talk to him myself. Surely he can't refuse to *talk* to me?'

'I think he may,' she said wearily. 'I think he has discovered something about us. Quite recently. I don't know, because he won't say; but he's changed.'

'He's not taking it out on you?' I said, appalled.

'No. He's being very kind and loving. But he's adamant about you.'

'He can't stop you from asking me down,' I insisted, feeling already that a life-line was being severed.

'No. But if you came, it would make everything ten times worse.' She started to cry in earnest.

'Darling, don't, please. I'm sorry.' I fumbled for words. 'There is nothing to be done about it. You mustn't upset yourself, it's the worst possible thing. It's simply—'

It was simply that I could not bear the bleakness which lay ahead.

'Please telephone as often as you can,' I added. 'I love you.'

I rang Josh late that evening, knowing that Claudia

would be in bed. He sounded in the halfway stage between drunk or sober. At the sound of my voice he went silent.

'Josh?'

'I hear you, Leo.'

'I'm ringing to ask how Claudia is.'

'The same as when you last saw her. Last weekend. Anyway, you spoke to her this morning, didn't you?'

'She rang to tell me not to visit you again.' I cleared my throat. 'I don't understand. Am I that much trouble?'

'It depends,' he said with irony, 'what you mean by trouble.'

'Well, do I get in the way?'

'Yes, boyo, you do,' he answered with sudden emphasis. 'I may not have much longer with her and I want her to myself. That's what it amounts to. Is that so difficult to understand?'

'No. But—'

'I don't want to talk to anyone else, or see anyone, or bloody *be* with anyone else. But ring me if you flog another painting, OK? 'Bye, Leo.'

The line went dead. His words left no room for manoeuvre; they were unequivocal. No doubt in his shoes I would have felt the same. There was to be no contact now: I could not even write to her. If this was indeed a punishment for my treachery, it was a particularly refined form of torture.

It was the end of September before she was in remission. Seeing her once more, holding her – (however delicately, like touching a precious piece of porcelain) – was as miraculous to me as an oasis in a desert. We lay side by side on the bed, hands lightly clasped where once we had made love, quarrelled, and grown inextricably together. Now we talked, and I tried not to let my hopes for her become conviction. Painfully thin, she was; but her skin and her eyes had cleared, and her hair shone.

'It's wonderful to feel like this,' she said. 'Not completely well, but so much better. It's like coming out of a dark cave into the daylight. I went to this place in Somerset: you are put on a strict diet and given therapy to learn how to cope with your illness. You are taught to befriend it.'

'Is that possible?' I asked sceptically.

'Well – here I am.' She turned her head to smile at me.

Who was I to argue with the results, however suspicious I might be of a method that had no claims to orthodoxy? I kissed her gently.

'How did Josh manage without you?' I asked.

'Fine. Sam was back at school, and Josh painted furiously; and Mrs Morse put in extra hours. I think it did him good to be alone for a while. It's been a strain.'

I did not raise the question of my banishment. Nothing contentious was to be allowed to spoil this day.

'Leo, I want to ask you something.'

I squeezed her hand.

'This remission may be just that; it may not last.' I started to speak, but she stopped me. 'We've got to be realistic. Perhaps I've beaten it. If not, if anything happens to me, will you keep an eye on Josh and Sam for me?'

'Must we talk about it now?' I said.

'There may not be another opportunity. Please, Leo, will you promise?'

258

'Yes, of course I promise. But how I am going to achieve it when Josh has written me off, I don't know.'

'He will be different if I'm not there,' she said. 'Is there some wine in the fridge? I'm allowed a glass now and then.'

We had barely two hours; she had escaped Josh's guardianship only by claiming to shop with a girl-friend.

'It's funny,' she said, 'serious illness gives you a whole new perspective on life. Each day, everything that's enjoyable is a bonus; things that you took for granted before it happened. It also,' she added, holding up the wine glass to the light, 'makes you think of missed chances. Did you know I wanted to act? The fact that it's much too late, anyhow, isn't the point. It's only now that I acutely regret not doing what I was cut out to do.'

'What stopped you?'

'I was the only daughter of a father who dis-approved, and a mother who failed to win that battle for me. Now she's dead, and Father's in a residential home when I should have had him to live with us. More regrets.'

'Do you regret us?' I asked.

She looked at me, giving me almost, but not quite, the curving smile.

'No,' she said. 'You taught me a valuable lesson: how *not* to act in everyday life, remember?'

When the two hours were up, I put her carefully in a taxi noticing with a stab in the heart the brittle turn of her ankles.

'Don't look so forlorn,' she said through the window. 'I'm getting better by the hour.'

I watched her drive away as I had done on so many occasions; disappearing from me, returning to the reality of her life and the claims it had on her. The next time I saw her she was lying in a hospital bed.

She was too confused by drugs to recognize me, but her eyes, for the few moments they were open, were their same arresting blue. I had slipped in at a time when I knew Josh to be elsewhere. I held her inert hand for a short while: it felt like a collection of small bones wrapped in flimsy paper. I did not stay for long; the memory of her remote and motionless on the high white bed, already in a world of her own, was not the one I wanted printed indelibly on my brain. There were many others from which to choose.

She died in December. Lack of communication with Josh ensured I did not attend her funeral. I doubt I would have done so, in any case; I am not good at controlling my emotions, and the graveside is no place for weeping lovers. I wrote to Josh; it took time to compose a suitable letter. Of the small amount of correspondence to pass between us, one had been my letter telling him of the sale of two of his pictures, and his reply: brief and ambiguous. ('Well done, Leo; you are a man of many parts. Cheers. Josh.'). The letter of condolence went unanswered. It was not the time to remind him he owed me money for re-framing, but I sent him an invoice the following spring. He posted a note in return, scribbled on a page from a memo pad: 'If I write you a cheque, it'll only bounce. J.'. I did no more about it.

I hope my grief went unnoticed. It seemed unbelievable that the previous Christmas I had cried openly for my wife. This time there was no-one to turn to: like a wounded animal I turned inward, seeking my bed at night as a lair in which to hide. I do not know whether Sophie realized a little of the despair I felt: I never have known with Sophie. I merely told her that Claudia's death had shaken me; I loathed Christmas anyway, and why didn't we spend it in a comfortable hotel? She pointed out that it would be worse this year for Josh and Sam, and why didn't we ask them to join us? I had difficulty in persuading her this was the last thing Josh would have wanted.

On the morning of Claudia's funeral, I stood by my office window and looked down on traffic and pedestrians moving sluggishly through the icy drizzle. A few minutes before I had expressed my dissatisfaction on the telephone to an old and trusted picture restorer. Whether the work he had carried out on a certain painting was really as below par as I maintained, or whether my peevishness was a product of private agony, I cannot remember. Whichever it was, when Zelda came in with my coffee, tears were streaming down my face unchecked. Grief has to go somewhere; inside one, it festers. But it was an inappropriate moment for it to burst.

She put the tray on my desk without a word and left the room, leaving me mistakenly to imagine she had not noticed.

'Poor Joshua Jones,' she said later when I had come downstairs to discuss various matters with her. 'It's a terrible day for him.'

I could not tell whether she was referring to the weather or Josh's plight. I ached inside as I used to do after a bout of blubbing in the school lavatories. 'Terrible,' I agreed neutrally.

'I sent the flowers,' she continued; 'yellow and white. I also sent a little bunch of my own. Roses: I remember you saying they were very much her flowers.'

I wished she would shut up. I was incapable of replying, merely nodded my head.

'It's a bad day for you, too, isn't it?' she added.

'Zelda, I really don't want to talk—'

'That's all right,' she said calmly. 'Why don't you get yourself a large drink and some lunch? You look fit for nothing.'

Suddenly I did not want to lunch alone. If I did so, it would be purely liquid and would do neither me nor the afternoon's business the slightest good.

'Zelda, do me a favour. Come and make sure I eat something, will you?'

We lunched in a wine bar, leaving Zelda's assistant to mind the shop. Zelda made no further attempt to probe into my life: we talked of hers instead. Her father had been curator of a musuem in Hanover; during the Second World War, he had been taken from his bed at dawn and shot, together with a lorry-load of fellow Jews. Her mother and brother had died in a concentration camp: Zelda, by a miracle, had escaped this fate and was brought to England, where she was adopted by a childless Jewish couple. I was ashamed that all these years of knowing Zelda had passed without my once bothering to enquire into her background. Whether she divulged these facts because she was in a mood to do so, or to take my mind off my own personal torment, I could not tell. Suffice it to say it was a salutory lesson: it did not dull the pain, but it placed it in perspective.

'I am over sixty,' she said at the end of lunch. 'I should be retiring.' She smiled sardonically. 'You'll be wanting to replace me.'

'If you mention it again, I'll kick you out forcibly,' I assured her in the same vein.

She said, 'Today is not the right moment to discuss it, I agree. By the way you didn't give me a message to send with Mrs Josh's flowers. I quoted "In loving memory"; it's harmless, don't you think?'

I had meant them to be anonymous; now I was incongruously pleased they were named. 'Thanks, Zelda.'

She removed her glasses and started to clean them with a small cloth tucked neatly in their case. Without them, her eyes gazed at me, large and dark and myopic: and I saw for a startled moment how she must have looked as a girl. I wondered, not for the first time, about the components of her present existence. But she was not prepared to throw a light on these: her confidences were over, and I was grateful for them.

It became obvious that Josh had gone to ground. I telephoned to find a newly-installed answerphone at the cottage, on which I left messages that were ignored. Meanwhile enquiries were constantly being made in the art world about his progress, including one from the owner of a redecorated mansion anxious to acquire two of his paintings, and willing to commission a new work. I was loath to admit that I had, for the time being, lost a serious artist: but that, in fact, was the truth of the matter. Despairing of the telephone, I wrote to Josh a letter gently pointing out that to lose the interest of the punters, let alone the backing of

Siegler's, was gross folly. Another note scribbled on a sheet of memo pad in return read: 'For Christ's sake get off my back. I know what I'm doing. J.' I gave up. To those who mattered I let it be known that Joshua Jones was suffering a nervous *crise* following the death of his wife: I hoped for his imminent recovery. This was only partly a lie; I could understand his behaviour. There were times when I myself felt a strong urge to become a recluse; to retire until the scar of Claudia began to heal, as Jane's had done eventually.

Little by little, the idea grew in my mind that I was playing a large part in Josh's disregard of the world. The possibility that he knew about the affair had always seemed remote to me, but a possibility it remained and grew larger in my mind. The idea was insidious, and part of me shrank from contacting him again. However, apart from business, Sam was on my conscience, and the promise I had made Claudia. When Josh extended this invitation out of the blue, I was dubious of it being an olive branch. But never in my worst nightmares had I envisaged gazing down the barrels of a shotgun in the small hours, with Josh on the other end of it.

Chapter Ten

We stand there, Josh and I, staring at each other without speaking. I am incapable of speech, paralysed by fear, rooted to the spot. Seconds seem like hours before he lowers the gun slowly and steps back a pace, his eyes still on my face. My knees start to shake.

'Having a look around, were you, Leo?' He grins unpleasantly. 'Having a little snoop? I thought you were an intruder: might have shot you to blazes.'

I give a nervous laugh. 'I was looking for garden tools, actually; thought I might have a go at the grass tomorrow.'

'You won't find them here.'

'No, I can see that. They're all rusted up.'

'Funny time of night to look.' He sounds fairly drunk and as if he is enjoying himself. 'It's a no-go area, the shed. Didn't I tell you? Stupid of me.'

'I'm sorry—' I begin.

'How did you find the key?'

'I saw it hanging in a cupboard. It looked the right sort of key—'

'Young Sam didn't tell you, then?'

'Sam?' I can hear my voice squeak up an octave. 'Sam had nothing to do with it.' He is silent, mulling over the information. I take a pull on myself, try again. 'Listen, Josh, I apologize if I've trespassed, but I wasn't

265

to know. I couldn't sleep, you see, so I decided to take a walk.'

I don't like the way he is handling the gun, leaning on it butt downwards and with the business end pointing more or less at my chin. 'I hope you know what you're doing with that weapon,' I add jocularly.

'Oh, I know what to do all right.' He glances over my shoulder at the shed's dim interior. 'Claudia spent a lot of time here. It was very much hers,' he says softly.

'I remember.'

I am suddenly acutely aware of the pottery jug. His eyes drop in unison with mine to the hand that clasps it.

'So,' he says in the same soft tone, 'not content with prowling, you do a little poaching on the side.'

Goaded into standing up for myself, I hold the relic out to him. 'Take it,' I say, 'if you want something you've ignored for months. I was fond of Claudia: I'd like something to remember her by. But far be it from me to take a begrudged memento.'

'Begrudged?' He spits the word out as though it tastes nasty. 'What a pompous git you are, Leo. And a slimy, treacherous little git at that.'

He steps away from me a further two paces, his bulk silhouetted against the pale sky, a bearlike figure in black and white by the light of the moon.

'Bugger a piece of sodding pottery! It's my wife I begrudge you.' He makes a noise between a choke and a roar. 'You thought you'd got away with it, didn't you? Fucking my wife behind my back. Well, think again, boyo, because I'm going to blast you off the face of the earth.' He spreads his feet unsteadily and, raising the gun, points it roughly at my head. 'I'm going to

266

shoot you between the eyeballs.' And, his finger on the trigger, he squints along the barrel.

It is astonishing how quickly one reacts in order to save one's life. I leap backwards into the shed, slam the door and drop to my knees. Outside there is silence, where I expect a burst of gunfire. I wait, trembling from head to foot, listening for some noise or other to warn me what will happen next. Thoughts race through my brain like wildfire. How does he know, and for how long? He must have found the letters. If he kills me, Sophie will be orphaned. How on earth have I got myself into this appalling situation and how am I going to get myself out of it? If I wasn't so frightened, I would feel ridiculous, crouched on the floor in a spider-ridden shed in the small hours. What is the best way to talk him out of his murderous intent: cajolery, denial of the whole affair, a plea for mercy? Sweat is trickling down my back, but my hands and feet are icy cold: strange, that.

With the door shut I feel more secure. I suppose he can charge in, but so far he has made no attempt to do so. He is drunk, and quite unhinged. I have to move; my left leg has cramp. Standing to one side of the door, I should be safe. There is always the window, of course, if he really means to kill me. His voice has been loud enough to carry as far as the house; there is the possibility that one or other of the family will wake and come to my rescue. I crawl to the side of the door and cautiously ease myself upright, ear to the wall, listening. There are faint sounds outside, the shuffling of feet, what sounds like a low groan, and a scraping that might be the butt of the gun on the stone step. Really, Josh is bloody erratic with a firearm: as likely to shoot himself as me. If I rush him, take him by surprise, there is a good chance of knocking the gun upwards to fire harmlessly at the sky. Anything rather than having to stay here until morning. Before I have time to decide on this manoeuvre, the door is flung open sharply: once again I wait with dry mouth and eyes tight shut for a salvo. Nothing happens, and when I open my eyes again Josh's face is within inches of my own. He is leaning his forehead against the lintel, forearm crooked over it in the classic pose of Greek tragedy. The shotgun is at his side, carelessly supported by two fingers. One green eye flickers disparagingly in my direction.

'Come out, you bastard,' he says in a monotone. 'I've decided you aren't worth the hassle of shooting.'

Slowly I emerge into the open and stand beside Josh's still figure. My instinct is to take the gun from what appear to be his nerveless fingers; but this might precipitate a further act of violence.

'Look, Josh,' I say in a reasonably firm voice, 'why don't we talk this through in the morning? You've got it all wrong, but this isn't the time or the place to discuss it.'

'It may not suit you,' he says, pushing himself upright, 'but it happens to suit me fine.' His face is twisted with pain rather than anger. 'How the hell d'you think it feels to know your wife is sleeping with someone else?' He kicks the gun into a leaning position against the wall. 'The torture of it. But no, you wouldn't, would you? You were blessed with a wife you didn't deserve. I tried to persuade her off the straight and narrow once, but she refused. You didn't realize that, did you?'

I ignore this last remark; I do not believe it. 'How do you know Claudia was unfaithful to you?' I ask tentatively. 'What proof do you have?'

'Oh, that's great, that's marvellous coming from you. As if you didn't know.' No-one sneers more successfully than Josh.

'But I *don't* know,' I protest.

He gives me a look in which I catch a glimmer of uncertainty.

'I suspected before I knew for sure. Instinct, the way she was with me: for God's sake, you have to be pretty bloody thick not to sense these things. Then she got ill, and I put my nasty suspicions down to that. I felt a proper shit for accusing her of things that weren't true. I was abject.' His stare turns to a certain loathing. 'We had that touching little scene over a drink, you and I, remember, where you played the Dutch uncle and I was overcome with gratitude. Little did I know at that moment,' he says bitterly, 'and when I did it was too late. You can't raise hell with a woman who's dying.'

'But where is the proof?' I fully expect him to pull my dog-eared letters from his pocket and grind them under his heel.

'What I don't understand,' he says as though he has not heard me, 'is your crass sodding stupidity, leaving messages for her on the answerphone. How the hell did you expect to get away with it?'

'I did not leave any messages.' This at least is the truth. Into my mind swans the recollection of a conversation with Marcus.

Josh brings his face close to mine and grips a handful of my shirt-front. 'Don't give me that,' he hisses on a wave of brandy. 'It was your damned voice;

269

d'you think I don't recognize your dulcet tones? "Please ring me to let me know time and place, *dar*ling . . . Last week was *won*derful, when can I see you? . . . I miss you un*bear*ably."'

His grasp shifts to my upper arms.

'I've waited a long time for this,' he breathes at me, 'getting you face to face. I've waited and waited, and one thing I'm going to have from your own lips is an admission.' He starts to shake me, backwards and forwards, helpless as a puppet, his hands digging into my flesh like a vice. 'It's not my one and only reckoning, but it'll do for now. So let's have it before I shake the teeth down your throat.'

'For God's sake, Josh, I've told you: I left no messages on your bloody answerphone!'

My words come out in a series of mechanical jerks. We are eyeball to eyeball, so near that I can see the dilation of his pupils. A last pull from his powerful hands brings our foreheads together with an audible crack, causing a ringing in my ears and an instant gush of carmine blood to flow from my nose.

He lets go of me; I fumble in my pocket for a handkerchief.

'Oh, Christ!' he says. 'I didn't mean to do that.'

'It'd be a lot worse if you'd shot me,' I mumble through a wad of cotton.

'Put your head back,' he advises.

'I don't like swallowing it; it'll stop in a minute.'

He wanders up and down restlessly, anxious to continue his unfinished inquisition. An element of farce has crept into the scenario, reminiscent of an adolescent brawl, which has little to do with the seriousness of our differences.

'Are you well enough to talk?' he demands, patience running out.

'I can talk all right, thank you,' I tell him coldly, 'and let me reiterate, once and for all, the messages you describe are not mine; and whoever's voice it was, it wasn't mine. If I wished to conduct a love affair with someone else's wife, that isn't the way I'd go about it. Credit me with a little more sense.'

Up until now, I have been able to be truthful. I am so amazed at this unexpected turn of events, I even allow myself a certain moral indignation.

'You ought to be more careful whom you accuse,' I add, 'and not jump to conclusions.'

Josh stops pacing and runs his hands through his hair in agitation. Uncertainty is now written all over him.

'It *was* your voice,' he says, 'I could swear.'

'Answerphones distort the voice to some extent. Or,' – a brilliant alternative suddenly occurs to me – 'someone might have been ringing the wrong number.'

Hope appears fleetingly across his face, then hardens into solemnity. He raises his head to look at me.

'Can you honestly say you didn't have an affair with Claudie?' he asks, so quietly I have difficulty in hearing him. 'Tell me: put me out of this agony. I can't live without knowing.'

The direct question I have been hoping to avoid: and no time for hesitation. The truth will be harder for him, whatever he may think; it will gnaw at his soul for the rest of his days. If I deny it, I deny Claudia. Jane flashes in and out of my mind with a 'look where it's landed you' expression on her face.

'Don't be ridiculous,' I say firmly, trying to flannel my way out. 'Whatever may have happened between you, she loved you.'

'That's neither here nor there.' He comes closer, his eyes still on mine. 'I want an answer.'

'No,' I say, 'I didn't,' and I feel the smarting of tears for a different reason than a crushed nose. Forgive me, beloved Claudia: I am not made for heroics.

My words have a startling effect on Josh. He throws his head back and gives a groan of anguish, like a hound about to bay at the moon.

'Then who the hell was it?' he shouts.

I hear a window thrown open in the house. 'Let's go back, Josh. It's time to get some sleep,' I suggest hopefully.

He does not answer; merely snatches up the gun, turns on his heel and walks rapidly away without a glance in my direction. I watch as he heads for the river, then stumble after him.

'They might have been someone's idea of a joke, those messages,' I call to him; but he has already crossed the lawn to be swallowed up by the inky shadows of the trees.

I am suddenly apprehensive for him, out there in the darkness in a possibly suicidal frame of mind. No sooner has the thought struck me than the double report of a shotgun shatters the silence. I start to run, while the upper windows of the house light up one after the other, and a small figure bursts into the garden from the kitchen. I swerve in my course to intercept it, catching Sam by the arm in mid-sprint.

'Wait! Don't go, Sam.' In my imagination, a body lies sprawled and lifeless in the undergrowth.

Sam wriggles furiously. 'Let me go! Something's happened to Josh!'

His upturned face is white and scared and indignant. I am vaguely aware that other figures have gathered on the terrace behind us.

'Stand still and listen,' I insist, breathing heavily from the unaccustomed exertion; and Sam quietens as I relax my hold on him. In the distance I have heard a noise; now there is the complete silence that precedes the dawn. Then comes the unmistakable sound of a voice cursing and swearing in the vicinity of the trees, and of dried twigs snapping underfoot; music to my ears. There is enough blame attached to me already without having Josh's death added to it.

Beside me, equally relieved, Sam shrugs. 'Oh well, he's all right. I suppose he's been potting rabbits.' He moves away in disgust.

'Are you going?' I ask.

'Might as well go back to bed.' He eyes me. 'You're bleeding. It's all down your shirt.'

'I had an argument with a door.'

'The shed door?'

'Yes, as it happens.'

'I thought it might be something like that. 'Night, Leo.'

Very little escapes Sam. Out of the corner of my eye, I see Da and Marcus hesitate for a moment before following him indoors. I am about to make sure that Josh has not shot himself through the foot when Sophie slips from the house and across the lawn; like a moth in her white floating dressing-gown, she walks swiftly to where the lower branches of the copper-beech sweep the grass, and vanishes.

All the old animosity towards Josh returns to me as I wait for her to reappear, envisaging with acute discomfort what they might be doing. When she does come into sight, she is with him; he has one arm round her shoulders and she seems to be taking a large proportion of his weight. He is limping badly: whatever injury he has done himself, it is bound to be exaggerated. Their heads are close together in whispered conversation, which somehow serves to fan my anger. I have a sudden desire not to be seen and step backwards rapidly as they near the house.

'Darling girl,' he is saying, 'what would I do without you?'

My foot slides from under me into a rose-bed and I subside half-sprawled across one of the bushes as I watch them negotiate the kitchen entrance. A flicker of white cotton robe and they are gone.

Heaving myself upright, I look to see what damage I have done Claudia's rose, and pick the thorns from my trouser-legs. A light appears in Josh's bedroom window above my head, denoting their arrival upstairs. Then the curtains are drawn across and shadowy figures can be seen behind the flimsiness of the material; elusive and maddening. I am conscious of being overwhelmingly tired, and at the same time full of a terrible loneliness. It seems I have been deserted by each one I have ever loved: Jane, Claudia and now Sophie, who has defected to the enemy. There is no doubt in my mind that this is Josh's other revenge, far more subtle than the threatening of my life. And even Josh, with whom I once shared a mutual admiration and affection, has shown his hostility and declared war. Who can blame him? The fact that I deserve every moment of this bleakness makes it no more bearable.

My despised bedroom, when I finally crawl there, seems a haven of peace after what I have been through. I realize I have lost the pottery jug: dropped, I suppose, during the confrontation by the shed. I shall go back for it in the morning. It is morning already: the grey mist of dawn lying over the garden, a yellow flush in the sky to the east. The birds are starting their infernal racket. The bridge of my nose is stiff and tender. Nothing, however, will stop me from sleeping. Undressing to pants only, I throw myself on the bed immune to its discomforts; my last thought before passing out is of Marcus. Later today, at some point, I shall seek him out: for I rather think, unless I am badly mistaken, we have a score to settle and one of some importance at that.

I am the last down for breakfast, having slept with weird and muddled dreams until ten-thirty. There is no sign of Josh but the others are there, and Sophie, in the same cotton robe, is making toast. She kisses me: her face is quietly glowing.

'I was telling Da,' she says, 'what happened to Josh. He tripped over a root and sprained his ankle, and the gun went off by accident. I don't think it's a bad sprain.'

'He shouldn't have a gun. Madness,' Da pronounces, spreading marmalade thickly on a slice of toast. 'He doesn't know the first thing about them.'

He is dressed for Sunday morning in varying shades of cinnamon, his halo of white hair brushed neatly. A powerful scent of after-shave surrounds him.

Sam leans his elbows on the work-surface next to

Sophie and waits for the toaster to pop up. 'What did you do for Josh's ankle?' he asks with interest.

'Soaked it in hot and cold water and then bandaged it. He can hobble on it,' she says, 'but he'll have to paint sitting down for a day or two.'

There is a proprietory air about her as she announces this, as if she is in sole charge of his well-being.

'For one awful moment,' Marcus says, 'I thought he'd shot himself.' He catches Da's eye. 'Had an accident; you know.'

'It's not a joking matter, boyo,' Da says.

'I wasn't laughing,' Marcus replies innocently, getting up from the table and stretching. 'God! Life is wonderful this morning, isn't it?'

And with this ambiguous statement he wanders into the garden.

'Gone to his head, this drama school lark, there's certain,' Da says severely. 'Why, whatever's happened to your eye, Leo?'

He has caught sight of my left one, round which a multicoloured bruise is spreading. 'I walked into a door,' I tell him, feeling foolish.

'The shed door,' Sam explains helpfully.

'Oh, Pa!' Sophie drifts over to examine it. 'I'll put some ice on it. You and Josh seem accident-prone. Why the *shed*?'

'It's a long story,' I say wearily, pouring myself some tea.

'You'll have a corker of a black eye,' Da says cheerfully. 'Think I'll take Josh a cup of coffee. Time he was up.'

'He *is* up,' Sophie says, opening the fridge. 'He's been in the studio for at least an hour.'

276

'Painting?' Sam asks, his face lighting up.

'Of course.'

'There's good news.' Da gets to his feet. 'I'll take him a cup there, then.'

'He left strict instructions not to be disturbed.' Sophie sounds embarrassed. 'I'm only allowed in because I'm sitting for him.'

I am glad to see she has the grace to blush.

'Aren't you going to eat anything, Pa?' she says, returning to me with ice-cubes wrapped in a tea-towel.

'No, thanks.'

'Then hold this on your eye as long as possible. I suppose you must have been as plastered as Josh or this wouldn't have happened.'

I am happy for her to believe in that solution. 'Stop being so horribly sanctimonious,' I tell her. 'One day it might happen to you.'

'Well, I'm off to buy the papers,' Da says. 'Like a drive, Sam?'

'No thanks, Gran'da. I've got a baby blackbird to feed.'

'By the way, Sam, Josh says will you lock up the shed and put the key in a different place. And you're not to let on where it is except to Josh himself. He was very insistent,' Sophie says.

'Oh, all right. Seems stupid to me. There's nothing much in that old shed, anyway.'

'I'm only the messenger,' Sophie points out. 'I suppose I'll have to be one all day.'

'Not if you want a lift with me,' I say. 'I intend to leave soon after lunch to miss the rush.'

Neither have I the least intention of going without her, if she but knew it.

277

'Then I'd better hurry; Josh wants me over at the studio.'

'That's right, dance to his tune,' I mutter under the ice-pack.

'Are you going to be there for *hours*?' Sam says. 'Won't we have time for a row on the river?'

'Later on, probably,' she answers; then, meeting his anxious blue gaze: 'I promise.'

Torn between the demands made upon her, unable by nature to disappoint: I can imagine this becoming a recurring pattern in her life, and hope I am mistaken. The kitchen is all at once empty of habitation apart from myself and a stray bee humming round the rose-bowl. Being here alone immediately invites memories of Claudia; I see her sitting across the table from me in a faded blue shirt, smiling in the way she had when we were left on our own. So vivid is the picture that I can make out the scattering of freckles across the bridge of her nose which appear with the sun, and the little lines by her eyes and mouth. Sometimes the memory of her seems frighteningly distant and misted at the edges, but this place brings her into focus with amazing clarity. I wish I had found the letters, for these too would bring her alive, but it is not to be. There is no likelihood I shall be asked to stay again, and remem--brance of her will be dependent on a badly-made pottery jug, if I can find it, and the painting I have of her back view.

In a few hours I shall be gone: I seem to have lived a lifetime in one weekend. I don't know where this leaves Josh and myself, but I cannot imagine us working in conjunction as we have done in a previous existence. It will be my loss more than his; he will have no difficulty in finding an interested art dealer of note with the introductions I have given him, and the propaganda I have spread around. He is no longer unknown. If he works, his will be a success story and I shall have lost a unique talent. I defy him, however, to find someone who will believe in him as I do.

The ice is melting through the towel and trickling down my chin. I dump the lot in the sink and look through the open windows at Marcus in the distance, lying on the grass above the river, a book held upwards against the sun's rays. I dry my face on a handkerchief and set out to spoil his fabulous morning.

'"What is honour? A word. What is that word, honour? Air. A trim reckoning,"' Marcus is declaiming. He looks up as I appear. 'Hello, Leo.'

'What's that from?' I ask.

'Falstaff. *Henry IV Part I*.' He lays the book face downwards. 'I've always wanted to play Falstaff. He's not just a buffoon and a fat lecher; he's intelligent and bothers to work things out and dispel myths.'

'Funny,' I say, 'there are a few myths I should like dispelled. Let's walk. I need to ask you something.'

He looks at me with wariness. 'All right. Which way?'

'The pub, to give us a purpose.'

We take the river path, less overgrown than in the opposite direction where Josh led me some forty-eight hours ago. In the green-brown waters of the river, small fish make ever-decreasing circles on the surface in their quest for flies. We walk side by side. There does not seem any point in delaying what I have to say.

'You left those love-messages on the answerphone, didn't you?'

He glances at me, his jaw sagging. 'How do you know?'

'Again, like Falstaff, I worked things out. It wasn't difficult. What in God's name possessed you to imitate my voice?' I ask, turning on him grimly.

He flushes. 'It was a joke. At least, most of it was meant as a joke.'

'Do you realize where it's landed me with Josh? He believes it was me and I don't think I've persuaded him otherwise. Your bloody joke has done untold damage.'

'I'm sorry,' he mumbles lamely. 'Honestly, Leo, I never thought anyone would take it seriously. Josh is so gullible. I didn't think—'

'Precisely. Well, you've got plenty to think about now. You're going to go to him and admit what you've done.'

'I can't, Leo! He'll murder me.'

'Quite likely. Murder is in his heart; only last night I was the prospective victim. Now he'll get the right man. Come on,' I say callously, 'we're both going to need a drink.'

I have shaken him; we proceed in silence, Marcus's face white with fear of his imminent fate. Inside, conscience niggles at me belatedly. I am, after all, guilty of a worse crime than some ridiculous jape.

'Cheer up,' I say quite kindly. 'Nobody's going to die. You can tell me how you thought up this infantile scheme over a glass of lager.'

Seated at a table in the pub garden, I wait for him to explain. He keeps his eyes on the beer, turning the glass this way and that.

280

'I never liked Josh,' he says. 'I think I told you. He resented me being around half the time. He resented anyone who shared in Ma's love, except perhaps Sam. Ma ran everything, did everything for him, put up with his bloody artistic temperament, which was just another word for egotism.' He glances up at me and away again. 'I longed for her to leave him, to find someone who'd look after her. And then, just before she realized she was ill, she told me that was what she might do. I asked her where she would go, and she said it wouldn't be a problem. That was what made me think there was someone else in her life, although she never actually mentioned it. It was then I had this brilliant idea –' he catches my eye '– well, it seemed brilliant at the time, of leaving incriminating messages on the answerphone. It would cause a crisis, and it needed a crisis to get Ma to make the first move.'

He pauses, sips his beer nervously. 'After I'd done it, it seemed pretty moronic but it was too late. But I thought it would be harmless enough if no-one believed it; no more than a joke. I really imagined Josh would put it down to some crank or other, playing silly buggers. Then Ma discovered how ill she was, and I wished I'd never thought up the bloody scheme, because it worked. Josh blew his top, I overheard them.'

'And you used my voice,' I say coldly, 'which is tantamount to forgery.'

He looks at me, colouring up again. 'I never thought of it that way. I'd got rather good at impersonating you, I was quite proud of it. Using it seemed to come naturally: it suited the style of the type I imagined might—'

He stops, acutely embarrassed.

'Might what?' I prompt.

'Might fall in love with Ma,' he finishes with a rush.

There is a pause in which the conversations of our fellow-drinkers can be quite clearly heard.

'In fact,' he ventures suddenly, 'I used to have this fantasy that you had: fallen for her, I mean. You fitted in with my picture of someone who'd give her a good life; sort of suitable. And you were always together, both of you, when you stayed down here. After she was pregnant, and Josh was being extra bloody, I wished it very much.'

'Was that your motive for leaving the messages?' I ask, amazed.

'Subconsciously, I suppose it was.' He sighs. 'Silly, wasn't it?'

'Not silly, no.' I am undone by the intuitive nature of these revelations, am at a loss for words. 'Misguided, perhaps,' I add. 'It's a mistake to try to manipulate people.'

'Yes,' he agrees more hopefully. 'I'm really terribly sorry, Leo. I didn't mean it to backfire on to you.'

'Apology accepted,' I tell him. 'It doesn't mean I'm letting you off the hook, though. Josh has to be told the truth.'

'Christ!' He swallows the last of his drink. 'I think I'll need something stronger than this.'

'A written confession will do,' I say, 'but it must be handed in today, before I leave for London. There's nothing to stop you bolting before me,' I suggest.

I feel magnanimous towards this boy who has favoured me as a stepfather above his own. Relief floods his face.

'That's a great idea. Thanks, Leo. I'll write it directly we get back.'

Returning by the same route, we discuss his acting career, his hopes and fears and aspirations. Where before I saw no resemblance to Claudia, now I recognize in him her movement and gestures. We pause to watch a swan sail majestically downstream.

'May I ask you something, Leo?'

'Of course. I don't promise to answer.'

'*Did* you love Ma?' He watches me from under his thick, dark lashes.

I am under no obligation to reply. I can brush it to one side, point out that such information has a right to privacy. But I have denied her once and have a hatred of doing so again. Besides, I think her son deserves to know his fantasies had a firm base. Across the river, in the shade of the weeping willows, I see the outline of her figure watching me. It is of course a mirage, the deception of light and shadow, gone in a moment.

'Yes,' I say at last. 'I loved her.'

Marcus says nothing, just smiles: but it is a contented smile.

Before we part in the garden, he says. 'Thank you, Leo'; although whether this is for trusting him with my confidences, or for allowing him to make his confession in writing, I cannot be sure.

'Would you like a lift back to London?' I ask.

'I think I'll hand over the necessary and run,' he says, grinning, 'thanks all the same.' Walking away towards the house, he stops and turns. 'I hope I'll see you soon,' he calls. 'Sophie and I plan to take in a film sometime.' And he waves a hand in salute.

I consider this statement and come to the conclusion I approve. Whatever damage Josh has caused Sophie this weekend, it has not stopped her dating his stepson. They are of an age and he is likeable: quite suitable, to coin Marcus's own phrase used in connection with myself. The thought brings a wry smile to my lips as I wander in the direction of the shed, in search of the pottery jug.

The shed is locked: Sam has obeyed orders. There is a broad patch of trampled grass in front of the stone step where Josh and I had our set-to. I look amongst the other sort of grass grown tall and rank against the shed itself, and further afield still, but there is no sign of my memento. I lift my head at the sound of a piercing whistle, like that of a doorman summoning a taxi, and catch sight of Sam swinging down the rope ladder from his tree-house. He runs towards me with the jug in his hand.

'I guessed you'd be looking for it,' he pants, holding it out. 'You said you wanted something of Mum's.'

'Thanks, Sam. I'm happy you found it.'

'It's not the best thing she made,' he says. 'It's a bit lopsided, isn't it?'

'It doesn't matter.'

'Pottery wasn't really her thing, anyway,' he says matter-of-factly. 'The garden was: she was great at that.' He grins so that his eyes light up the way Claudia's used to do. 'Mum was funny, always starting something new and not finishing it. She should have stuck to gardens.'

I look round at the sadly-neglected lawn and the clematis grown out of control.

'Sam, where is the mower kept? And the rest of the garden tools, ones that haven't rusted?'

'In the garage.'

'I'm going to see whether I can do something about this wilderness. Will you help me?'

For the next hour we work at it, taking the Flymo repeatedly over the grass until, although it looks ragged, one can see the semblance of a lawn emerging. Sam rakes up the cuttings and sacks up the dead wood from the climbing plants. I am no gardener; I am far from sure that what I am doing is right. But at the end of it, it resembles a more fitting memorial to Claudia than at the start. There is a glow of satisfaction to see it so, and a tinge of sadness, for this may be the last opportunity I have of making a gesture of love. Sam fetches iced drinks from the house and we sit with our backs to the wall and the sun on our faces. The sweet smell of grass-mowings lies heavily on the air. He takes the little jug from the step where we have left it, and runs his finger over the frieze of wild strawberries painted on the glazing.

'Mum did a better one than this, a saucer with an ivy leaf pattern,' he says. 'It was one of the things she chose for the time-capsule.'

The warmth is making me somnolent. 'What is this time-capsule?' I ask, out of friendliness rather than interest.

'Don't you know? Well, you choose a dozen objects which are sort of typical of the age you live in, and put them in a box and bury them. Then hundreds of years later someone will dig them up and find out what life was like all that time ago. Archaeologists and what-not.'

He slaps a hand on a bare leg to squash a mosquito.

'Surely the box would rot?'

'Mum found a deed-box like solicitors have, made of metal; the same as cash-boxes, only bigger.'

'And what objects made up the dozen?'

He reels off his own list, much of which has a bearing on wildlife: the discarded skin of a grass snake, a well-preserved skeleton of a mouse, snapshots of river birds. Claudia's choice he thought boring in contrast, consisting of needle and cotton, a paperback and various small household items.

'Oh, and she put in a bundle of letters,' he adds. 'It seemed a bit pointless to me. I mean, they wouldn't *tell* people much in the future, would they? Except how much stamps cost.'

My eyes, which have been threatening to close, fly open.

'I don't know,' I say slowly. 'It depends what was in them. Did she,' I ask, 'say anything about that?'

He shakes his head, squinting into the sun. 'Only that they were important to her. Chronicle of a trip to the moon, she said, or something like that. I didn't understand what she meant, but Mum was always saying weird things. She wasn't interested in space travel at all,' he remarks idly.

'Were there many letters?'

'Don't know: I didn't really notice. There was a little bundle of them with an elastic band round them.'

In silent contemplation I imagine my letters buried beneath loam and leaf mould, awaiting some chance excavation in another century. Or perhaps more likely in the not-so-far distant future when the woodland is cleared for building purposes. I am convinced the letters are mine, to judge by her elusive description of them. The situation is ironic: the letters are safe and yet quite beyond my reach. There is no possibility of Sam divulging the whereabouts of his black box: he has made that clear. The fact that I am irrevocably parted from them brings a rush of nostalgia, a longing to re-read them at leisure.

'Do you ever get the wish to dig up the treasure and have a look at how it's doing?' I ask with small hope of a satisfactory reply.

'No, I don't,' he says emphatically. 'It took us hours to dig that deep; we had blisters on our hands.' He looks at me sternly. 'And don't think I'm giving away where it is. We swore each other to secrecy, Mum and me, and I'm not cheating.'

'Quite right,' I agree hurriedly. 'It was just an idle question.'

Sam looks thoughtfully at the jug in his hand and says, 'Was this what you and Josh were having a row about last night?'

'A row?' I prevaricate.

'Josh was shouting, it woke me up. And I guessed you were with him because you'd asked me where the shed key was kept.'

'Ah. No, it was nothing to do with the pottery and it wasn't a row exactly, just a slight disagreement. He'd had a drink too many, I think.'

Sam glances at me. 'He's painting again properly, isn't he? That means he'll drink less and you'll be able to sell his paintings and we won't have to sell the house. Which is a good thing, because there isn't enough running-away money to last me more than two days, and, anyway, we decided I shouldn't do that.'

This all comes out in one long sentence, at the end of which he adds, 'Josh doesn't usually stay furious for long.'

'I expect he's forgotten all about it this morning,' I agree, although I doubt the validity of this statement. I have no idea on what terms we shall part after the revelations of last night.

'So you will go on helping him, Leo?'

'Certainly,' I assure him, 'if that's what he wants. He's a very fine artist.'

He gives a sigh of satisfaction and drains the last of his coke. 'Are you going on gardening?'

'No, I think not.' I get to my feet and glance at my watch. 'One o'clock. Let's put the tools away and see if Sophie is back from the studio. It's time for something to eat.'

He picks up the rake and removes strands of grass from the prongs with his shoe. 'I wish you weren't going this afternoon; I wish you could stay for a bit,' he says without looking at me.

Looking down on the thatch of russet hair and the freckled face half-hidden, I am touched by the sudden crack in his independence. Forget the painting, forget the pottery: I have only to watch this boy of Claudia's to bring her vividly to life.

The last crunch of wheels on gravel, the final wave and we are on our way: over the stone hump-back bridge that crosses the river before the village, and up the narrow lane flanked by cow parsley and dog roses. I expected that enormous sense of release one experiences when an ordeal has ended. Instead, glancing down at the cottage over my right shoulder, I feel a loss: that, and an awareness that nothing has been settled. There is no clean-cut finality to what has occurred: merely an uneasy truce in which, I suspect, Josh has the upper hand. I cannot see this changing. It is guilt that causes it; and even had he absolved me from it unequivocally, I shall never be rid of it. Weighing up the injuries he has or has not inflicted on me and mine does not help. There is no winner in this game we have been playing, but if there were I would undoubtedly come a poor second.

Apart from Sophie's enthusiastic remark – 'What an amazing weekend' – and my concurrence, for 'amazing' is one way of describing it, we have fallen silent; each occupied with our own private thoughts. What she is recalling I dare not imagine: she looks no different from two days ago, when we were about to enter the lion's den. She has the same serene profile, the same air of innocence. It is only I who expect to find in those doe-like eyes a certain knowingness that was not there before. Her hair stirs in the breeze from her open window as it did on the downward journey. Any change in her is imperceptible; although she does look particularly well. What am I looking for, for God's sake; *seduced*, stamped across her forehead? I let my mind wander back in relief to safer ground, to the last hour or so of this angst-ridden visit, where she was spreading butter on slices of bread in the kitchen, and Marcus was adding the ham.

'It's only sandwiches for lunch, I'm afraid,' Sophie said. 'We were to have the rest of Da's paella, but the cat got at it.' I looked around me nervously. 'It's all right, Pa, she's on Josh's bed, sleeping it off.'

'Good. I love sandwiches,' Sam said.

'No washing-up,' agreed Marcus.

He seemed relaxed: almost too relaxed. I raised my eyebrows and mimed the writing of a letter. He nodded, giving the thumbs-up sign.

'What *are* you two doing?' Sophie asked.

'Sophie, will you take a note to Josh for me as soon as possible?' he said. 'I've got to leave in a hurry after lunch.'

'All right. I'll do it when I go over with something to eat. No, don't put the top bread on, I've got to add lettuce. And stop picking.'

We ate in the shade of the trees where, a few hours earlier, Josh had stamped around in a fever of uncertainty and sprained his ankle.

'Josh isn't joining us?' I queried, secretly thankful to be spared the stress of meeting him.

'He won't stop for anyone or anything,' Sophie said. 'He's painting flat out. It's terribly good,' she added, her eyes shining. 'You're going to be pleased, Pa.'

'If I'm ever allowed to see it,' I said, hearing the peevishness of my tone.

'Back to his old form?' Da said, lowering the financial pages of *The Sunday Times*. 'There's hoping it's the start of better things.'

'Exactly,' she said excitedly. 'The end of his mental block.'

They did not appear to have heard me; I stared malevolently at the patches of blue sky between the leaves above me, feeling unfairly excluded.

Lunch being finished, everyone except for myself and Da drifted away; Sophie to the studio, pampering Josh to the last, Sam on his own business and Marcus to prepare himself for a hasty getaway. Da was to drive him to catch a bus to Petersfield and from there the train to London. I poured the remainder of a bottle of white wine into our glasses.

'Ta, Leo.' Da lifted his glass to me. 'Something bothering you, is there?'

'No,' I said shortly. 'Should there be?'

His little eyes sparkled with intelligence. 'The opposite, I was thinking. You should be pleased your protégé's pulling his finger out at last.'

'We can thank Sophie for that, if it's so. Nothing to do with me.'

'It's everything to do with you, boyo, so there's no need for you to have your nose put out of joint. More than it has been, that is,' he said, glancing at my bruise. He offered me one of his slim cigars, which for some reason I accepted. 'Whatever went on between you and Josh last night, it's cleared the air. Am I right?'

'I'm far from sure, Da.'

'It can't have been easy for you these last two days. Proper little bugger Josh is when he's a mind to be, and I've seen him giving you a hard time.' He gave me a light, and the smoke from our cigars rose pungently in the warm air. 'Don't back out because of it, Leo, that's all I ask,' he said. 'He can't get back to where he was without you. He needs you, and he bloody well knows it.'

I did not answer at once. The old man did not know the true story. He might suspect, but did not have the least idea of the emotions involved, the wounds inflicted and as yet unhealed. In his view, Josh had no problem that could not be solved by a good kick in the pants; and any ruffled feathers of mine could be easily smoothed and soothed into place by a little soft-talking. Da had everyone's interests at heart; it was best he should be left in ignorance.

'There's no ill-will between us on my part,' I told him. 'I've no desire to wash my hands of him. He knows where to find me if he wants to do so: I shall be there.'

He sighed with relief, exhaling smoke like a dragon. 'There's good of you, Leo. I'm off soon to the sunny south; there's bargain flights to Marbella should be made the most of. I'll be going with a lighter heart, knowing you'll be looking after the business side of things.'

I opened my mouth to speak and shut it again. There was no point my telling him I had better things to do in a busy life than cosset recalcitrant artists, however talented. He spoke instead, adding a minor bombshell of a rider.

'The green eye of the little yellow god,' he said thoughtfully. 'That's what Josh has been suffering from. Let's hope he got it off his chest about Claudia.' He eyed me in a tolerant manner. 'Not so easy for you, is it, Leo?'

Marcus came back at that moment carrying a grip and an anorak, and wearing a haunted expression. He shook my hand and said goodbye before hustling Da towards the Jaguar and freedom. I stood there in the sunlight letting the cigar peter out between my fingers. I was glad they had left; I had underestimated Da's perspicacity and would have been at a loss for words.

In my bedroom I packed the last of my things in a hold-all and pulled the zip shut. Now I was about to escape,

I saw the room for what it was: a small dark place in need of a coat of paint or new wallpaper, but innocuous enough. All houses had them, rooms that were used as an overflow only when the others were occupied. I would have been tempted to think I had imagined its grim atmosphere, and the unnerving happenings within it, if it had not been for the picture with its broken wire stacked against the wall. Tonight I would be sleeping in my own bed, and tomorrow the familiar confines of the Gallery would enclose me for much of the day. Taken up with my own affairs, the weekend would fade to no more than a macabre incident and be given merely the odd passing thought. It was not so easy to leave behind the shades of Claudia that hung like mist about the house and garden, and the river-bank.

This musing was interrupted by Sophie standing in the doorway with a note in her hand.

'It's from Josh,' she said breathlessly. 'I'm more or less packed, and I'm going to have a quick row on the river with Sam because I promised. I shan't be late.'

'What's it about?' I asked, taking the paper from her.

'I don't know, it's for you. I expect it's a written goodbye. He said to apologize for not being there to see us off. See you soon.'

I watched her trotting across the lawn with Sam, each of them carrying an oar, before opening the folded paper; a sheet from a sketch pad, by the feel of it.

Leo,

it started baldly,

Well, here's a turn-up for the books. I wonder if you bribed young Marcus to take the blame? I'm sure

he's perfectly bribable. Difficult to know who's lying, isn't it? You'll never know how close I came to shooting you last night. Only the resulting mess and the idea of Wormwood Scrubs prevented me. I don't think I believe a word, you sod, but it no longer matters. Revenge is sweet and I'm painting, painting, painting. And let's face it, I need you, although don't think I'm going to crawl with gratitude as in the past. You owe me one, Leo, so how about getting off your ass and making arrangements for a show in, say, nine months' time? You won't regret it.
Josh

My instinct on reading this ambiguous missive was to tell him to get stuffed, which was the kind of language he understood. The thinly-veiled abusive tone of it stared up at me out of his beautiful italic handwriting. I saw how managing his affairs henceforth would be. Secure in the strength of his position where I was concerned, he would become one of those infuriating artists who demand a say in every detail of their professional lives. They are a pain, and one has to have a very sound reason for keeping them on the list of regular gallery artists. But my reason lay in a promise to Claudia, made at a time when I could hardly refuse her; and although I doubted very much I was under an obligation to Josh any longer, there was always Sam. He could not be so easily tossed aside. It seemed that Josh and I were inextricably bound together in a loveless marriage for the unforeseeable future. I tore the paper into pieces and dropped them in the waste-basket.

Through the window drifted the sound of voices

from the river; careless, excited voices of children at play. Sophie was a mere six or seven years older than Sam: the realization turned in me like a knife. I tried not to think of the sweetness of revenge.

Da and Sam were there to see us off; Da asking me impossible questions about the Volvo's power of acceleration, and comparing it unfavourably with his Jaguar. Sam was silent, a smile fixed to his face as if he was determined to keep it there. If I had not known better, I would have suspected him of being close to tears.

'Don't forget I'm coming to stay with you,' he said gruffly, leaning in at the window.

My mind is still on Sam as we sweep down the hill into Midhurst's sleepy main street and past the ruins of Cowdray Castle.

'I can't think how Josh is going to manage if he's working full-time again,' I comment as I slow down for a gaggle of tourists crossing the road. 'How can he possibly paint and look after Sam and the house?'

'Oh, that's all being taken care of,' Sophie says airily. 'One of Josh's sisters is coming to stay for three weeks until he can find local help. And there's always Mrs Morse; Sam likes her because she lets him eat hamburgers and chips for every meal.'

'When was this arranged?' I ask, bewildered.

'It was Da; he's a great organizer.' She turns her face to catch the breeze. 'Isn't it good that Josh is painting seriously?' she says. 'It's what you wanted.'

'If he really is serious, yes. I wouldn't know,' I reply, adding a little unfairly, 'You're in a better position to judge.'

My choice of words is unfortunate, but it is too late; I can see the pink rising up her cheeks.

'If you hadn't had a row,' she says, 'I expect he would have let you judge for yourself.'

'It was Josh's row,' I say childishly, 'not mine. Anyway, how do you know about it?'

'I heard it. We all heard it.'

'He'd been drinking.'

Her chin tilts, a sign in Sophie of obstinacy. 'He only drinks because he's miserable. You can't expect him not to mind about Claudia.'

'I don't expect anything of the sort. But the argument had nothing to do with Claudia's death.'

'No,' she says matter-of-factly. 'I suppose it was to do with you and Claudia. That's what I meant. He's bound to mind.'

My hands jerk on the wheel, then steady again to bring the car back to the correct side of the white line. The shock of her words leaves me breathless.

'I presume Josh has been filling you up with a lot of nonsense,' I say, resorting wildly to pomposity.

'No. He never mentioned it. I worked it out for myself.'

'But how—?'

'Oh, Pa,' she says quite kindly, 'you were so obvious; the way you spoke to her on the phone, and brought her name into the conversation as often as possible, and always being late home on Fridays. The way you looked at her, and wanted me to like her.'

'You didn't,' I say sadly.

'I hated her,' she admits. 'Do you remember her visiting me in hospital after I'd had my tonsils out? I wanted to chuck that vast bunch of primroses back in her face and scream at her to go.'

The high embankments of the Haslemere road flash past us as I think wretchedly of the mess I have made of things.

'It shows my lovely nature that I managed to restrain myself,' she says, rescuing the moment with humour. 'You did have an affair with her, didn't you?'

I let my breath go in a deep sigh. 'I suppose you dislike me for it, just as Josh does.'

'Never that.' She shakes her head. 'I minded terribly at first, I was furious and miserable. But that was a year ago and I was younger and didn't understand. I've grown up, and I can see that things happen sometimes whether you want them to or not. It must have been awful for you when she died – first Ma and then Claudia. I don't hate her any more,' she adds.

'If Ma had lived, it wouldn't have happened,' I say, desperately wishing the statement to be true. 'I can't justify my actions. But I'll try to explain, if you like.'

'I don't think so, thank you. We'd both get horribly embarrassed.'

On the outskirts of Haslemere, I bring the conversation round to mundane matters by saying, 'Like to stop here for tea?'

'Not unless you want to,' she answers. 'I'd quite like to get home. Marcus and I have a vague plan to go to a film this evening.'

My spirits lift a little. 'I rather like Marcus,' I venture cautiously.

'He's all right,' she agrees, 'even if he's a bit young.'

'What's become of Smog?' I ask of this experienced woman.

'Oh, we broke up weeks ago,' she says cheerfully. 'He began to get serious, so that was that.'

'Poor old Smog.'

'He found someone else straight off,' she says. 'Besides, you know me, Pa. I want to concentrate on dancing. That's why older men are best; they understand. I don't want my life complicated in any way. But Marcus thinks like I do, so that's fine.'

I wonder whether all this wisdom pouring out of her has been acquired in the last forty-eight hours. ('I've grown up now and I can see that things happen whether you want them to or not.').

'Older meaning Josh?' I enquire.

In profile I can see she is wearing Jane's inscrutable smile, and the patient expression of a mother dealing with a difficult child.

'You're not still worrying over that?' she says. 'Just because he flirts and I pose for him.'

'Not if that's all it amounts to.'

'Don't tell me you're worried for my virginity?' she asks incredulously.

'Is that such an odd thing for a father?'

'Only that I lost it ages ago.' She puts her head back and laughs. 'Darling Pa, don't look so shattered. One has to lose it some time or other.' She sobers up and says, 'I have an admission to make, though. It seems the moment for guilty secrets. Remember when I went to stay with Smog's parents? Well, we slipped away and went to Spain for a weekend, Smog and I; to Madrid and Toledo. That's where – well, I'm sorry I lied.'

'I don't see that it makes much difference,' I say. 'It's possible to sleep with someone in Yorkshire.'

She looks at me fondly. 'You know, Pa, you really can be very funny when you try.'

'I'll take that as a compliment,' I tell her, managing a smile.

We lapse into silence. I need time to digest these revelations of hers, flung at me without warning. My chief emotion is one of failure as a parent. Where was I, that I failed to notice her transition to adulthood? Jane would not have missed the signs, would have been with her every step of the way from a safe distance. My lack of observation cannot be excused; concentration was centred elsewhere, on my own convoluted problems. I was aware of Sophie, but the awareness was blinkered. I thought I had done my best, but it was not a very good best. And yet, come to think of it, there is little wrong with her; she has achieved the transition alone and remained amazingly unaltered and unscathed. I take a swift glance in her direction, at the long dark hair blowing in the wind, and thank God.

Among her confidences there has been no mention of the part Josh has played in all this: I doubt I shall ever learn the truth now. Perhaps it does not matter; but it will always be my own private and painful enigma, and Sophie is the last person to put paid to my imaginings.

'Do stop fussing, Pa,' she says out of the blue.

'I haven't said a word.'

'That's the trouble. It's silent fussing and the vibes are fairly whizzing around.' She puts a hand on my knee, and I cover it with mine. 'Listen: I love you; that hasn't changed. And whatever I've done for Josh, it's made him work again, which is what we all wanted. So why worry?'

'I'll stop,' I promise, squeezing her fingers. 'Perhaps I should be proud of you.'

'I'm quite pleased with myself,' she admits modestly.

The heavy stage curtains slowly close, and Sophie slips between the gap in the folds to curtsey to the applause. It is her end-of-term performance at the ballet school and the last time she will dance as a student. Around me resound the enthusiastic stamps and calls of fellow students and the more reserved clapping of the guest audience. Her smooth head bends demurely; then she straightens and accepts a bouquet of roses in long white arms, putting out a hand to her partner who stands beside her. My throat constricts; there are three more curtain calls before the audience finally releases them and we rise, filing out eventually into the warm night air. Sophie will not be joining me: there is a leaving-party planned for them.

In the car I switch on the light and look through the programme once again. There was nothing demure about Sophie's performance. The ballet which she has just danced is new and entitled *Secrets*. For two people, it appeared to be an explicitly choreographed portrayal of a young girl's introduction to love.

It is the first time I have seen her perform in modern dance; the others have been classical and traditionally dressed. In this, her frock, made of some diaphanous material, barely covered her, clung to her body at every move; and the movement was erotic in its passion, assuming contortions of which I had not thought the human frame capable. Certainly it comprised some highly original interpretations of the act of love. But it was not the concept of the ballet which held me transfixed: it was Sophie herself. Gone was the

300

technically competent but uninspired performance; and in its place was a woman in thrall with her lover. It is odd and a little frightening to see your child on fire with lust, all inhibitions melted away. To be honest, I feel shy at the thought of facing her in the morning.

Slowly I stuff the programme in my pocket and start the engine, no longer in any doubt. My enigma is solved. I do not feel anger or pain: it is a relief. It happened, it has become a fact and, as such, I am able to put it behind me. Strange that it should be Sophie, after all, who has given me the answer.

THE END

The Fifth Summer
Titia Sutherland

Every summer the Blair family went to Italy – to the villa
in The Garden, a lush wilderness of cypress trees and
bougainvillea tumbling down to the sea. Phoebe, who
owned the villa and lived close by, loved the Blairs – of all
her summer guests they were the ones who gave meaning
to her life. She was possessive, enigmatic, manipulative,
but Will and Lorna never really minded – until the fifth
summer.

Something was wrong even before they arrived. There
was a tension, a distance between Lorna and Will,
something strange that Lorna could not quite define. The
children were equally off-balance – Debbie overweight
and rebellious, Fergus tortured and falling in love for the
first time. And into this uneasy gathering of friends,
family, and lovers, burst Bruno Andreotti, handsome,
greedy, selfish, much loved by women but giving nothing
of himself to any of them. Bruno was to prove the catalyst
that blew the fifth summer apart, making Will and Lorna
and the two children reassess and finally rebuild the
structure of their lives.

'THE STANDARD OF WRITING IS HIGH, EACH
CHARACTER IS WELL DRAWN, RELATIONSHIPS AND
FEELINGS ARE BELIEVABLE. YOU CAN PRACTICALLY
FEEL THE WARMTH OF THE SUN ON THE PAGES'
Sue Dobson, *Woman and Home*

'SUTHERLAND SCORES FULL MARKS . . . A FIRST NOVEL
OF PROMISE AND SOME DISTINCTION'
David Robson, *Sunday Telegraph*

0 552 99460 X

BLACK SWAN

Out Of the Shadows
Titia Sutherland

The house was one of the most enduring influences in
Rachel Playfair's life. It was really too large for one
woman, but she liked the memories it held, the graceful
garden, and even the amiable resident spirit who lived on
the top floor. When Rachel's authoritative and somewhat
pompous son tried to persuade her out of her house, she
decided to make changes in her solitary life. With three
children who needed her only spasmodically, and a small
lonely granddaughter who needed her quite a lot, she
made plans, first of all to take in a lodger and then, with
the help of the unhappy Emily, to research the past of her
house. Both decisions were to shatter the structure of
Rachel's tranquil life.

The lodger proved to be a beguiling but disturbed man
who was instantly fascinated by his cool landlady, and the
delving into the past reopened a moving and poignant
wartime tragedy that held curious overtones of events in
Rachel's own life.

'THIS SENSITIVE PORTRAYAL OF A MIDDLE-AGED
WOMAN'S UNEXPECTED SEXUAL PASSION TURNED
INTO A GHOST STORY I COULDN'T PUT DOWN'
David Buckley, *Observer*

'AN EVOCATIVE STORY . . . GENTLY TOLD, ENVELOPS
YOU COMPLETELY'
Company

0 552 99529 0

BLACK SWAN

A SELECTED LIST OF FINE WRITING AVAILABLE FROM BLACK SWAN

THE PRICES SHOWN BELOW WERE CORRECT AT THE TIME OF GOING TO PRESS. HOWEVER TRANSWORLD PUBLISHERS RESERVE THE RIGHT TO SHOW NEW RETAIL PRICES ON COVERS WHICH MAY DIFFER FROM THOSE PREVIOUSLY ADVERTISED IN THE TEXT OR ELSEWHERE.

☐	99313 1	OF LOVE AND SHADOWS	Isabel Allende	£6.99
☐	99565 7	PLEASANT VICES	Judy Astley	£5.99
☐	99535 5	WRITING ON SKIN	Sara Banerji	£5.99
☐	13649 2	HUNGRY	Jane Barry	£6.99
☐	99648 3	TOUCH AND GO	Elizabeth Berridge	£5.99
☐	99593 2	A RIVAL CREATION	Marika Cobbold	£5.99
☐	99587 8	LIKE WATER FOR CHOCOLATE	Laura Esquivel	£5.99
☐	99602 5	THE LAST GIRL	Penelope Evans	£5.99
☐	99622 X	THE GOLDEN YEAR	Elizabeth Falconer	£5.99
☐	99488 X	SUGAR CAGE	Connie May Fowler	£5.99
☐	99610 6	THE SINGING HOUSE	Janette Griffiths	£5.99
☐	99590 8	OLD NIGHT	Clare Harkness	£5.99
☐	99391 3	MARY REILLY	Valerie Martin	£4.99
☐	99503 7	WAITING TO EXHALE	Terry McMillan	£5.99
☐	99606 8	OUTSIDE, LOOKING IN	Kathleen Rowntree	£5.99
☐	99607 6	THE DARKENING LEAF	Caroline Stickland	£5.99
☐	99529 0	OUT OF THE SHADOWS	Titia Sutherland	£5.99
☐	99460 X	THE FIFTH SUMMER	Titia Sutherland	£5.99
☐	99620 3	RUNNING AWAY	Titia Sutherland	£6.99
☐	99650 5	A FRIEND OF THE FAMILY	Titia Sutherland	£5.99
☐	99130 9	NOAH'S ARK	Barbara Trapido	£6.99
☐	99549 5	A SPANISH LOVER	Joanna Trollope	£6.99
☐	99636 X	KNOWLEDGE OF ANGELS	Jill Paton Walsh	£5.99
☐	99592 4	AN IMAGINATIVE EXPERIENCE	Mary Wesley	£5.99
☐	99639 4	THE TENNIS PARTY	Madeleine Wickham	£5.99
☐	99591 6	A MISLAID MAGIC	Joyce Windsor	£4.99